EXIT STAGE
DEATH

HAVE YOU EVER WONDERED HOW BOOKS ARE MADE?

UCLan Publishing is an award winning independent publisher specialising in Children's and Young Adult books. Based at The University of Central Lancashire, this Preston-based publisher teaches MA Publishing students how to become industry professionals using the content and resources from its business; students are included at every stage of the publishing process and credited for the work that they contribute.

The business doesn't just help publishing students though. UCLan Publishing has supported the employability and real-life work skills for the University's Illustration, Acting, Translation, Animation, Photography, Film & TV students and many more. This is the beauty of books and stories; they fuel many other creative industries! The MA Publishing students are able to get involved from day one with the business and they acquire a behind the scenes experience of what it is like to work for a such a reputable independent.

The MA course was awarded a Times Higher Award (2018) for Innovation in the Arts and the business, UCLan Publishing, was awarded Best Newcomer at the Independent Publishing Guild (2019) for the ethos of teaching publishing using a commercial publishing house. As the business continues to grow, so too does the student experience upon entering this dynamic Master's course.

www.uclanpublishing.com
www.uclanpublishing.com/courses/
uclanpublishing@uclan.ac.uk

AVA ELDRED

EXIT STAGE ~~DEATH~~

uclanpublishing

Exit Stage Death is a uclanpublishing book

First published in Great Britain in 2025 by
uclanpublishing
University of Central Lancashire
Preston, PR1 2HE, UK

Text copyright © Ava Eldred, 2025
Cover design by David Wardle, 2025

978-1-916747-58-6

1 3 5 7 9 10 8 6 4 2

The rights of Ava Eldred to be identified as the author
of this work has been asserted in accordance with the
Copyright, Designs and Patents Act 1988.

All rights reserved. No part of this publication may be reproduced,
stored in a retrieval system, or transmitted in any form or by any means,
electronic, mechanical, photocopying, recording or otherwise; or be used to train
any AI technologies without the prior permission of the publishers.
UCLan Publishing expressly reserves this work from the text
and data mining exception subject to EU law.

Set in Kingfisher by Becky Chilcott.

A CIP catalogue record for this book is available from the British Library.

Printed and bound in Great Britain by Clays Ltd, Elcograf S.p.A.

*For anyone who knows exactly
how many ways you can measure a year.*

PROLOGUE

I'D NEVER STOPPED TO THINK ABOUT HOW MURDER investigations and musical theatre are actually pretty similar until I was caught up in one when I was trying to focus on the other.

If that makes it sound like I'm being flippant about what happened at Camp Chance last summer, I need you to know one thing right up front: I'm *never* flippant about musical theatre. Until last year's camp, I would have argued that there was nothing more important.

But then – murder investigation.

That would make even the most single-minded of people reassess.

Think about it, though: All the elements are there.

For each, you need a killer main character – not to be confused with an actual killer, although sometimes they are one and the same. In most cases, you're just looking for...well, not a hero, because we were all still normal teenagers – or as normal as Camp Chance kids could be – but someone to root for. Someone you want to win.

I'll let you decide who ours was.

Next, an inciting incident.

Example: A creepy phantom schemes to get closer to an opera singer. Eventually kidnaps her.

Example: We find a dead body beside the lake.

How you react to that is where your plot comes from. What takes you from your first song to your finale, and the kind of shape you're in when you get there. But that's getting ahead of ourselves.

First, you need your act one climax.

Somewhere in the middle comes the moment you've been anticipating since the overture, since the first clue, even if you didn't know it yet.

The revolutionaries wave the red flag.

The green witch flies.

The couple kiss at the Life Cafe.

The couple kiss under the Washington Heights fireworks.

The two of us, desperate for something good in the midst of all our fear, kiss on the main stage.

You'll need a script, and a cast willing to play the parts. The romantic lead. The true crime detective. The unlikely suspect. The red herring. The innocent new girl who is changed by the events. The villain.

A director, guiding them to where they're supposed to stand. How they're supposed to react.

Throw in a good twist and you're almost there.

As for the thing that takes a show from a script on a page to really being *theatre* – that transforms a crime investigated secretly into a *show* – you need an audience.

Which is where you come in.

One last thing that helps, when it comes to both musicals and murder: ask questions.

What if two rival gangs went to war on the streets of New York?

Why were they the victim?

What if the tudor wives formed a girlband?

What was the motive?

What actually *is* a jellicle cat?

Are the rest of us in danger until we figure this out?

Who lives, who dies, who tells your story?

By the end, it felt like the most important thing was that it was *us* – or, I guess, me – who got to tell ours.

So. Nothing else for it.

Curtain up.

CHAPTER 1

THEN

SCENE 1 — A MOVING COACH, SOMEWHERE IN THE BRITISH COUNTRYSIDE.

Morning. Summer.

A teenager wearing a bedazzled Phantom of the Opera mask takes centre stage, trying to belt her way through 'Let It Go', ignoring the fact that:

   1. The rest of the people on this coach have no way of escaping.

   2. She can't technically hit those notes.

Downstage right, LIVI CAMPBELL
lifts a hand to her mouth to hide
her smile. She loves this. Loves every
over-the-top, way-too-loud, nothing-
close-to-subtle, bedazzled-phantom-mask
minute of it.

The song reaches its climax.
It's an overture.
A beginning.
Lights up.

If you really concentrate, you can pinpoint the moment.

For a long time, I couldn't work out how to articulate that; the feeling of atoms shifting – of the world being one thing, and then, in the next second, another thing entirely. The only way I could describe it was that my body *knew* when I was on my way back to camp; knew on a cellular level that things were about to get good again. I'd always put it down to relaxing – to letting everything go (pun, considering the soundtrack, not intended) rather than gaining anything. Stripping back the armour to find Livi underneath. Then my classmate who had a shellfish allergy gave a presentation where they said that they felt something physical when someone nearby was eating sea creatures – like the world was giving them warning. Telling them to pay attention.

I loved that.

Not the fact that they had a possibly fatal allergy, that filled me with anxiety, but the rest of it – the idea that the whole universe was rearranging itself to give them a sign. *Telling them to pay attention.* Those were the exact words they'd used, and that was it. *Exactly* what I felt when the coach crossed the invisible threshold from reality to Camp Chance.

Be present for this bit. Keep your focus. Something is about to happen.

Pay. Attention.

And then, without even a ripple of recognition from anyone else, because this was *my* feeling, *my* universe . . . it happened.

If you really concentrate, you can feel the air change.

It's hardly ever as obvious as a newbie in a phantom mask who hadn't learnt yet that holding back, knowing when to keep something for later, is as much a part of performance as knowing when, literally in this case, to 'Let It Go', but really, could there be anything more Classic Musical Theatre?

In *A Chorus Line*, they don't form the kick line until the very last song.

Elphaba only belts in *Wicked* right at the moment it becomes uncomfortable that she hasn't yet.

A quiet Camp Chance coach? Anyone who knows anything would be waiting for it. And then there she was, Elsa in someone else's costume, bursting into song, and that was my cue to come out of hiding.

To be reborn.

To awaken the part of myself who *didn't* find it a bit intense that a fifteen-year-old in a bedazzled *Phantom of the Opera* mask was currently trying to belt their way through 'Let It Go', with apparently no awareness that we were *trapped on a coach* and also that *they couldn't hit those notes*.

No matter, I thought. *They'll learn to sing it properly.* That was what we were all there for, after all. I'd come to camp as a complete novice and, after four summers, was only just starting to feel like I'd really found my footing – and even now, it still came in waves. Performing was about allowing yourself to be vulnerable, right? About being able to get it wrong before you got it right. That was the whole *point* of Camp Chance.

I looked around the coach for anyone I recognised from previous years, spotting a few veteran campers huddled together near the front, although none of my regular circle. I'd been devastated at the end of last summer when most of my closest Camp Chance confidantes left the forest closer to eighteen than seventeen; closer to adults than being allowed back in next time the rainbow gates (seriously) opened to welcome another cohort. Sure, being here made me feel more *with-my-people* than pretty much anywhere else in the world, but the thing I hadn't been brave enough to admit yet was that I was scared this year . . . that when it came to Camp Chance, I'd actually never felt so alone.

```
LIVI doesn't notice LOUIS sliding into the
empty seat beside her until he's already
there. Until she's jumping as he speaks.
```

LOUIS: Livi Campbell.
LIVI: Louis.

Her cheeks redden. She looks pleased to see him; surprised by how pleased she is. LOUIS smiles. He's noticed. He gets it. A friendly face is a good thing. Besides, he's cute. Sandy blonde hair, and a smile that wouldn't look out of a place in a boyband - a smile that right now is directed solely at her.

LOUIS: You good?

LIVI nods.

LIVI: I'm on my way home. Of course I am.

LOUIS leans closer, serious; somehow doesn't cringe at her theatrics. Livi tenses, as if on alert for whatever he's about to say.

LOUIS: Have you heard?
LIVI: If you don't tell me what I'm supposed to have heard, how will I know if I've heard it?

LOUIS: We have a couple of celebrities in our midst.

My heart dropped.

It wasn't entirely unusual at Camp Chance for the children-of-famouses to be given a place because their rich West-End daddy paid for a lighting rig, or their casting-director mother promised to come to the showcase. They always showed up for a singular summer, usually got all the best parts, and disappeared at the end of the month with no promise to keep in touch, no real lessons learnt, no *idea* of the magic they'd been part of – not really. And this year, more than ever, I did not want them there. This could be my *last* year – one last summer fling before my parents forced me to 'grow up' and 'pick a real career'. Their words, of course, not mine. According to them, drama school was a waste of their money, and since I had no hope in hell of paying for it myself, I was at their mercy. This summer was my final chance to prove to them that I could do this – that if they let me really commit to performing, I might just make it. I'd been planning for this summer for years. Everyone knew that the seniors got all the best parts in the showcase, and I was finally a senior. Ready. Poised to work like hell for the whole of camp, then know that I'd earnt it if, when casting went up, the first name on the list was mine. It wasn't that I thought I was the best and, don't get me wrong, it was not about winning. I'd stand in the wings and be the first to give an ovation to *any* long-time camper who played the lead. We *all* deserved it. But the lead should go to someone who knew all the best camp legends without having to be told. Who wouldn't set foot in the star dressing room because of the superstition, who only hung out by the small lake because the big one had bad energy ever since Brown-Haired-Georgina pushed Blonde-Georgina in it because they both wanted the same part. Besides, I'd spent such a long time hearing from the counsellors that I was going to be the 'one who made it out', that I was supposed to 'believe in myself' because I had 'what it takes', and I wanted to live up to that. To prove that they'd been right to back me. That I *was* one of the lucky ones who got to take the thing she loved most in the world and make a life out of it. It would be their success almost as much as mine, and I didn't want to let them down.

The leads were for the people who became themselves at camp – had *been* becoming themselves for years – working, and waiting, and then working some more.

I was not letting *any* child-of-celebrity take that away.

'Who?' I asked, trying to keep my voice measured, but if the way Louis smirked was anything to go by, I was not succeeding.

'Aaron Wilson,' he said, looking completely smug to have been the one to tell me. Understandable. My jaw dropped.

'You're joking.'

Statement, not question, because he had to be. Aaron Wilson was like . . . *famous* famous. Louis shook his head. Apparently not a joke.

'Nope. He's sitting at the front of the coach.'

I immediately craned my neck to look, tried to pretend I wasn't, then decided I didn't care and committed fully. *Aaron Wilson!* His parents were Hollywood royalty and the word on the street, or at least in the entertainment press, was that Aaron was primed for the same. And now he was *here*. Suddenly I didn't hate the idea of celebrity children at Camp Chance at all. Imagine *Aaron Wilson* as my scene partner?! I was practically vibrating at the thought.

And then I remembered.

'Wait, you said a couple. Who else?'

'Juliet Stone?' Louis said, a question, as if he'd been told she was famous but didn't recognise the name. And there was the heart-drop again, because I had no such luck. I knew exactly who Juliet Stone was. The opposite side of my coin. My 'competition', because theatre, by its very nature, *was* a competition. Only one person could play each part, and even when you factored in understudies you were looking at a maximum of about four per coveted character. The odds were stacked against us, which meant we couldn't afford to be stacked against each other. Nobody wanted to be the one with the reputation; the one who wasn't happy for her peers. I was all about actors supporting actors; all about smiling and saying congratulations, knowing that my time would come. All about the idea that if *they* could do it, *I* could, if I just worked harder; got better. All about all of that, unless, apparently, the actor in question was Juliet Stone.

I didn't want to compete with her.

'Are you sure?'

'Who is she?' Louis asked, nodding.

'She makes theatre on the internet,' I said. 'She's got hundreds of thousands of followers; her whole thing is that theatre should be for everyone so she makes it for free and uploads it in digestible little chunks.'

'And we . . . *don't* like that?'

Louis sounded confused by my less-than-enthusiastic tone, which I guess made sense. On paper, of *course* I agreed with Juliet's philosophy. The more people who could access theatre, the stronger the industry would become, right? After the true terror of the pandemic years, when I'd had no camp, no trips to the West End, no new musicals at all, anything that helped it recover was something I was on board with.

Well, almost anything. There was something about what Juliet was doing that was a sticking point for me. I tried my best to explain.

'No, of course that's a good thing,' I began. 'But shouldn't theatre happen . . . you know . . . in a theatre?'

Louis smiled, although whether that was because he agreed with me or just because he could see what angle I was coming at this from, I couldn't be sure.

'Livi, if your TikToks are to be believed, you watched at least as many livestreamed shows as the rest of us over the last few years. Actually, let me revise that – *way* more.'

Ah. The smile was because he thought he was getting one up on me. His eyes were twinkling, daring me to argue. I smiled, held up my hands.

'Now that I can't deny.'

'But?'

Louis and I weren't particularly close, but even he knew me well enough to know I wouldn't let it go that easily.

'But that was when we had no other choice!' I could feel myself getting animated. 'Obviously I watched livestreams when the theatres were closed, but the minute they reopened I bought a ticket for *Jersey Boys*, that's how desperate I was. I wanted to show my support the very first chance I could. Show theatre how much we missed it.'

'You hate *Jersey Boys*.'

'I know!' I practically shouted.

The two girls in the seat in front of us turned to look at me. *Oops.* I gave them an apologetic smile and turned back to Louis, cheeks burning with the thought that Juliet herself might have heard me. That would have been mortifying.

'I wonder what she's doing here?'

The look on his face told me there was more where that came from, the worry lines between his eyebrows suggesting I wasn't going to like it.

'Don't shoot the messenger,' he said, holding his hands up, 'but I heard she's been offered a part as soon as she turns eighteen, on the proviso she has some proper training first.'

'What part? Who told you that? Camp – *our* camp – is the proper training?'

'Livi, keep it down,' Louis hissed, and I grimaced. He was right. This coach was loud, but the thing about multiple years of vocal training was that my voice carried even when I wasn't trying.

'Sorry,' I said. 'What part? Who told you that?'

'I heard it from Leah, who heard it from Sam,' he said. Leah and Sam were two campers I'd known for ever; had enough history with to count as casual friends, but who had never been part of my inner circle. It made sense that they hadn't told me. It wasn't like we spoke in the eleven months between camps.

'A heads up that us girls have no chance at showcase lead would have been nice,' I said, and Louis looked confused.

'That's what this is, Livi. Me giving you the heads up. And it isn't like us guys have it any better with the movie star being here. But anyway, Juliet might not be interested in getting the lead, or any of that. Maybe she's here to keep her head down and get in shape for whatever this part is.'

I scoffed.

'Like that'll matter to the counsellors! Maybe she'll be brilliant and I'll have to eat my words. Maybe she'll audition and blow us all away and get it fair and square. Maybe I'll walk away from here knowing we all did everything we could and the best girl won, but I don't think it's going to matter what she does at all, Lou. Can *you* see them giving up the chance to tell the press Juliet Stone is the principal girl in the summer showcase?'

Louis didn't answer, which was all the answer I needed.

Great. I turned my head to the window, pressed my cheek to the glass. I'd thought proving to my parents that I could do this would be the hard part; thought getting whichever part I deserved fair and square would be easy in comparison, but already the summer wasn't going as scripted. In the least-Livi move imaginable, I spent the rest of the journey in silence.

> The coach pulls into Camp Chance —
> through the rainbow gates that are
> the wrong side of cringe but which the
> campers love anyway. LIVI, who has been
> scowling since her conversation with
> LOUIS, begins to physically thaw —
> stretching; shaking out the tension.
> The girl with the phantom mask is
> silent now; awed.
>
> Even the air feels different — quiet.
> Charged. The perfect conditions for
> magic to brew.
>
> LIVI smiles to herself.
>
> **LIVI (*under her breath*):** Welcome home,
> Liv. Now, let's get to work.

CHAPTER 2

THE AIR WAS STICKY WHEN YOU STOOD STILL IN IT, so I kept moving towards the luggage collection area, desperately hoping to meet the forest breeze I'd spent the past year missing. No such luck – it was thirty-two degrees in the shade, and most of my fellow campers had stopped where they'd landed and were turning their faces up to the sun.

Well, if you can't beat them.

I was careful not to spend too much time in direct sunlight usually, knowing full well that the freckles I did my best to keep hidden would explode into life after five minutes of exposure, but the warmth did feel nice, and besides, there was make-up for that.

'Welcome to Camp Chance!' Celestia Sinclair was practically shouting every time a new camper got off the coach. It was probably supposed to be encouraging, but Celestia was an overwhelming presence at the best of times, so I smiled at one of the girls who looked like she was about to cry when faced with this human personification of a rainbow. Or a particularly over-excited puppy wearing bright pink Crocs. *So* Celestia. Former child star turned Head Counsellor at Camp Chance, she was pure sunshine . . . until she got comfortable with you, when she turned into a strict taskmaster. It wasn't because she was *horrible*. More because it was her job to make us all the best we could be, and I guessed that was how she'd been trained – tough love only from the directors and choreographers that had shaped Celestia's career.

'She calms down,' I assured the girl, who looked around my age. *Weird*. Aside from the occasional celebrities, we didn't really get new kids older than about fourteen, and this girl had to be sixteen at least. 'She can't possibly sustain that energy for the whole summer.'

The girl smiled back, grateful, I thought, for the interaction. I didn't tell her that if you asked most people around here, they'd tell you Celestia's vibes only got worse. It didn't seem fair to deprive her of the long-held Camp Chance tradition of finding that out for herself. I left her looking for her bags and moved on, stopping outside the reception cabin where Sophia was standing with Oliver.

'Hey!' she said, stepping away from him when she saw me, going in for a hug. 'Welcome back!'

For eleven months of the year, I was not a hugger. Quite the opposite – I tensed up if anyone touched me outside of a theatrical setting. Dance classes and rehearsals? Fine. Classmate trying to say hi? Absolutely not. I'd just never felt like a person who could pull casual hugging off. Never quite felt like I was reading the 'wrap your arms around them now' cues right. At Camp Chance, though? I opened my arms to Sophia gratefully. It felt good to be back with people who knew me.

'Thanks!' I said. 'Good to be here. Excited to get stuck in! Get to work!'

The expression on Sophia's face told me she knew exactly what I wasn't saying. *Excited to prove that I have what it takes. That I can do this.*

'Breathe, Livi,' Sophia laughed. 'There's time enough for all that.'

Of everyone at camp, I knew Sophia *got it*. Two years ago, she'd been in the same position, after all. The star camper. The one to watch. Except when the showcase came around, it wasn't her name at the top of the cast list. I don't know if it knocked her confidence beyond repair or maybe she was just never good enough in the first place, but when she left Camp Chance and started auditioning for drama schools, Sophia had been rejected by every one.

So.

She came back here, where she still got to be a star, and started working as Celestia's deputy. I hated that the industry could do that – could twist fate around so that someone who really deserved it, like Soph, ended up answering to someone who'd had their chance and let it make them spiky, like Celestia. It made me pity Sophia a bit, which I felt weird about. I loved having her here but, make no mistake, I was not going to end up like that.

'Remember to have some fun, Livi,' Sophia said, and I nodded along. It was impossible for me not to have fun at Camp Chance. Working hard *was* my fun. Sure, I also liked the parties – singing around the campfire was my favourite serotonin hit and staying up chatting until the embers went out made me feel a part of something like I never did back in London, but getting stuck in to some scene work with a partner who was equally passionate about acting? Nailing a dance routine after getting it wrong for hours? Hitting the high note every time? That was where I came alive. I was planning on having a *lot* of fun this summer.

CELESTIA: LISTEN UP, campers!

Her voice is high pitched, excited. In another scenario it might be described as screechy, but here it works. The gathered crowd, turning in her direction, are excited too. CELESTIA waits for the chatter to fade. Carries on.

CELESTIA: Welcome to Camp Chance! Welcome back to our veteran campers, and to our new recruits . . . welcome home.

She pauses, as if waiting for applause. The silence is awkward; goes on just a touch too long before LIVI starts clapping, despite what CELESTIA has said not technically making sense. It doesn't really help since only about three people join in. In fact, it makes the whole thing worse.

CELESTIA: For the next three weeks, you'll be trained by professionals at the top of their game in singing, dancing, acting and, most importantly, how to do all three at once.

She stops, as if she's made a joke, and LIVI laughs loudly. Once again, her efforts to people-please make it more awkward. For everyone.

CELESTIA: You'll all have chosen your specialities already, but it isn't *just* performing on the cards this summer. We'll have groups focusing on lighting, and set design, sound, and producing. You'll have guidance, of course, but everything that happens on stage during the final showcase will have been devised, built, and pulled off by all of you. *The silence, if silences can do such a thing, transitions from polite to awed. It happens like that every year, no matter how many times the assembled campers have heard it. Lived it. It is cool. They are the ones doing this. Making it happen.*

CELESTIA: On to a few ground rules, beginning with the most important. Camp Chance is a safe space. We will not tolerate discrimination of any kind against our campers. Zero — it's an automatic ticket home.

The silence, if silences can do such a thing, shifts from awed to serious.

CELESTIA: While you're here we want you to be able to be yourselves completely. We also have some campers with public presences and, for safety reasons, it's important that they're allowed to be here in private, without the press descending. That's why we say no photos which

identify your location and no video can
be posted, at all, for the duration of
your time here. At the end of the summer,
I can't stop you, but while you're my
campers, I want you present and focused,
not worrying about how you look on
someone else's social media. Got it?

The assembled crowd nods, and CELESTIA
smiles. She has them in the palm of her
hand, which happens to be her favourite
place to have people.

Celestia: Great. You'll learn more as
we go through, and if you ever want clarity
on how things work at Camp Chance you can
ask any of my counsellors at any time. For
now, though — who wants a tour?

Picking up my bags, I headed away from the rest of the group, keeping an eye out for Aaron and Juliet. I'd yet to set eyes on either, but I wasn't in any huge rush. Camp Chance was a small place. We'd run into each other before long.

'Where are you going?' Celestia called after me, and I gestured vaguely into the distance.

'To unpack!'

Celestia grinned. She knew as well as anyone that I didn't

need a tour; that her 'welcome home' spiel might have been stilted and weird but I *felt it* entirely. I knew this place like the back of my hand. Like the whole of my heart.

Better than either of those things, if I was being really honest.

'I'll be in my cabin,' I said, picking up my bag and walking towards the 'living area' without a backwards look.

Living area was not a particularly accurate description, since so little of the 'living' that happened at Camp Chance took place in the cabins. The stages were my living area – and the rehearsal barn, and the campfire, and the clearings you wouldn't know were there unless you'd been spending summers here since what felt like the beginning of time. I felt a pang in my chest. Without my friends, who was I going to meet by the willow trees – the small ones at the back of the site, not the ones everyone knew about – when I needed to vent? Who was going to lift me up when we'd been rehearsing for nine hours and I had nothing left to give, but needed to give a little more?

Who was I going to be sharing a cabin with?

I stopped short as the plaque on the door answered that question for me. Daisy Wright – a newbie, I assumed, since I didn't recognise the name . . . and Juliet Stone.

OK, then.

That felt like a test; a chance for the universe to prove me wrong. A chance for *Juliet* to prove me wrong, which was probably even worse.

Great.

CHAPTER 3

I WAS BUSYING MYSELF WITH UNPACKING MY SUITCASE into the far too small chest of drawers that Camp Chance provided when I heard the latch on the door click, and by 'busying myself with unpacking' I mean I was pretending to unpack but really on full alert, ready to turn around and do some casual *'Oh, you're my new roommate? Cool!'* acting when Juliet walked into the cabin.

Game face on, Livi.

Except the girl standing in the doorway looking lost was not the freakishly self-assured person I'd seen on social media telling the camera that the future of theatre was digital. It was the girl I'd met getting off the coach.

Powers of deduction told me this must be Daisy.

I took her in properly this time – light brown hair that hung just below her shoulders, and a kind face, wearing far less make-up than a lot of the Camp Chance girls got up early every morning to paint on before rehearsal. The bare-faced look suited her – she looked fresh when she smiled, as though nothing phased her, even though when the smile wavered I could tell she was probably nervous to be here. *Excellent* cheekbones, too. Who needed bronzer when your face just looked like that?

'Hi, again,' I said with a wave, pleased to see her. Daisy felt like the kind of person I could be fast friends with.

By which I mean, Daisy did not feel like a threat. I wasn't proud of what my insecurity had done to me.

'I'm Livi,' I said, holding out a hand for her to shake. Her palms were cold, despite the hot weather.

'I know,' she said. I tried not to show that I was thrown by that.

'How?' I asked.

'You're a Camp Chance legend,' she said, as if the answer was obvious. And while it was true that I'd been around long enough, and was good enough, to be one of the campers the counsellors might use that word about, I was failing to see how a complete stranger knew that. It freaked me out a little, actually.

'In what sense?'

'You're all over the YouTube channel!' she said, again like it was obvious, and now I thought about it . . . it actually was.

'*Oh!* You've been watching the past showcases?'

'Of course!' Daisy said. 'As soon as I found out this place existed, I watched everything I could get my hands on! I never dreamt I'd actually be good enough to – sorry, I'm fangirling, aren't I?'

'It's fine,' I assured her, since the object of her fangirling was camp itself rather than me. It was so much better than fine.

This was exactly what I'd needed from the summer – someone who would show Camp Chance the same reverence I did.

Who would *get it* eventually, even if they didn't know the history yet. I was starting to like Daisy Wright already. I gestured for her to come further into the cabin, and pulled the door shut behind her.

'You're in all of them,' she continued, like I didn't know that. Like I didn't watch them myself every time I needed to remember that the drudgery of school, and sub-par dance classes, and nights studying acting techniques from videos on the internet, was not my real life. This was.

'I've been coming here a long time,' I said – which was definitely part of it, but not the whole story. To say I worked hard would have been adding a little more to the picture, but still not everything. The truth – the bit I couldn't say out loud to this stranger yet – was that I was *good*. I knew that, logically, Celestia and co wouldn't have said I was good if they didn't think it was true, and I trusted their judgement implicitly. Besides, as much as it wasn't in my nature to believe so unreservedly in my own talent... I'd heard myself. I *knew*, even when I was unsure, that I might actually have a future here.

'Is it your last year?' Daisy asked, and the glow of the compliment vanished immediately. *Unspoken rule, Daisy! Never acknowledge to a senior that they'll soon be leaving, or ask what their plans are after the summer.*

'I'm trying not to think about that,' I said, my voice falsely bright. I was about to turn back to my half-unpacked suitcase when the door opened again.

It pained me to admit that Juliet Stone was even prettier in person. Her shoulder-length pink hair didn't look washed out like it did on most of the girls in my school who had tried it. She made it shine, somehow. It looked like it had grown out of her head that colour. She lifted a small hand, smiled a small smile.

'Hi,' she said. Small voice. Everything about her was surprisingly *small* given the energy in her videos. I wondered if she could turn it on whenever she needed to, and decided that she had to be able to, right? I could already tell she was a brilliant actor.

'Hi,' Daisy said back, rushing towards Juliet with a hand outstretched. 'I'm Daisy.'

'Jules,' Juliet said, which on anyone else could have been cringe, because she knew that *we* knew exactly who she was, but which she somehow pulled off.

'I'm Livi,' I said, and Juliet turned her small smile, small hands, full attention to me. She was *magnetic*. It was like I was the only person in the room. I knew that couldn't be taught, and I should have been jealous of it, but I wasn't. Who *was* this girl? How was she doing that?

'It's so nice to meet you,' she said.

'Likewise!' I meant it. 'What brings you here? You know – you've had loads of success already! No offence to Camp Chance, but what more are you looking for?'

No offence to you, Juliet Stone, but can't you leave something for the rest of us?

I kept my smile pasted on. Juliet grimaced.

'I don't have any actual training. That's fine when I'm making my own stuff, but if I want to start doing more mainstream work, I thought I should know how to function on a set. I've never really been in a theatre rehearsal room, or like . . . part of a cast. I want to make sure I'm doing it right when the time comes, and not just waltzing in like an idiot from the internet.'

Good answer. Damn this girl. Was I going to have to like her?

'Talking of success, though,' she said, leaning in conspiratorially. 'I spied Aaron Wilson getting off the coach. Does he come here?'

'Not usually,' I said, slipping easily into the trap of gossiping with Juliet.

'He was sitting near me,' Daisy piped up. 'He seemed really nice.'

'Oh yeah, I'm sure he's media trained to within an inch of his life to *seem really nice*,' Juliet said, and I let out a surprised laugh. She turned to look at me. 'Sorry, that was so bitchy. I get bitchy when I'm intimidated. *Aaron Wilson*. He's like . . . a proper star.'

'You're intimidated by him?' Daisy asked.

'By his family, yeah.' Juliet shrugged (small) as she answered, as if revealing her vulnerability to two people she'd just met was no big deal at all. I envied that. 'I sort of hate that he's here,' she continued, and now she was talking as if she was letting us in to a secret. 'I wanted to come and learn in private, you know? No pressure. And now Aaron Wilson has rocked up.'

Now you know how we feel, I wanted to say. Might have said, if I was feeling as loose-lipped as Juliet clearly was.

'He might want the same thing,' Daisy pointed out. 'I doubt you go places like this lightly when you're Aaron Wilson.'

'No, you come looking for attention,' I said. I felt bad as soon as it was out of my mouth, it sounded so unlike me, but Juliet looked at me like '*exactly*'. It made me feel warmer than it should have, which, if I'm honest, was why I'd said it. I was already craving her approval. We all had something to prove here, I realised. Perhaps I shouldn't judge Juliet too harshly on the video thing until she showed me what she was really made of. Perhaps, with her penchant for talking about her feelings, and her honesty about the things she thought she lacked, she was even the sort of person I could be friends with.

'So, who do you already know?' Daisy asked, her attention back on me having unpacked the final thing from her practically miniature suitcase. *How did everything she'd need for a whole summer fit in there?* 'From other years, I mean. There must be loads of you, right?'

I decided to take a leaf out of Juliet's book. To show them something real. Something I didn't like admitting.

'There are a few,' I said. 'Sam Chambers has been around a bit – tall half-Filipino guy, floppy brown hair, looks like a typical leading man and knows it. We're not really friendly though. We've always run in different circles. Louis, too. He was the guy sitting next to me on the bus, and he's really nice, although again, we're not close. I know Leah, she's the pretty Chinese girl I saw you talking to, Daisy, and some of the others have definitely been here before, but . . .'

Deep breath.

'But I don't really have any friends left here. Everyone in my friendship group aged out last summer or decided not to come back because they're focusing on exams, and . . . I'm feeling pretty alone here, if I'm honest.'

'Well, now you know us,' Daisy said without skipping a beat, and Juliet gave me another one of her small but mighty smiles.

'So,' I said, feeling like this room assignment might actually have been a stroke of genius on Celestia's part, 'how do you feel about a campfire party?'

'Like I can't believe we've spent the last ten minutes talking when we could have been doing that!' Daisy . . . cried. She cried. It was way too over the top, but I knew she was nervous and overcompensating because I'd *so* been there, so I flashed what I hoped was a reassuring smile.

'So, let's go!' I said, ushering them out of the cabin, Daisy in front of me, Juliet bringing up the rear.

'Show me to this "typical lead" of a man!' Juliet said as she swung the door shut behind her.

'Oh, don't you worry,' I promised. 'I can guarantee he'll be waiting for you.'

CHAPTER 4

Night. The Woods.
What were just trees and empty clearings
the last time we saw them light up as
LIVI, DAISY and JULIET enter. It's like
the moment in Wicked when everything
turns emerald. You thought that stage was
green before?

You thought Camp Chance was pretty,
in a 'fresh air and nature' kind of way?

Now it's beautiful.
Spectacular.

As if the forest itself is putting
on a show.

We see the festoon lighting strung between the trees long before the girls reach the campfire. Here's the thing about sharing a camp with a whole team of wannabe set designers — you can guarantee a gorgeous setting for a party. They must have been working all afternoon.

Smoke machines in various colours mark a path for our leading ladies to follow — LIVI in front, DAISY and JULIET following a step behind. A soundscape plays — a beautiful mashup of all the shows performed in last summer's showcase. LIVI shivers. Goosebumps.

DAISY: This is unreal!

LIVI turns to face her. Throws her arms wide.

LIVI: Welcome to Camp Chance, baby!

If it feels like all eyes are on the girls as they enter the clearing, it's because they are.

I was under no illusion that any of the stares were aimed at me. Apparently word had spread that Juliet Stone was here, and subtlety was not something Camp Chancers were naturally very good at – nobody even tried to hide the fact that they were looking. I had a quick glance around of my own, but it looked like our other celebrity was yet to join the party. *Still time*.

I spotted Sam sitting on the other side of the fire, his arm around Leah, who had been at Camp Chance as long as I had. They were sitting right beside the magic tent – once a showcase prop the year Celestia got really into circus acts after she saw Pippin on Broadway and made us perform practically the entire show – but far more famously a notorious Camp Chance hookup spot. The fabric door was hooked back so I could see nobody was in there, but the way Sam kept glancing over at it, in a way I bet he thought was subtle, suggested it wouldn't be long. Sam and Leah must have been in touch over the year, I thought. They looked very cosy for two people who hadn't seen each other since last summer. I raised a hand to them both, more to be polite than because I actually wanted to say hello. Sam returned the wave. He always had been good at playing the nice guy – *playing* being the operative word. Leah was too busy giving him heart eyes to even have noticed. Good for her, I guessed.

'Good to see you,' I mouthed, mostly sincerely, as I slid into a seat and Sam gave me a thumbs up.

'Same!'

As he turned his attention back to Leah, not that I cared

about who he spent his time with, I took the opportunity to look around at the people I'd be sharing stages with for the rest of the month. Bedazzled mask girl was back with a whole new outfit – this one a cross between Annie from . . . well, *Annie* (red dress) and Glinda from *Wicked* (completely insane wig that I was sure I recognised from the costume department). The bedazzled mask was still in her hand. Maybe it was some sort of safety blanket. I had no idea, but either she was having some trouble settling on an identity or she really liked attention. Knowing most of the people who came through Camp Chance, knowing myself, probably both. Good for her. One of her new friends was making a valiant effort to follow suit with a Heathers uniform, but it looked half-hearted in context, when there were at least three others that I'd seen around the fire. I rubbed the tattoo on my forearm almost subconsciously. It was hardly my place to judge when I'd had my own love for musical theatre permanently inked into my skin, completely illegally with a fake ID that looked nothing like me, and much to the dismay of my parents, who's first question was how I was ever going to get a job with a tattoo – like it was the nineties or something. I'd gone for a lyric from my favourite show, *Next to Normal*. 'There will be light'. It reminded me that no matter how dark things got, there was always a way back to this contentment. To the light, if you like. As long as I had theatre, I'd be all right.

I'd lost track of Daisy and Juliet already, not at all interested in joining the circus that was quickly forming around my new friend. *Friend?* I was reserving judgement on that one, but I had to admit that she was kind of hypnotic; was making me question everything I'd decided I knew before I met her. Either way, I couldn't stand all the gushing. They'd find me again when they wanted to, I knew. Until then I'd be OK here alone.

Or . . . not alone? I didn't notice Louis sliding in beside me again until he was already there, the slow grin spreading across his face a surefire sign that he'd already had his fair share of the spiked punch that was always a feature of Camp Chance parties.

'Having fun?' I asked, rhetorical, but I guessed that wasn't obvious since he answered in earnest.

'The best time! Even better now you're here.'

I rolled my eyes, smiling as I did it.

'You're a liability,' I said, but when he went to reach for my hand, I let him. Inched my fingers towards his. Encouraged it. Finding someone to spend the summer falling into was as much a part of Camp Chance as the performances – for most people, anyway. It was an unspoken acceptance that these relationships were just for the summer, so we didn't overthink them. We didn't have time. *Try it, and if you don't like it you can stop.* I wasn't entirely sure I was interested, but Louis was *cute*, and *nice*, and clearly liked me, and besides, it was my *last* summer. I wanted to experience everything camp had to offer. I'd be stupid not to see what happened, wouldn't I?

'You love it,' he said in return.

'We'll see.'

I meant it.

'So, when does the singing start?' Daisy asked, joining the circle on my other side, and I turned away from Louis for a second.

'Just as soon as someone starts it.'

'Shouldn't that be you?' she asked, grinning. 'Camp Chance royalty Livi – god, I don't even know your surname and I already feel like we're friends!'

'Livi Campbell,' I supplied.

'Leading lady Livi Campbell, would you be so kind as to lead us in a song?'

I had never been one to turn down an invitation to sing, so, after a quick toss-up between *Six* and *Rent*, during which I decided the answer was definitely both . . . I did.

The key to a successful Camp Chance singalong was that everyone should feel involved – no solos, nothing with notes that some of us couldn't hit in either direction. I began with 'Seasons of Love', pretty confident that everyone would know the words; that we were all the kind of people who *jumped* to answer when a maths teacher asked how many minutes there were in a year. We didn't need to type '(24x60) x 365' into our calculators, we'd known that since the first time we listened to *Rent*. We learnt from musical theatre songs the way other kids did from books.

Our voices took a second to find their place in the ensemble, but as we slid into instinctive harmonies and unwritten riffs, I felt something click. *This* was what I lived for.

The air was thick with smoke by the time the singalong finished. I'd be able to smell it on my hair for days, I knew, but I loved that. It was a tangible thing – I was really here again. This was really happening, if my hair smelt like smoke, and I was bone tired but couldn't stop smiling. I picked up a strand and sniffed it. Of *course* that was the moment Aaron Wilson, who I hadn't even noticed arrive, caught my eye. Raised an eyebrow. Smiled.

Great. Now the actual Hollywood celebrity thought I was some sort of weird hair sniffer. I smiled back like nothing out of the ordinary was happening, hoped it was dark enough that he couldn't see my cheeks redden, which I knew from the sudden heat of them they had.

It wasn't *just* the weird hair sniffing that was making me react like that. No – I was also struck by the fact that in the probably hundreds of photos of Aaron Wilson I'd seen in my life, he'd never seemed *quite* this good-looking. Obviously, I'd known he was hot – it was part of the reason (the other part being his very famous parents) that the press were ready to pounce every time he so much as breathed in a way that wasn't what they were expecting – but in person, he seemed *vibrant*. Alive. A whole world away from the boy who faked his smiles for the cameras and walked as quickly as he could past any waiting crowd. He was, if I had to guess, just over six feet tall, and his dark skin looked like it knew all about very expensive skincare. He stood out in the gathered company – Camp Chance tried their best to be inclusive, and were miles ahead of what I thought of as 'the real world', and definitely more progressive than the actual theatre industry outside of like ... every production of *Hamilton*, but the fact remained that the majority of campers here were still white, or white passing. It was a huge systemic issue, and one I'd seen Aaron's parents talk about in the press more than once as a reason why they moved away from theatre and into movies. I smiled back at him and he did this thing that was somewhere between an eyebrow raise and an actual eye-sparkle that said something like 'we'll unpack the hair sniffing later', then he turned back to whoever he'd been talking to before. I recognised the boy as Luke, one of the technicians who had been coming to camp almost as long as I had. He was a sweet boy, or at least he seemed it from the very few conversations we'd had, but from what I knew, he definitely wasn't interesting enough to warrant the way Aaron Wilson was looking at him right now. A look that, if I was a worse person, I could have sold to a tabloid and probably paid for an entire year of drama school. If it was happening anywhere else, I might have thought about it for more than a second before dismissing the idea as impossible. Because it was happening at Camp Chance, my sacred space, where aside from the showcase nothing that happened behind the rainbow gate had real consequences on the other side of it, I knew I couldn't have done anything about it even if I'd wanted to. Which I didn't. Honestly.

It would have been *really* easy, though. He was being so obvious.

Aaron's sexuality was no secret, but seeing him with an actual partner would be news all the same. I loved that he felt comfortable enough here to be who he was. To flirt openly. To sing along, *in harmony*, with the spirited rendition of 'Do-Re-Mi' now happening on his side of the circle. He *got it*. Maybe Aaron Wilson was about to be the second celebrity to prove me wrong today.

Dotted around the dwindling fire, I could see some of the younger campers beginning to flag. Bedazzled mask girl was clutching her bedazzled mask a lot less tightly than she had been all day, her eyelids drooping. I hoped one of her new friends would notice before she dropped it; would stop it from falling on the ground and shattering in a hundred different directions. It was a thing of beauty, I had to admit, even if she would probably be embarrassed that she ever wore it by the time she arrived back next summer. I could tell she *would* be coming back next summer – it was easy to spot the ones with the real passion. The ones who were in it for the long haul. They were the ones with the custom *Heathers* uniforms, the *Six* crowns. The bedazzled phantom masks. Mine had been an exact replica of Elphaba's act two hat. I wasn't too proud to admit it ever existed, but it hadn't been on my camp packing list since the end of that first summer. I didn't need it any more.

I looked around the fire for Louis, found him propped against a tree on the other side in what looked like a deep conversation with Leah and Sam. I was too far away to hear what they were saying, but could guess from the way Louis was gesticulating that it was something to do with how happy he was to be here. Or maybe I was just projecting.

'Ready to go?'

Juliet appeared by my side as I turned in the direction her voice had come from. She was smiling, her pinky-purple lipstick still perfectly applied even though it was somehow also all over the punch cup she was holding. Everything about her seemed so *curated*, but I didn't think it actually was – she carried herself so naturally. I hated being jealous of other performers, but I had to admit that I really *was* with her. She was completely authentic, I thought, and wasn't that supposed to be the end goal? She made it hard to remember why I'd been so wary of her.

'Yeah, where's Daisy?'

Juliet pointed across the clearing and my jaw dropped when I followed her finger with my eyes. *Daisy* was talking to *Aaron Wilson*. It looked, from the way they were leaning their heads together, laughing, that they'd been talking for a while.

'How did that happen?' I asked, incredulous, and Juliet laughed.

'I know, right? She had about two sips of her punch and just went over! Said he seemed "sweet" on the coach and why should we treat him any differently just because he's famous!'

'Good for Daisy,' I said, raising my barely touched drink to clink against Juliet's almost empty one.

'Good for Daisy!'

As if she'd heard her name, Daisy looked up and waved in our direction. Excusing herself from Aaron, as if she was the coolest girl in the world and his celebrity didn't phase her at all, she joined us.

'What?'

'You're friends with Aaron Wilson now?' I asked, and Daisy grinned.

'Yeah, I think I might be.'

'Shall we?' Juliet asked again, and now I looked more closely I could see the dark circles under her eyes. She was tired. I guess we all were. It had been a long day.

'One second,' I said, grabbing a napkin from the drinks table and pulling a pen out of my pocket. 'I'll catch you up.'

Was I sure I wanted to do this? I tried to swallow down the sick feeling as I scrawled out the note; tried to decide what I was actually asking.

Oh, just do it, Livi. One last summer, remember? One last chance for going after the things you want, experiencing it all.

I took one last look at the message before I folded up the napkin.

'*Meet me in the rehearsal barn at midnight.*' That would do. I could explain the rest later. I crossed the campfire in the direction Daisy and Juliet had left in and, as I passed, I dropped the note into his lap.

Your move.

'Good first day?' I asked as Juliet lazily wiped her make-up off, already lying under her duvet.

'Really good,' she said, discarding the cotton wool pad and closing her eyes. 'I didn't realise how natural it would feel to be making things with other people instead of just on my own in front of a camera. Didn't even realise I was missing it.' Her speech was slow and sleepy, but I couldn't resist engaging her on this; couldn't pass up the chance to dig into why Juliet did what she did.

'What made you start?'

Juliet didn't open her eyes to answer.

'Vlogging? The internet stuff?'

'Mmm.'

'I was sick of people like me not being able to access good art because of where we live, or because we don't have any money,' she said. I was willing to bet the money thing wasn't an issue for her any more. I'd seen some of the sponsored posts she did; knew that these things *paid*.

'I totally agree,' I said, 'but don't you think theatre needs to be experienced live? Isn't it about making that an option rather than turning your back on it entirely?' My heart was pounding as I spoke. It was low level, sure, but I'd never been good with confrontation. Juliet opened her eyes. Shrugged a small shrug.

'No.'

No?

'I think you can get as much from filmed theatre as you can

from live. What makes it theatre? It's not just that it happens in person, right?'

'Well, no,' I said, 'but don't you think—' I was cut off as Daisy came out of the bathroom, scrubbed and changed, and pointed towards the open door.

'All yours.'

'What time is it?' Juliet asked, smiling to let me know she was letting me off the hook. But I didn't want to be let off the hook. I wanted to talk about it; to show her she was wrong – that there *was* still something to be said for sitting in the dark of an auditorium and having a collective experience. I wanted to make sure I was as right as I thought I was. I'd been known to go miles down a rabbit hole in the past before realising that the other side of the argument also had some good points, and I was making a conscious effort not to do that any more. Not with this. Not with something as important as theatre.

'11.36,' Daisy said.

Crap. That changed my focus fast. For my plan to work, I needed them asleep in the next twenty-four minutes. That clearly wasn't going to be a problem for Juliet, who could already barely get a sentence out, but Daisy, with her sunny personality, seemed like the kind of girl who'd want to stay up talking, bringing the sleepover vibes but with less gossiping about boys and more about *Bonnie and Clyde*. The musical obviously, rather than the actual historical figures. Any other summer I'd have been right there with her, but this was not any other summer. Luckily, I was a very good actor. I turned to face her.

'Don't feel you have to wait up for me to get ready,' I said, forcing out a yawn despite the fact that I felt wired. 'You know what camp is like – we're going to need all the sleep we can get before rehearsals start tomorrow. I don't want you to be lying awake waiting for me, only for me to fall asleep in seconds.' I smiled, one of my sweetest, to really hammer home the *I'm just thinking of you* vibe I was going for. It seemed to work, since Daisy returned the smile and started climbing into her bunk.

'God, do they work us that hard?' She asked. 'I'm a bit nervous.'

Oops. Too far?

'You'll be totally fine,' I promised. 'It is hard work, but it's so worth it. You're going to love every second, I know you are.'

That seemed to do the trick.

'Thanks, Livi,' she said. 'I'm glad you're here – clearly you love it because you keep coming back, so that's a good sign.'

And now I felt like a terrible person.

Closing the bathroom door behind me, I looked in the mirror. Hair looking good – I'd had it blow-dried yesterday so I didn't have to touch it much during the gruelling first week, and I had to admit the stylist had done a great job. I'd never dyed my hair – the chocolate-brown tone of it might have looked like it came out of a box but it was completely natural, and one of my favourite features. I did look a bit tired, so I pulled a concealer out of my toiletries bag and made quick work of hiding the dark circles, giving my face a bit of a lift. It was part of the job, I reminded myself. I had to know how to look after myself if I was going to be an actor and have my face on underground posters promoting my shows. A tiny slick of mascara, the ghost of a layer of lip gloss, and I was done. I pulled my pyjama bottoms on over my leggings and put a hoodie over the T-shirt I'd already been wearing, just in case Daisy was still awake when I left the bathroom.

I didn't have to worry about that. They were both asleep when I crept back into the room.

'Daisy?' I whispered, just checking. She barely stirred.

'Juliet?'

Nothing.

Show time.

I opened the cabin door as quietly as I could and stepped out into the almost-midnight air, closing it behind me with a barely audible click. I realised my mistake as soon as I was out of the door. I forgot how absolutely *freezing* these woods got at night, but I couldn't risk going back in for a jacket and waking Daisy or Juliet. Then we'd be back to square one, except I'd have been caught red-handed and have to come up with a lie, so that would be more like square minus... some huge number. Square Not Good.

I'd stay cold.

I was pretty impressed with how quietly I managed to navigate my way past the rest of the cabins, my quick footwork from a lifetime of dance classes carrying me past the rooms where my fellow campers were sleeping... or doing god knows what else. I was sure I saw the back of Aaron's head through the window of what I assumed was Luke's cabin. Good for them. They wouldn't be the first out-of-place campers I saw on this journey, I could almost guarantee it.

I could see the light on long before I reached the barn and I felt a grin spread across my face, my heart rate picking up. It had worked. It was like I was a moth and the light spilling from underneath the wooden door was my flame, completely magnetic, pulling me so fast I almost tripped, until I was running up the steps and pulling open the door, practically launching myself into the rehearsal room, and he was standing there.

'Chambers,' I said, forcing a smile.

'Livi Campbell,' Sam said back, matching it.

CHAPTER 5

Rehearsal Barn. Midnight.

Lit by uplighters, because theatre people know nothing better than smoke and mirrors. They know how to draw the eye to where they want you to look. They're good at hiding what they don't want you to see.

Anyway.

LIVI and SAM. Centre stage. Where they belong. But that's getting ahead of ourselves.

SAM: How was your year?
LIVI: Stop talking. Doesn't matter.

She walks towards him, still smiling.
Holds out her hand for a reluctant
high five. Awkward.

LIVI: We don't have time. We're here to work.

Spotlight on SAM as he raises his
eyebrows, followed by his hands.
A surrender.

SAM: Well, clearly you have a plan, Miss Campbell. Go on then, how do you see this working?

How I saw this working was as follows:

If this was my last year as a performer, I wanted to step back onto the coach at the end of the summer knowing I did *everything* I could. That I was the best I could possibly have been, no matter if I got the lead or not. That, if it didn't work out, it wasn't because I hadn't tried hard enough, it was because someone else was better and deserved it more. There were always going to be people better than me. I couldn't control that. What I *could* control was how I responded. How hard I worked. And for that, I needed a scene partner. I needed Sam. Unfortunately. Just like we were tonight, once our cabin mates were asleep, Sam and I would meet here to rehearse. We'd go as long as we could until one of us was falling asleep, or the sun was coming up, or both. Or until we got caught, I suppose. It was a risk, and I had no idea what the counsellors would do if they found us, or if what we were doing was technically even against the rules, but we needed all the help we could get.

If you asked the counsellors, Sam and I were the epitome of leading man and lady last year. Paired together for everything, almost universally praised for our performances on stage. We were so good I didn't think any of the staff even realised that we were constantly performing *off* stage, too. Pretending we could tolerate each other. Pretending I *hadn't* completely misread the signals and – well, anyway. We were *good*. We were just waiting for our senior year to get the parts we deserved. Now the competition had stepped up – of *course* the counsellors were going to see Juliet and Aaron as the leads before we'd even begun.

That's why I wrote the note.

One last summer.

One last chance to experience everything.

I had a hunch that Sam Chambers felt the same, despite the fact that right now he was looking at me like I'd lost my mind.

OK . . . I can turn this around.

'Juliet and Aaron are going to walk out of here at the end of the summer and have the careers they were always going to have,' I said. 'She's got a role lined up, although she hasn't told me what, and he's from a literal Hollywood family. They don't need this, Sam. We *need* this. Think about it – it would make life easier with your family, right? If you got the lead?'

I knew the pressure Sam was under from his mother's family back in the Philippines, where the legacy of successful musical theatre actors ran stronger than maybe anywhere in the world. It was what they'd always wanted for Sam and, in a rare case of the stars completely aligning, it was exactly what he wanted too. No pressure. Not like they were all counting on him or anything.

'You know it would,' he said, still sounding confused. 'And it would prove a point with yours too, right?'

Everyone who had been around Camp Chance long enough to have had even the briefest conversation with me knew the deal with my parents. It wasn't that they weren't supportive – they'd been paying for me to come here every summer for the last few years after all, and were pretty understanding that acting class took priority over homework, but sometimes it felt like they were using all that support as their ticket out when the time came to really dedicate my life to theatre. Like because they'd been onside while they could pretend it was still a hobby, it meant they didn't have to be when I tried to make a life out of it.

'*We've supported you for ever,*' it was like they were saying, '*but don't you think the time has come to grow up?*'

The plan had *always* been to smash this senior showcase; to prove that there was no back up option. And now Aaron and Juliet had come along, and probably ruined that without even trying.

'Right,' I said in answer to Sam's question. 'And here's the thing. I've spent the past four summers listening to everyone here tell me I *can* do this, and I do believe them. I want to believe them, I mean. I want to be the person they all think I am and make them proud, but even without this plot twist I was worried about falling short, and *with it* . . . well, no offence to our celebrity guests – it's not even about them, I'm sure they're both lovely people – but we're going to need all the help we can get, Sam. Why aren't you saying anything?'

It came out snappier than I'd intended, and Sam held his hands up again.

He was still looking at me like I'd lost my mind . . . but like maybe he was willing to lose his too?

'Woah, why the aggression?'

'If that's what you call aggression, you've lived a very sheltered life,' I said, which made him smile and, I thought, choke back a laugh. One point to me. 'I'm just saying, we don't have time – are you in or not?'

'I know,' he said, the ghost of a laugh playing across his lips. 'You don't have to be so . . . Livi. I already agree with you.'

Oh. OK.

'So, you're in?'

Sam didn't answer. Instead, he made his way over to the grand piano in the corner; made a show of running his hands along the lid, of lifting it, of pressing down on one key, another, one more, before he sank onto the stool, poised his hands to play, and finally looked up at me.

So dramatic.

I loved every second. Hated that I loved it.

'I'm in,' he said. 'Now, where do you want to start?'

It was impossible to predict this early in the summer what direction Celestia and Sophia would go in for the showcase this year. Impossible, that is, unless you were me. Unless you'd seen the direction they went in every other summer and honed perfect powers of deduction to work out that last year had leant towards the traditional, so this year we could count on the material being more contemporary. That last year the ensemble pieces had been male heavy, so this year it was the girls turn. That they were both pretty basic and followed the trends of the wider industry, so we'd be belting high and loud, two things that were thankfully well within my wheelhouse. I pulled out the music folder I'd been prepping for pretty much the whole year and put it down in front of Sam, admittedly the far better pianist of the two of us in that he could play a little bit and I couldn't at all.

'Let's start with these,' I said, hoping he wouldn't notice that they were all very Livi-focused. His smirk as he flipped through told me he already had.

Sam put his fingers to the keys, and we began.

First run through, first song. My voice wasn't warm yet but I sang through it anyway, trusting that it would come. Knowing that the only way to get better was to never quit, even when it was past midnight, even when I'd been up since six, even when Sam was looking at me like *are you sure you want to do it again*?

Screw him. I was sure. With every pass of the song (it was

'Heart of Stone', from *Six*, because that was the first piece in the folder rather than because I particularly liked singing it), I could feel myself getting stronger. Shedding the year. Leaving it all on the stage, as they say. Coming back to Livi.

It took longer than I would have liked, but it was always like this on the first day back, I reminded myself. It was a muscle, and yes, I made sure to keep mine exercised back at home with weekly singing lessons and drama clubs, and Saturday dance workshops, but none of them were the same as being here. The expectations were so much lower, my classmates so much less experienced. They were doing it for *fun*, and it *was*, but it was so much more than that to me. If I cracked on a note in a class back home, the teachers would be encouraging, supportive, tell me it *didn't matter* or that I could *try again*, not quite understanding that on stage there was no *again*. In front of an audience, you didn't get a second chance. I had to be good *all* the time. I didn't want them letting me off for fumbling a dance move or missing a line. They told me I had potential, as if that was enough, but if you asked me, potential meant nothing at all unless someone was teaching you how to reach it. I had never been one of those performers who got it right every time, no help needed. So yes, I wanted to do this for ever, but the unspoken worry, the thing I'd never told *anyone*, was that I was scared I'd never be good enough. That I'd do whatever it took to get there, in the hope that putting in the hours would work. Try to ignore the ever-present fear that it wouldn't.

Somewhere around the sixth time through the song, which

made me laugh considering what I was singing, I felt it happen. I was my best self again, emotionally if not technically. All that was left to do now was take it even further.

Make my best even better.

'Aren't you tired yet?' Sam asked as 2 a.m. approached, and I looked at him like he was from another planet. *Tired?* This was the most alive I'd felt in a long time. My voice was on fire, my acting choices spot on, and my chemistry with Sam, which was the bit I'd been the most worried about after a year away from pretending to like each other, was electric. He made a *perfect* scene partner. I'd chosen well, for both of us.

But also, yes, I was tired.

'A bit,' I admitted, and that was Sam's cue to close the lid of the piano and spin his legs around on the stool so he was facing me.

'Do you really think we can do this?' he asked. 'Do you really think we can get so good that the leads go to us rather than them?'

'We have to get so good that the counsellors don't have a choice,' I said sharply.

Did I really think we could? I wasn't ready to answer that.

'Livi, we're on the same side. No need to snap!' He sounded confused, which was fair since I hadn't actually meant to be snappy. It was just my natural reaction to him. A defence mechanism after what had happened last summer, when I'd tried to kiss him at the closing night party, and he, who had been linked with so many other campers of all genders, apparently decided that Livi Campbell was where he drew the line. He'd rejected me. Everyone had seen, or at least that was how it had felt. There was no coming back from that, no matter how well we acted like there could be.

'I'm sorry,' I said, my tone more even. 'We have to get so good that the counsellors don't have a choice,' I repeated. 'No snapping here.'

He smiled.

'And what if Juliet and Aaron get that good too?'

'Then we know we tried,' I said. It sounded like a weak alternative. I really hoped it wouldn't come to that.

CHAPTER 6

IT FELT LIKE I'D BARELY PUT MY HEAD ON THE PILLOW when the site-wide alarm went off at 7 a.m. the next morning, ready for the first official day of camp. I put my best 'refreshed and ready' face on – it involved a lot of concealer, three different types of highlighter, and saying how excited I was to get started at every opportunity, so Juliet and Daisy wouldn't think for a second that I'd actually got started last night.

If you asked me, it was foolproof – even if it did bring with it a heavy serving of guilt.

If I was honest, their lack of suspicion was probably more to do with the fact that they were dealing with their own stuff than my excellent acting.

'I'm so nervous,' Daisy said when I passed her going into the bathroom, and she held up her hands to show me that they were visibly shaking.

'You've got this,' I promised her. 'They don't let people in if they don't think you're good enough.'

I meant it sincerely – she had to have *something* to have even made it onto the coach, but the look on her face told me I may have touched on an insecurity.

'Sorry, I feel like I just made it worse,' I called after her as she walked away, and she turned back to smile at me but didn't say I hadn't. *Great.* Not the start to the day I wanted.

By the time I'd finished getting ready I was running too late for a sit-down breakfast, so grabbed a coffee and a pastry on my way to the first music rehearsal. All the performers were included in this one, a chance for Celestia and Sophia and the rest of their crew to see who suited what – which kids were the ones to watch, who they wanted to pair with who in the hope of creating magic. Once they'd established all of that, we'd be split into much smaller groups based on our strengths, coached by the experts in our chosen fields, prepped and primed until we were the best that they could make us, then unleashed on the showcase audience so that the counsellors could show off all of their hard work. There was almost as much at stake for them as there was for us.

Almost.

I could not be late.

I caught Sam's eye as I walked into the rehearsal barn. We'd cleaned up after ourselves perfectly – you'd never know we were there just hours before. He smiled at me and I returned it quickly, before forcing my face back to a neutral expression. Our secret had to stay a secret, and besides, I wasn't going to forget our past that easily. We needed each other, that was all. I spotted Juliet walking in just after me – she'd already left by the time I peeled myself out of bed this morning, so I hadn't had a chance yet to feel her vibe; to see how committed she was to being Juliet Stone here. Capital J, capital S. How committed she was to being the star.

Sliding into a front row seat between Daisy and Juliet, I picked up the running order for the rehearsal and felt a wave of relief rush over my body when I saw the song list. At first glance, almost every single one was already in my folder. I'd judged it *exactly* right. I felt really good about the rest of this summer. I wanted to turn round to find Sam again, to see if he'd noticed the same, but I didn't dare. No matter. The warm glow that seemed to be spreading up my back, to my cheeks, pulling my mouth into a grin would be enough until we got a chance to talk.

```
Rehearsal Barn. Morning.


CELESTIA is standing on a makeshift stage
(podium made out of shipping pallets) at
the front of the room. As she speaks, the
excited hum that had filled the room a
moment before is swapped for silence.
It has officially started.

CELESTIA: Welcome to your first rehearsal
of Camp Chance!
```

It is so basic it might as well have been scripted, but more than one camper has visible goosebumps.

CELESTIA: It all starts here. From here on out, you'll rehearse for eight hours a day, exactly as you would if you were working professionally. Like I told you yesterday, it won't all be singing and dancing – at Camp Chance, our aim is to give you a complete overview of all the ways you might be involved in the theatre, so if you change your mind about performing . . .

Or if it doesn't happen for you, the campers fill in silently.

CELESTIA: If you change your mind about performing, you know there are other options. You'll have classes in stage management, and technical theatre. You'll learn about costumes, and design, and producing. You've already declared your areas of interest, and those will take up most of your time, but you have

nothing to lose by branching out a bit.
Seeing what you find.

SOPHIA: Now, though, let's get to work
with our first piece of music.

*The campers open their folders as if
it's choreographed.*

The work begins.

Daisy, despite her insecurities, was really good. She was tentative in her performance, sure, but I thought she had *it*. The thing that made the difference between theatre being a hobby and a lifestyle. When she looked in my direction, I gave her a thumbs up – and meant it. I was pleased for her. I loved watching people find their place here.

Most people, anyway.

But even Juliet seemed so far to be less of a threat than I'd thought. There was no denying she had star quality – it was a struggle to keep my eyes off her and on my own music – but she seemed distracted, and a lot less interested in spotlight-hogging than I'd worried she would be. It was as if her mind was elsewhere – she was looking around the room as if trying to work something out. As if she was waiting for something to happen.

'You all right?' I asked her in the first break, and it was like watching her turn Juliet Stone back on. The switch was almost seamless, but I saw it. She was definitely distracted.

'I'm fine,' she said with a smile. 'Just tired. I don't sleep well in unfamiliar beds.'

Well, *that* wasn't true, since she'd been out for the count when I left to meet Sam *and* when I came back. I decided to drop it for now. Maybe she was just nervous. Most of the theatre she made involved her alone in her bedroom, after all. She was as new to working with an ensemble as I was to uploading monologues to the internet.

I'd keep an eye on her. I may not agree with all of her philosophies, but the last thing I'd want is for anyone to come to Camp Chance and not get the most out of it. If you were here, you'd feel the magic. I'd make sure of that.

But how does that sit with the fact that you don't want *her to get the lead?*

Simmer down, I told the voice in my head. It wasn't that I didn't want her to get the lead if that was what she deserved. I just felt bad for the rest of us, who had been working our butts off for years to get these specific powers-that-be to notice us. It didn't seem *fair* for Juliet to walk in, so much more poised and polished than any of us, and steal the chance away from under our noses without even trying. *Shake it off.* I tried to force my body to relax, but I felt tense. Conflicted.

'All right!' Sophia bellowed when we finally reached the end of the rehearsal, voices tired, eyes drooping, hearts full. I could only speak for myself, but by the expressions on everyone else's faces, I was pretty sure they all felt the same. 'Well done, campers! You made it through the first rehearsal, but don't get complacent. There are many more where that came from. The key now is keeping up your stamina, so I advise you to have your dinner then get some sleep.'

A laugh swelled from the veteran campers. Everyone knew that the second-night party was the stuff of Camp Chance legend. Once the counsellors were done with the formalities, and we'd started settling into life as it was going to be for the next month, everyone could take a breath. Relax for a night. Start getting to know the people who, by the end of the summer, could be as close as family.

Nobody was getting any sleep. Not for a good few hours yet, anyway.

'Why are they laughing?' Daisy asked in a hushed voice.

'There's a party,' I told her. 'I wasn't going to go . . .' True, I wasn't. I knew it wasn't good for my voice, and I thought I should probably get some rest in before I met up with Sam later.

'Oh *please*, Livi,' Daisy said, and as I looked at her, I saw how the night could unfold. We'd stay up chatting around the fire, talking about how much we loved theatre, and how nobody in our 'real' lives would ever really understand. There would be singing, obviously, and dancing, probably, and definitely a whole lot of laughter. She might introduce me to Aaron Wilson. Besides, she looked like she genuinely wanted me to be there, and I really liked being included. It wasn't something I felt a lot from my friends back home. I was never around long enough to really feel like part of a group – always rushing off to the next class, or the next practice. Here I could *belong*, if I just gave myself the chance to.

I didn't want to let Daisy down, but, more important than that, I didn't want to let myself down either. I wanted to walk out of here on the last day of camp knowing I did it all.

One last summer.

Experience everything.

'Fine,' I said, smiling.

I was going to the party.

CHAPTER 7

Woods. Night.

Cabins are lit from within and we see various campers through the windows. Hairbrushes, being used both as hairbrushes and microphones; make-up being swapped; singing in showers and mirrors, the voices just as strong as the ones on the soundtracks they are singing along to.

A 'Getting Ready' montage brought to life.

If the vibe of the official welcome party was decadent and dreamlike, tonight's festivities were a lot more... downmarket. The second-night party was supposed to be a secret, but since it had been happening as long as I'd been coming here, and by all accounts a lot longer than that, there wasn't a counsellor in the whole forest who didn't know what was going on.

Still, we played pretend. It was what we did best, after all.

It went like this:

After dinner, everyone headed back to their cabins as if they were taking Sophia's advice and turning in for the night. This usually social group were barely looking at each other as we said goodnight and vaguely directed calls of 'see you in the morning' were thrown around, until everyone was out of the counsellors' earshot.

Somewhere between the dining hall and the cabins, the plan was hatched.

A senior would volunteer, or more likely be nominated by consensus of the others, and that person would be our captain for the night. This year it was Sam. Of course it was Sam. Our leading man personified, he'd be the one to keep watch until the coast was clear of counsellors – and, as soon as it was, to spread the word. For that he'd need his cabin mate. In this specific situation, one Aaron Wilson.

When Sam gave the signal, Aaron would run to the nearest cabin and knock three times. That would be the cue for whoever was inside to take the metaphorical baton – to run to the next cabin and do the same. Once each person's knock was done, they'd hotfoot it to the campfire where Sam would be waiting, throwing together a makeshift drinks table with whatever we'd all been able to sneak in in our cases. As people arrived, they'd be given a job – lights, music, starting the fire. By the time the last people rocked up at the clearing, it would be transformed into something if not as surface-level gorgeous as last night, then at least a rustic kind of magic that felt more *us* than the show we put on under supervision.

I was halfway through doing my make-up when the knock came. I looked at my clearly unfinished face in the mirror, wondering if you could tell. You absolutely could, but I didn't have time to fix it. Personally, I didn't think the counsellors would even care if they caught us sneaking out, but that wasn't in the spirit of the night. Besides, there was always the chance that if you were the one caught, they'd choose to make an example of you. Punish you. Take away your chance of playing the lead; prove to you that in the real world it was never *just* about talent. Everything you were, everything you did, could play a part.

Not that I'd spent a long time worrying about just that or anything.

I sighed and turned off the tap. Time to go.

'You guys leave now – go to the clearing,' I told Juliet and Daisy as I walked back into the bedroom where they were both trying on jackets. As the longest serving camper in the cabin, it was my job to do the knocking – to be the one to pass the baton on. 'I'll be right behind.' I didn't wait to make sure they'd listened as I opened the door and grinned at Leah, who had clearly been the one to knock, as she flew off in the other direction having seen me coming, knowing her work here was done. I could smell smoke in the air already – Sam was making quick work of that fire. I knocked hard on the door of the next cabin along, pressed my face to the window to make sure they'd heard me. Louis waved, then gestured for me to wait. I saw him jogging to the door.

'Excited?' he asked as he pulled on his trainers, ready to take over, to rally the next cabin. He'd done something different with his hair, I noted. It suited him.

'Yeah,' I said, surprised to find I meant it more than I'd thought I would. I needed this; to let out some of the tension I was clearly holding from the year gone by, and from my hopes for the summer. It would do me good to relax for a night.

'Well, I'll see you there,' he said, taking my wrist in his hand briefly. The warmth of his fingers made me smile. I was getting used to Louis faster than I'd expected.

'Go!' I said, pushing him away in the direction he should have been running. The smile was still on my face when I walked back past our cabin towards the fire and saw Juliet rummaging in her suitcase – *wait*, why was Juliet still in the cabin? I barged back through the door and she almost jumped out of her skin.

'Sorry! Sorry, it's just me!' I shouted before she could scream or do something else that made us even more likely to get caught. 'What are you doing here? We need to go!'

'Sorry!' Juliet said, slamming the lid of her suitcase shut like whatever she'd been looking for was definitely not for my eyes. 'I forgot my camera! I just came back for it! I'm ready now.' She held it up, as if to prove herself. That made sense. Of course she was filming all of this, ready to twist it into a piece of theatre for her channels when she got home at the end of the summer.

I didn't know yet how I felt about that, but I also didn't have time for her excuses – if we took much longer, I was sure one of the others would come looking for us and the whole game could be up. I'd be watching, though, I promised. If anyone was going to break Celestia's golden 'no posting until we left' rule, I thought it might be Juliet Stone.

'Livi!' Daisy called as I walked into the clearing, Juliet on my heels. We'd been running too fast to say much, but still, Juliet had seemed quieter than usual. I was pleased to see Daisy, knowing she'd carry the conversation as far as we needed her to. She always seemed to know what to say. I looked to her right and saw she was sitting next to Aaron. I felt my cheeks warm. This was going to be a fun night.

'Hey!' I said, walking towards them. 'I'm Livi. Campbell.'

'Aaron Wilson,' Aaron Wilson said, like that was a normal way to introduce yourself. Which, for him, I guessed it was.

'Nice to meet you.'

I sank into the empty seat on Daisy's other side. I didn't see where Juliet went.

'So, what brings you to Camp Chance?' I asked, and settled in, elbows on knees, as I leant forwards to let Aaron tell his story.

```
AARON smiles, warm, as if he doesn't mind
telling this at all.

AARON: Nice to go somewhere nobody is
sticking a camera in my face.
```

> Silence. Nobody had expected an honest
> answer. Aaron breaks it with a laugh.
>
> **AARON:** It's fine. Actually, it's not
> fine, that's the point - I've stopped
> pretending it's fine and started telling
> it like it is. It's nice to go somewhere
> I can just be Aaron, and not Aaron
> Wilson.

I mentally scrubbed the 'Wilson' I'd added to his name in my head.

'That must be hard,' Daisy said, leaning over, and he gave her a smile like *yeah, you get it.* I was a bit jealous. I *got it* too. Why was she getting all the Aaron Wilson smiles?

The Aaron *smiles,* I reminded myself. *He's just* Aaron.

'It's fine,' he said again, then grimaced as if he was so used to saying that, he was going to have to correct himself every time. 'It's a bit of a first-world problem, isn't it? I don't know if I want to be a famous actor, and I sort of want to figure that out . . . not in public. If that's as hard as if gets, I'd say I'm doing all right.'

I looked at him, my eyes widening so much that I knew I should be embarrassed. I probably looked like they were about to pop out of my head. He *didn't want* to be a famous actor? What was he doing here, then?

'I didn't mean to say that bit out loud,' Aaron said quietly, planting his hand over the top of the plastic cup he was holding, as if he was afraid another sip of whatever was in there would loosen his lips even more. Which was weird, because I'd read in an article that he didn't drink, so I was pretty sure it was just Coke.

'We won't tell anyone,' Daisy promised, and I remembered my own promise from the night before. If it happens at Camp Chance, it's sacred. Besides, he was nice. I wasn't going to be the one to tell the press he wasn't interested in the path they'd chosen for him, and probably ruin his life.

'Can we change the subject?' he asked.

Happily.

Aaron was so easy to talk to. We fell quickly into a deep analysis of the shows we loved, and I was relieved to find that even though he (maybe) didn't want to *work* in theatre, dissecting other people's work to within an inch of its life was still very much on his list of hobbies. I could feel some of the younger campers – the girl with the bedazzled phantom mask, which she still had in her hand; one of the three Heathers from last night; another girl I hadn't noticed before hovering on the edge of our group. At first, I'd assumed they were waiting for their moment with Aaron, ready to swoop in and ask for a selfie that I hoped he'd be comfortable enough to refuse but expected he would not. I felt protective of him suddenly – wanted his camp experience to be everything he needed – and if that meant shielding him from excited fans, I was up for the challenge. But that moment had arrived and passed more than once and the girls hadn't made their move, their eyes instead flitting between Daisy and I as if they were waiting for something from *us*.

Ah. They were looking for Juliet.

I had no idea where she'd gone, so shielding her wasn't an option. Not that I would have even if she'd been right here, probably. I knew Juliet could handle it, would probably even enjoy it, so I decided instead to relax. To enjoy the company. To stop thinking about the phantom mask, which I could see out of the corner of my eye and which, if I'm honest, was starting to creep me out.

I was so relaxed I was practically horizontal by the time Sam came over, eyelids heavy, stupid grin on his face that I assumed was something to do with Leah, since they'd been forehead to forehead in intense conversation all night.

'Are we still on for later?'

'Sam, shut up,' I hissed, extracting myself from the conversation I'd been having with Daisy, Aaron and Louis, who had joined us just a minute ago, always gravitating back to my side eventually in a way that made me feel warmer than it should, to give Sam my full attention. 'It's meant to be a *secret*, remember?'

'Livi, chill,' he said, clamping a hand down on my shoulder. I shrugged him off. 'None of them are listening. None of them care what we're talking about. I could probably start screaming about our secret plan right now and barely get any of them to raise their eyes.'

'Don't try it,' I said, but I knew he was probably right. Off-stage, I wasn't the kind of person who commanded attention like that. Sam could be, but he knew how to turn it on. Flying under the radar here was the best move for both of us and, unlike the girl singing 'Let It Go' on the coach, who was still hovering beside us, we'd been playing this game long enough to pull back as masterfully as we went full out.

'So that's a yes?' he asked, serious suddenly. 'We're still on?' I nodded quickly. Of course we were.

'I'll meet you there the minute Aaron falls asleep,' Sam said. I looked over to where Aaron and Daisy had been joined by Luke, who had his hand on Aaron's leg in a way that suggested not that much sleeping would be happening. *Fine,* I thought. *As long as he's distracted, I don't really care how.*

The younger campers were already starting to drift back to their cabins, too tired after their first full day to let false bravado carry them through in an attempt to prove their cool. I knew this meant the rest of us wouldn't be far behind – it wasn't like we were waiting for the juniors to leave so they didn't see us flaking before midnight, but there was some level of credibility to uphold. You didn't want to be the first. Now, though, I was more than ready for a cup of tea under my duvet; a little break before I got back to it with Sam in – I checked the time on my phone – forty-three minutes.

Taking my time check as what looked like their cue, the girls who had been hovering started drifting towards me like three musical-theatre ghosts, moving en masse without speaking.

A laugh threatened to bubble up from my chest, but I squashed it down. I didn't want to be rude to them. I'd been exactly like them once.

'Hey,' I said, as I caught Phantom Mask Girl's eye. 'Looking for Juliet?'

She looked confused for just a second.

'No,' she said. 'We were waiting for you.'

OK?

'Oh. Well then . . . hi?'

'I'm Chloe,' the girl said, thrusting out her hand. 'This is Tasha and Kitty.' Chloe gestured at her friends, standing slightly behind her as if to make it very clear who was leading . . . whatever this was.

'Livi.'

Chloe grinned.

'We know who you are. That's why we wanted to talk to you. We've seen you on the YouTube videos. We wanted to ask you about how to make the most of our time here.'

Who knew that YouTube channel got so many views?

'Of course,' I said, my smile matching Chloe's now. I could talk making-the-most-of-Camp-Chance for ever.

'Who do we need to impress?' Kitty asked. She was softly spoken, and I had to strain a little to hear her over the chatter of the party. She'd have to find her confidence, I thought, if she wanted to impress here. She'd have to find her voice, literally. It wasn't my place to tell her that, though. The only way that would ever really sink in would be for her to learn it herself.

'It's not about impressing anyone but yourself,' I said, and all three girls leant a little closer, like these were the pearls of wisdom they'd tracked me down for. I almost laughed. It was very cute. I saw a lot of myself in the three of them. That felt like the kind of thing they wanted to hear, so I told them so.

'I can't believe you think we could ever be as good as *you*,' Tasha said. That actually *wasn't* what I'd said, but it was close enough, so I smiled.

'Of course you can,' I told her. 'All you have to do is *your* best. That's all you can control, so focus on that instead of what everyone else is doing and you're halfway there.' I wished it was as simple as that; wished I found it easier to take my own advice, but they seemed satisfied – seemed to be taking what I'd said and forming a plan. My gaze wandered to my watch. Being gushed over like this was making me feel a little awkward. A huge adoring crowd? Sure, I'd relish that any day. The stage lights would probably mean I couldn't see their expressions anyway. But a small group like this? It made me shudder. I was much more comfortable with attention when I was pretending to be someone else. To be fawned over like this felt . . . exposing. Like at any second they could look just a little too closely and see through it all. See that most of the time, I didn't feel anywhere near as confident as I pretended to be.

Taking my time check as a sign, Daisy caught my eye.

'Time to go?' she mouthed, and I nodded, saying goodbye to the girls and rejoining my roommate. I was glad for the excuse to leave, and not only because it meant she was hopefully tired enough to be asleep before I had to go out again.

'Definitely. Where's Juliet?'

Daisy shrugged. 'I have no idea. I haven't seen her since just after we got here.'

Weird. I hadn't seen who she'd been talking to, but it didn't seem like the Juliet I knew to disappear off with someone on the second night. Then again, it *was* only the second night. 'The Juliet I knew' was still an almost-total stranger. I had no way of predicting where she'd gone.

'I'm sure she'll catch us up,' I said, already walking out of the clearing in the direction of the living area. 'She might be back in the cabin already.'

She was not back in the cabin already. There was no sign that Juliet had been here at all since I'd seen her rummaging in her suitcase earlier in the evening.

'Good for her,' I said aloud, and really what I meant was good for *me*. If Juliet was spending night two in someone else's cabin, or even if she was still at the party and made it back before we turned out the lights, clearly it meant she wasn't as single-minded about any of this as I was. I busied myself pulling my hoodie over my head, so Daisy wouldn't notice my smile.

'I wonder who she's with?' Daisy asked, yawning as she climbed into bed without changing.

'I didn't see who she was talking to,' I said. 'Could be anyone really. We don't even know if she likes guys or girls.'

We don't know her at all. She could be anywhere.

'Do you think we should wait up?'

'No!' I knew I'd answered too quickly, but I hoped Daisy hadn't noticed. Waiting up was the *last* thing I needed her to do. If Daisy waited up, there was no way of me sneaking out unnoticed. I needed a plan.

'We don't want to embarrass her,' I said, heading in the direction of the bathroom, hoping that leaving Daisy alone for two minutes would lull her into such a deep state of tiredness after the day that she'd be asleep by the time I came back in. 'If she's off with someone, we should wait for her to tell us. We don't want to be sitting here gawping when she comes home if she's not ready for us to know.'

And if there's an ulterior motive here? Well, that's just a bonus.

I wasn't proud of it.

I was still thinking entirely of myself when I walked into the rehearsal barn at 12.10 a.m., the quickest I could get there after Daisy finally fell asleep, to find the lights off, the room empty. The air was cold, like nobody had been here in hours, so I knew I hadn't missed him.

He wasn't coming.

He'd probably had a better offer – gone back with Leah, or more likely taken her back with him, since I knew his cabin was empty, Aaron making no attempt to hide away with Luke. Except, thinking about it, I'd seen Leah through the window of her cabin on my way over here, and she looked like she was alone. Must be yet another girl who ranked higher than me then. I should have seen this a mile off. Of course, when it came down to it, Prince Charming went where the princess asked him to, not the desperate peasant girl who wanted to spend the whole night doing chores. I was basically Cinderella, except nobody was forcing me to work myself to the bone. I was doing that by choice. What an idiot. Sam wanted the cool girls; the ones who went with the flow. Pretended they were above it all. I'd been too intense. Cared too much. I shuddered. Even thinking about last summer, how badly I'd misread the signs, made a lump form in my throat.

I slid down the wall and sat with my back against it, the barn still in complete darkness.

Was this all too much? I knew not everyone was as serious about all of this as I was, but I'd thought Sam was a good bet. I thought he was committed. And now here I was, alone again, because everyone else had learnt how to be chill and left me in the dust, scrambling for my place in an industry that had so far shown me no evidence at all that it wanted me. Celestia's career had basically *finished* by the time she was my age, she'd already had that much success. But that said, Sophia had been primed for greatness when *she* was 17, everyone at camp telling her whatever she wanted was hers, and it just hadn't happened. Maybe I'd be somewhere in between – flying under the radar until I was ready, then emerging like a butterfly into...well, who knew what. I knew I had no control over what happened once I really put myself out there, but I *did* know that I wasn't going to leave it up to chance. I'd be as ready as I could, controlling the only bit I could – my own commitment. *God, Livi, do you think you might be overthinking this just a touch? He's probably just lost track of time. Have you ever tried not jumping to the most dramatic conclusion possible? Besides, you were late too.* I pulled myself to my feet, shuffled over to the light switch. The spill from the lamps outside the door beat me too it. I almost jumped out of my skin when the door opened, and their soft glow cut a slice across the floor of the barn.

'Livi?'

I gasped, even though I recognised the voice immediately; knew exactly who had walked in.

'Sam,' I breathed, and it came out sounding like a sigh of relief. I tried to pass it off as a *'oh thank god you're not a murderer'* sigh, but I knew, and I thought he probably did too, that it was more a *'oh thank god you came!'* one.

'Sorry I'm late,' he said, crossing the room in a few huge strides and turning on the light, since I was still standing next to the switch doing nothing.

'I thought you weren't coming,' I admitted in a small voice, not really sure where the vulnerability came from. *Get it together, Campbell.* Sam put a hand on my shoulder, just like he had at the campfire, although this one felt a lot more reassuring. I shuddered. Hated the way he laughed as he took it back; hated that I wasn't quite sure if he was mocking me or trying to show he was on my side.

'Of course I was coming. I promised, didn't I? I just got caught up at the end of the party – didn't want to run off when people were still milling around and make them all suspicious. I got here as quickly as I could. What time is it? *Woah*, twenty-past . . . sorry, I thought it had only been a few minutes.'

That made complete sense. It *had* basically been Sam's party. Of course it would be noticed if he left before the end, even if our fellow campers just thought he was flaking out early to go to sleep.

'Oh.'

Sam let out a little laugh and wrapped his arm around my shoulders, pulling me into his side. I stiffened.

But didn't pull away. *Crap*.

'Livi, I've got you – I promise. If I say I'm going to be somewhere, I'm going to be there. Give me a chance to get it right next time before you leap straight to "*he's abandoned me and I'm going to die alone*".'

'I wasn't quite that far along,' I protested quietly, and Sam laughed again, planting a kiss on the top of my head.

So.

That was weird.

'What the hell are you doing?'

Sam froze. Stepped away from me without meeting my eye. Looked like he'd rather be *running* away from me.

Talk about mixed messages.

'Sorry. I didn't mean to . . .'

He trailed off, as if he couldn't even bring himself to say what it was he hadn't meant to do. That was how much he wanted to avoid it – two seconds later and he couldn't even think about it without physically cringing to himself. Which made me feel just *great*. I wasn't stupid, though. Of course I knew he hadn't meant to kiss me. He must have had more to drink than I'd noticed at the party.

'I'm not Leah,' I said, as Sam tried to bore a hole into the floor with his eyes.

'Trust me, I know you're not.'

'Sam, I don't know what that means.'

'Why are you so *snappy* with me, Livi?'

'Well, why are you so *confusing*?'

He didn't answer. Could barely look at me as he walked over to the piano and opened the lid.

'Where do you want to start tonight?' he asked, and I was too thrown to make that decision suddenly, so I took a deep breath, relinquished just a *tiny* bit of control, and said, 'You choose.'

CHAPTER 8

THE CABIN FELT STILL WHEN I OPENED THE DOOR just after 3 a.m. The rehearsal had been a good one, both of us fired up by the party. OK, fine, maybe I was a little bit fired up by the weird head kiss and needed to work out some serious nervous energy before I could possibly fall asleep. Either way, we'd made it through three whole songs, polished them to perfection, and could put them to the back of the folder. Ticked off the list. Success all round.

That was when I realised my mistake.

Juliet was back in her bed.

Which meant she knew I hadn't been in mine.

Crap. How had I missed that? Well, I knew how – I'd been so desperate to get to Sam that I hadn't spared a thought for how it would look if 'Jules' came back and found me missing. That was a lot to unpack, so I decided not to. No time for my weird feelings about Sam Chambers to be resurfacing. Not tonight. Tonight, I had to come up with an excuse; what I'd say when she inevitably asked.

I feared the thought would keep me awake, but I hadn't even had a chance to think of a *bad* excuse, let alone the one I'd use, before my head hit the pillow and I was out for the count.

Juliet was still asleep by the time Daisy and I left for breakfast the next morning.

Good. Gave me a little more time to work on my story.

We were among the first to reach the dining hall and we grabbed a table near the French doors, grateful for the warm breeze cutting through the soupy summer heat. Slowly, and then with a little more speed, our fellow campers started pouring in, pouring coffee for their probably fuzzy heads, pouring their hearts out to their roommates and new friends, snippets of conversation floating on the air towards the table where Daisy and I had settled in with a perfect view of the door.

'Well, *I* heard he's only got eyes for one boy,' someone was saying as they passed, and I followed the direction of her eyes to see who she was talking about.

Ah. Aaron and Luke had just arrived. I smiled in their direction, and Aaron waved. I felt my cheeks redden as I raised my hand to wave back. It wasn't *normal* yet that Aaron Wilson was at *our* camp, as much as we were pretending it was.

I felt a presence at my shoulder and turned to see two of the girls from the night before, Tasha and Kitty, standing there.

Wiping my mouth to get rid of the crumbly pastry I knew was stuck to it, I smiled at them.

'Hey!' I said, but the girls didn't return my energy. On second glance, they looked sort of worried. 'Is everything OK?' I asked, and Kitty pushed Tasha forwards, designated spokeswoman for ... whatever was going on here.

'We can't find Chloe,' Tasha said. 'She didn't come back last night.' I raised an eyebrow. *Not unheard of on the second night – I'd suspected Juliet of a late-night dalliance of her own, after all – but definitely unexpected, especially for someone as new to camp as Chloe.*

What I *wasn't* going to do was shame her for wherever she'd spent the night, so I wiped the smile off my face; made my expression serious.

'Wherever she was, I'm sure she'll tell you when she's ready,' I said. 'Camp is a really great place for experimenting – it's safe, and you're with like-minded people. You know there's support around. If that's what Chloe's doing, you just have to stand by her. A lot of people figure out who they are here through nights just like the one Chloe had last night.'

'No,' Kitty said quietly. 'You're not listening. She'd *never* go off with someone and not tell us.'

I stopped myself from pointing out that they couldn't possibly know what she'd *never* do after being friends with her for two days, but I had to admit that I also didn't know Chloe. Who was I to say that my theory was the right one?

'OK,' I said, turning my attention to Kitty. 'So what do you think has happened?'

Neither of them answered. At first I thought it was because they didn't *have* an answer. The much more logical explanation was that Aaron had just joined the group and rendered them completely speechless.

Classic.

'Good morning, good morning!' he sing-songed as he slid into a seat at our table. When none of us responded, he looked at Daisy.

'What's up?'

'Their roommate didn't come home last night,' Daisy said quietly, gesturing to where Kitty and Tasha were still standing. 'They're worried.'

'We're sure everything is fine,' I said, trying to regain some control over a situation which felt like it could descend into chaotic panic at any second. 'We're just going to work out who she might have been with, and we can go from there.'

```
Dining hall. Morning.


AARON looks around the room, LIVI and
DAISY following his gaze, lingering on
the door for a second as JULIET enters,
raises her hand to wave at them, and
heads for the breakfast bar. When AARON
turns back to the group, he isn't
smiling.
```

AARON: Nobody else is missing.
DAISY: What?

She leans closer, as if that might change what he's said.

AARON: Whoever she was with, they're not missing. Everyone except Chloe is here.
TASHA: You know her name?

She gapes at him, awed. AARON smiles.

LIVI: Well, who knows who she was with last night then, but she must have left them and gone back to the cabin to get ready.
DAISY: She's cutting it fine.

Breakfast was mandatory at Camp Chance. Whether you sat down to eat or grabbed something to take away, every camper was ticked in by one of the counsellors, to make sure we were eating enough to sustain ourselves before a day of rehearsal. By not turning up, Chloe was risking her first red mark of the season. If she made it to three, there was no chance of an exciting showcase role.

'I'm sure she knows what she's doing,' I said, which didn't seem to ease Kitty's nerves in the way I'd hoped.

'Do you think she's OK?'

'I think she's fine. Look, someone else must be missing. We can work out who she's with.' *Who she's risking it all for*, I added, silently.

'Nobody else is missing,' Aaron said, more forceful this time. 'I have a photographic memory and I already know everyone here by face if not name. Since Juliet just walked in, Chloe is the only one not in this room.'

I gave my own cursory glance around the room. I knew more people than he did, I'd be able to spot what he hadn't.

Except Aaron was right. Everyone else was accounted for. So where *was* Chloe?

'Liv, I'm getting worried,' Daisy said.

The truth? So was I. One of the most magic things about Camp Chance was how safe it felt; how for three whole weeks the only things we need worry about were dance steps and keeping our voices in top condition; making new friends, keeping old ones. The whole point was that we got to feel *settled*. As someone who almost never felt like that in my life away from here, that feeling was sacred. I'd do anything to push the worry away. Including pretend like I wasn't feeling it at all.

'You have no reason to be,' I said, cocking my head in the direction of Tasha and Kitty, hoping Daisy recognised the signal for '*shut up and stop freaking them out!*'.

'Girls, Sophia incoming,' Aaron muttered, right before Sophia was gripping the edge of our table, surrounded by a cloud of perfume way too sweet for this time of the morning, and leaning towards us in a manner I'd describe as forceful.

'Where's Chloe?' She demanded, zeroing in on Tasha and Kitty. The girls froze.

I had to make a quick decision – say something before Daisy did. Before one of the others dug a hole and threw Chloe into it.

Now, Livi. Say something now.

'She's . . . not feeling well,' I blurted out. 'She's back in her cabin. She asked – well, begged actually – not to be disturbed. I think it's . . . a stomach bug. She just needs to, well, you know . . . get it out. I'm sure she'll be back on form before rehearsal.'

Sophia looked at me like she didn't trust me; like it made no sense that I'd be the one to answer her question when Chloe's friends were standing right there, but what could she say to that? She tried to act like a mini-Celestia and throw her weight around a bit so we knew we were meant to defer to her, but at her core she was . . . nice. Sophia was really nice. She wasn't going to punish Chloe for being sick. Or me for being the one to tell her. She walked away without another word.

'You're really good,' Aaron said, looking at me with admiration. If I couldn't actually *see* my cheeks blazing red, I could pretend it wasn't happening, right?

'Thank you.'

'Thank *you*,' Tasha said. 'But what do we do now?'

'We should actually go and check your cabin,' Daisy said, scraping her chair back from the table so fast I thought she was about to go flying backwards off it. 'You girls go back to your table, and don't let on to anyone that Livi lied.'

I appreciated her concern, even if she was definitely speaking loudly enough for everyone around us to hear.

'Livi lied about what?'

Juliet's voice was soft, but my *god* she knew how to use it – to make everyone listen, to cut through the noise. I hadn't heard her approaching at all, but there was no question that She Was Here, inserting herself into the group with her question, all eyes on her. Daisy looked at me like '*was that my fault?*'.

I shrugged. It wasn't that I minded Juliet knowing what was going on, more that I wished everyone would stop saying *Livi* and *lying* so close together in their trained-to-project voices. Nobody made a move to speak, so I guessed that was my cue.

'Their roommate, Chloe, is missing,' I said, gesturing to Kitty and Tasha. 'I needed to buy some time, so I said she was sick in her cabin. By the time Sophia has time to check, we'll have found her. A harmless lie. In fact, shall we all just stop calling it a lie?' My voice had risen by about three octaves. *Calm down, Livi.*

'So where do you think she is?' Juliet asked, turning her attention to Kitty and Tasha, who didn't quite know what to do with the spotlight on them.

'We don't know,' I said, trying to pull Juliet's, and everyone else's, focus back to the fact that we were on borrowed time if we wanted to find Chloe before the counsellors did. 'We're going to check her cabin now. She's probably there.'

'I'm coming with you,' Juliet said. It wasn't a question.

'Lead the way,' Aaron said. Quite how Juliet had become our

leader just by turning up I didn't know, but we didn't have time to argue about it. I stood up.

'We'll find you before rehearsal,' I said to Tasha and Kitty. 'And we'll have Chloe with us, I'm sure of it.'

'Let's go,' Daisy urged.

'Livi,' I heard a voice calling from behind me as we made our way out of the dining hall trying to look as natural and non-suspicious as we possibly could. 'Aaron!'

I turned to see Sam rushing towards us and tried to push down the sick feeling rising through my body before my breakfast threatened to make a reappearance, as I remembered last night. The weird kiss.

'Where are you going? To rehearse?'

Oh, god. I'd created a monster. Were our late-night sessions not enough for him? Did he really think I was having secret little side-things with anyone and everyone? I raised an eyebrow. *Really, Sam?*

Aaron was talking before I had a chance to decide what I wanted to say.

'Chloe is missing,' he said. 'You know, the first-year girl? With the phantom mask?' *Oh great.*

'*What?*' Sam asked. 'I saw her last night. How can she be missing?'

'Well, we *all* saw her last night,' I said. 'And I think *missing* might be an overstatement. She's probably just in her cabin, which is where we're heading now.'

'We all saw her last night, but nobody seems to have seen

her since,' Aaron muttered. I hated the anxiety that bloomed in my stomach when he said that.

'No, I mean late last night,' Sam said. The way we all stopped walking and turned to face him looked choreographed. My body was flooded with relief. Sam knew where she was. Everything was *fine*. As much as I hated that he was going to be the one to save the day, what really mattered was that it *was saved*, right?

'Where?' I asked.

'By the lake. Right at the end of the party.'

'What were you doing by the lake at the end of the party?' I was sure I didn't want to know before the question was even fully out of my mouth. Sam looked at me like '*well, you asked...*'

'Looking for somewhere private to hang out with Leah,' he said with a shrug.

Wonder how Leah would feel to know you left her to hang out with me?

'And what was Chloe doing there?' Daisy asked. *Oh yeah. Chloe.* The reason we were having this conversation in the first place. *Focus, Livi.*

'I have no idea,' Sam said, his expression apologetic. 'Once we saw that the clearing wasn't empty, we moved on.'

'Was she alone?' Aaron, this time, gesturing for us to start moving towards the lake as he spoke. Sam nodded.

'Looked like it, yeah. Like I said, we didn't stick around to find out what she was doing, but it's not a big clearing. I think I would have noticed if there was anyone else there.'

'Fine,' I said, stomping across the forest with a little more force than was strictly necessary. Or comfortable. 'Let's go.' I didn't want to think about why the idea of Sam and Leah looking for a private spot was so irrationally annoying to me.

I could tell the clearing by the lake was empty before we even reached it. I didn't know what I'd been expecting – that Chloe would still be here, having spent the night alone in the freezing cold when she had a perfectly good bed just steps away?

'She isn't here,' I said. *Stating the obvious, much.*

'It was worth a try,' Juliet said, and I gave her a small smile to reassure her.

'Where now?' I asked, already turning in the direction of Chloe's cabin. Beside me, Aaron stilled. It was hard to describe what changed in his demeanour, but it was as though he stiffened without actually moving; was overcome by . . . panic? Whatever it was felt palpable. I gulped, tense.

'Aaron, what?'

He lifted his hand without moving the rest of his body an inch, and my eyes snapped to where he was pointing. He was right, there was something there – tangled in the weeds at the side of the lake, sparkling in the glorious early morning light. My brain was telling me to run towards it, but my body froze. What the hell was going on?

'What is that?' Sam asked, apparently not sensing the tension at *all*. Lucky him. He was striding towards the object, hand outstretched, before my body caught up.

'No!' I called, like an *idiot*. 'Let me.'

I wish I hadn't.

I reached into the weeds and pulled out Chloe's phantom mask.

I didn't say anything.

I didn't have to.

That was when Aaron started screaming.

I had never seen a dead body before. That sounds like a completely obvious statement when you lay it out like that, but it was my first thought as Aaron and Sam ran towards the other side of the lake, where Chloe's body was curled up in the overgrown bushes like she'd simply lay down for a nap. *I have never seen a dead body before.*

I am seeing a dead body now.

She's dead, right?

This is really happening?

```
Clearing by the lake.
Morning.


AARON and SAM pull CHLOE'S unmoving body
from the bush and lay her on her back, on
the grass. DAISY shouts that she is going
for help and exits in the direction of
the breakfast hall. JULIET sinks to the
```

> *ground, unable to take her eyes off the scene. LIVI squeezes her own eyes shut as AARON and SAM start performing CPR.*
>
> *Nobody speaks.*
>
> *Time stops? Speeds up?*

If my life were a musical, this would be one of those moments where the stage goes dark and the lights would focus in on me, tight and claustrophobic, as if I was the only one in the scene, even though the others haven't moved an inch. What I mean to say is that it felt like the world was caving in, my ears ringing in a way that I thought might mean I was about to faint, but I couldn't hang on to that notion for longer than a second before it was gone, a fleeting thought, making way for the next horrific realisation, which was that *Chloe* was *dead*. Actually dead.

I couldn't look at the body without feeling sick. I couldn't look away from the body.

She was still wearing her outfit from the party, and I hated that. Hated the thought that she'd got ready for a fun night; had probably looked in the mirror and thought '*yes, I look nice*'. She was supposed to pose for photos with her new friends in those clothes, and dance around the clearing, and still be able to smell the smoke on them for days, if not weeks. She wasn't supposed to die in them.

God, Livi, why are you so fixated on the clothes?

I knew why. If I focused on what she was wearing, I didn't have to look beyond that – to her face that looked like she was just sleeping, eyes closed, make-up running down her cheeks like she'd just forgotten to take it off before bed. Her hair was fanned out behind her, tangled and wet. *So, she'd been in the lake.* That was one question answered, I supposed. She'd fallen in, managed to drag herself out but it had been too late?

I hoped she hadn't known what was happening. I hated the thought of her alone and scared in the one place she wasn't supposed to feel either of those things.

She also wasn't supposed to be *dead* though, so it was fair to say a lot had gone wrong here.

```
It seems like for ever and like no time
has passed at all before DAISY is back,
CELESTIA and SOPHIA in tow.
LIVI is breathing in a very deliberate
way; specific, like she learnt it from a
meditation app, or a podcast on how to
bring yourself back to the moment.
Stop spiralling.
Breathe, LIVI.
Breathe, JULIET.
JULIET still hasn't taken her eyes off
the scene. She's in visible shock.
```

CELESTIA: Clear a space!

```
She runs towards the body, takes over from
```

SAM without missing a single compression, a single beat. LIVI opens her eyes just in time to see SAM slump to the ground, exhausted. That is her cue to move.

LIVI: Are you OK?

She crouches beside SAM, who reaches out to brush his fingers across hers but does not speak.

LIVI: Sam, I need to hear you speak. I need to hear you say something.

Sam shows no sign that he's even heard her.

DAISY: What do you think happened?

She sinks down beside them, still breathing heavily from her run.

JULIET: I guess she fell? Slipped? Had she been drinking?

LIVI: I don't think so? Yeah, there was alcohol there, obviously, but we all know not to take it too far. Nobody who's

serious about being here would ever risk a hangover, and Chloe is . . . was, definitely serious. She can't have just drunk too much and slipped. Her friends would have noticed, right? Made sure to help her? Besides, we saw her right before we left and she seemed completely sober. I don't buy that we walked away and she got wasted . . . and whatever happened, if she fell in the lake, she managed to get herself out.
DAISY: Do you think she did? Fall in the—
LIVI: Her hair is still wet. She must have been so *cold*.

The sound of LIVI's voice seems to remind CELESTIA the campers are there. She does not turn to face them; does not take her attention off Chloe for a second.

CELESTIA: Aaron, everyone, go to your rehearsals and stay inside. You've been a real help, but you're done here. Sophia, go to the gate and wait for the police.

Her tone leaves no room for argument. Nobody tries.

As I went to stand, I saw the bedazzled mask lying where it had been forgotten. I picked it up gently. I hadn't known Chloe well, but I'd seen enough to be sure that she wouldn't want it discarded; that she'd want to know it was looked after. I'd give it to her friends, I thought. They'd know what to do. Its edges were sharper than they looked. I snagged my finger on the side and tried to wince quietly rather than gasping in pain. *Ow. What was that?* I knew that if Celestia saw that I'd taken the mask she'd make me give it back, and I really didn't want to do that. Didn't want to hand over this thing that had become so synonymous with Chloe in the short time I'd known her, and watch the police turn something that represented so much love into something clinical; forensic.

I didn't look back as we started walking towards the rehearsal barn. 'God, what a crappy ending. That poor girl. Nothing she could have done. A horrible accident.' Daisy's speech was stilted, like she didn't know what to say but felt like she should be saying something.

'Was it?'

I didn't know I was going to speak until it had already happened.

Aaron, Sam, Juliet and Daisy turned to look at me.

'Was . . . what?' Sam asked.

'Was it an accident?'

'Livi,' Sam said, his voice serious. 'What are you saying?'

I felt sick as I pulled the slip of paper out from where I'd found it, attached by a pin – no wonder it had hurt my hand – to the underside of Chloe's mask. I skimmed the handwritten words, but couldn't bring myself to read it out loud, so I handed it to Aaron.

> Chloe's death was no accident – everything went according to script. You're in the middle of your own murder mystery now, but the rest is still to be written. You have until the end of camp to find me, or she won't be the only one. You already know where it happened. You know when. If you're paying attention, it's pretty obvious how. All you have to work out is who I am, and why I did it.
> Before I do it again.
> Tell no one, or you might be next.
> I'll be watching.

So.

That was pretty unambiguous.

CHAPTER 9

Shellshock. Silence.

LIVI, JULIET, DAISY, SAM and AARON walk away from the lake as instructed, towards the rehearsal barn as instructed, doing everything they've been told to do, exactly as instructed. Never let it be said that actors aren't great at following direction.

LIVI looks around. Doesn't miss a beat. Slides the mask into the side of her billowing cardigan, then wraps it around her as if she's cold.
It's 32 degrees.

LIVI: Let's just . . . this is between us, right?

JULIET: Absolutely.

LIVI: Just until we know what's going on.

That's the end of it. They enter the rehearsal barn co-conspirators. In what? None of them quite know yet.

Walking into the rehearsal barn was like being hit by a wall of sound. *Everyone* was there, clearly having been herded up by the rest of the counsellors before they could find out what was going on, because the rumours ranged from completely wild (aliens by the small lake – said with a completely straight face by one of the design kids) to . . . well, still completely wild (a reality TV crew had arrived and they were keeping us here until they decided which of us were going to be the stars, suggested by Leah). I looked around for Chloe's friends, once and then again. If I was right, Kitty and Tasha were the only campers not there. That was small mercy at least – I was glad they were being told away from everyone else.

Or questioned?

The thought sent a shiver down my spine and my hand drifted almost involuntarily to the mask, still clamped to my side. I'd somehow forgotten about the note for a second, but Kitty and Tasha being missing had brought it right back to the forefront of my mind. Could they be in danger?

Or *were* they the danger? I felt sick, suddenly.

A glance at Juliet suggested she wasn't feeling much better. She'd gone completely pale, hiding behind her curtain of pink hair.

'You OK?' I asked quietly, and her head snapped up as if she'd completely forgotten anyone else was there.

'Fine.'

'It's OK if you're not,' I tried. 'Probably really normal, actually, considering what—'

'Livi, I'm *fine*,' Juliet snapped, pulling her phone out of her pocket in a very clear signal that the conversation was over.

Fine.

Bitch.

I sighed. If anyone was being a bitch in this situation, it was definitely me. We'd just seen a *dead body* and I was irritated that Juliet wouldn't *talk to me*? Hugely unfair, I knew. I'd meet her where she was. Make more effort. She didn't want to talk? Fine. We could not talk next to each other. I was not going to give up on Juliet Stone that easily.

Not before I'd worked her out.

```
At the front of the room, SOPHIA claps
to call the room to attention and
the usually rowdy group fall silent
immediately, more intrigued to find out
what's going on here than to continue
their own conversations.

That is to say, it feels big.
```

SOPHIA: OK, listen up.

She stops, even though everyone is listening up, as if she isn't sure what she's supposed to say next, as if she doesn't know the script for this bit. Poor SOPHIA.
She takes a breath. Shaky.

SOPHIA: OK. Unfortunately — god, unfortunately? Get a grip, Soph.

The campers are looking at her like she's unravelling in front of their eyes, which, if you asked SOPHIA, she'd probably say was accurate. Another deep breath. Another.

SOPHIA: OK. You're probably wondering why we've gathered you all here.

Sniggers from the crowd. SAM turns in the direction of the perpetrators. Glares. Says nothing. It's enough.

SOPHIA: Sorry, I'm not very good at this. You're not stupid. You've all worked out

by now that something is going on, and if
it's turned me — *me*, of all people — into
a stuttering wreck, it can't be good.
You're all adults.

*This isn't actually true, but nobody
corrects her.*

SOPHIA: I'm just going to say it. A body
has been found in the lake. Sadly, despite
the best efforts of Sam Chambers, Aaron
Wilson and Celestia, it was too late.
They weren't able to save Chloe.

If I'd expected carnage, I was proven entirely wrong. It was like nobody dared move a muscle. None of us knew how to react, even the four of us who had known before Sophia started speaking where her monologue was going to end; that it wasn't going to be good. That there was no changing the outcome.

A few people shifted their bodies in Sam and Aaron's direction, trying to pretend they weren't looking at them for a reaction. They were giving nothing away at all, faces completely stony, staring straight ahead at Sophia as if that couldn't possibly be the punchline.

As if this was all some sort of joke even though they'd *been there*.

Louis was trying desperately to catch my eye, and I felt bad as I turned my back and pretended not to see him. I'd have to deal with that later. Louis had never met a secret he didn't immediately want to share. He *could not* find out what we knew.

I reached out my little finger and grazed the side of Sam's leg, just letting him know I was there. If he felt it, he didn't let on. Despite the circumstances, I was embarrassed. What was I *doing*? Had I forgotten who he *was*?!

'Are we in danger?' Luke asked from the back of the room, and that, it seemed, was what everyone needed to snap out of the stupor and begin to panic.

And *there* was the carnage.

'Was she drunk?' One of the lighting girls, who's name I didn't know, called before Sophia could answer.

'Who found her?'

'Why was she alone *anyway*?' Leah piped up, which was a stupid question since *all of us* walked around alone here *all the time*.

'ARE WE IN DANGER?' Luke shouted again, and that snapped Sophia into action.

'NO.' She met his volume, maybe even increased upon it a bit, and everyone immediately shut up and turned back towards the front of the room.

'Nobody is in danger. This was a tragic *accident*, but it *was* an accident.'

I felt my hand drift back to my side, clutch around the mask where it was nestled in the crook of my arm.

'Had she been drinking?' Leah, this time, picking up the

script where the lighting girl had apparently decided not to.

'You'd all know that better than I would,' Sophia said, a fact rather than an accusation. She was right. We'd been the ones at the party. It should have been us who noticed when Chloe went missing. 'We'll want to talk to everyone who was at the party last night, especially anyone who spent any time with Chloe. The police will be finished at the lake shortly, and they'll be heading up those interviews, but in the meantime, if there's anything you want to share, we'd really appreciate it if you could let Celestia, myself or any of the other counsellors know. We'll make sure it's kept confidential, and we'll pass it on so that the police can decide what to do with it.'

Anything like the fact that it was murder? I wondered. *Anything like the fact that the killer left a note saying as much?*

I kept my mouth shut, obviously.

Obviously? We *were* doing the right thing here, weren't we? The note had said that *nobody should find out.* Were we supposed to take that at face value? Was the person behind this expecting us to lie to the police? Wasn't that *illegal*?

'Livi,' Sam interrupted my thoughts with a hiss. 'Stop thinking so hard. I can practically hear you.'

'So what happens now?' I almost jumped out of my skin when Juliet spoke from right beside me, her voice soft but perfectly projected as ever, and the whole room turned to look in our direction.

'We carry on,' Sophia said, defiant. 'Not as normal, because nothing about this is normal, but we *do* carry on. Classes will go ahead, but there will be more restrictions on moving around the camp than usual as the police begin their searches. If you're not scheduled to be in a class, you'll be in here or one of the other buildings learning what you can from each other. We have to stick together – Chloe was one of our own, and the next few days and weeks are going to be difficult, but she wouldn't have wanted us to give up, or go home. So.'

Despite not being a typical sentence ending, '*so*' seemed to be where Sophia had decided to stop, which was everyone's cue to begin talking among themselves. I heard the words 'conspiracy theory' and something about 'claiming on the insurance' from some of the sound kids who *definitely* didn't know anything about insurance or, for that matter, how to be sensitive when one of their fellow campers had just *died*, so I ushered the rest of our group into the corner furthest away from the drama hunters. It was the closest we were going to get to privacy for a while.

'This is so messed up,' Juliet hissed, as if this was all somehow my fault. 'We can't just *hide a murder*.' Daisy nodded so vigorously in agreement that I actually worried for her neck.

'So what are you saying?' I whispered back with just as much venom. 'We tell Sophia? The police? Even though the killer has *literally threatened us* if we do?'

'Nobody is suggesting that,' Aaron said, putting out his hands as if to separate Juliet and I from each other even though neither of us had actually made a move to touch.

'Aren't they?' That was Daisy, tears in her eyes. 'Are you sure we shouldn't tell *someone*? What if the police find out we kept it from them? I'm pretty sure that's a crime in itself . . .' She trailed off and I looked to Sam for some back up, even though I'd had the same thought minutes before. He was still staring into the middle distance, but instead of the usual contrived and deliberate leading man look on his face, he looked haunted.

Crap. I'd have to deal with that in a minute. Right now, though, I needed to stop Juliet and Daisy from doing anything completely idiotic.

```
LIVI: Think about it. The note said we
have until the end of camp to find them
or there will be more. Doesn't that
suggest that if we find them, there
won't? That us finding them is the best
way to keep everyone else safe?


She's whispering, but this camera is
excellent at picking up low sound levels,
luckily for us.


DAISY: Since when are we trusting what
killers say?
AARON: Actually . . .


Everyone turns to look at AARON. In an
even more pronounced way than everyone
```

*is always turning to look at AARON,
I mean.*

AARON: Actually, in true crime cases, when the killer is engaging anyway, what they say they're going to do is almost always what they actually do.
DAISY: So we're meant to trust them because they're talking to us?
AARON: Sort of.
DAISY: That's *so stupid*.
JULIET: He's right.

So. She's changed her tune. Everyone turns to look at JULIET. In an even more pronounced way than everyone is always turning to look at JULIET.

AARON: Go on . . .
DAISY: Yes, go on.
JULIET: He's right. But, Livi, you are too, as much as I hate the idea of not telling anyone who might actually be able to help. But trusting what the killer says is all we *can* do. They've already told us that if we don't find them, if we tell *anyone*, there will be more.

They couldn't have known it would be us
that would find that note, but we have
to assume they do know *now*. That they're
watching. So let's just . . . follow the
script. Play our parts. I don't see what
choice we have.

JULIET really is great at projecting.

SAM (finally): Juliet, *be quiet*. You're
right, OK. You're all right. You've all
got good points. We're completely trapped
by this psycho, so we'd better just get
on with it, find out who they are, and
once we do, we never have to speak to
each other again if we don't want to.

Silence.
Then.

JULIET: Well, *that* was dramatic.

It *was* quite dramatic, but it was what we needed to break the tension between us. Without talking about it, the five of us huddled closer, lowered our voices even further. Sam looked straight at Daisy, who I thought might be about to really cry this time, something we could all definitely do without.

'Look,' he said gently, 'we're not going to agree on this, and I think that's completely normal, in as much as nothing about this situation is ever going to be normal. But we're huddled in a corner with Aaron Wilson and Juliet Stone, so people are looking at us, and a camper has just shown up *dead*. Even without . . .' he paused, and leant in even further, 'what we know, I don't have to tell you that the last thing we need is people looking at us. I know strangers become mates at a mad speed here, but if we keep breaking off to whisper like this when we had nothing to do with each other before this morning, it's going to look suspicious. So. Let's just go to our rehearsals, stay in the background, and see what we can find out.'

He looked straight at me when he said 'stay in the background'. I thought I should probably have been offended, but he had a point. Blending in wasn't exactly my favourite camp pastime. *Noted*.

CHAPTER 10

I DIDN'T SEE ANY OF THEM AGAIN UNTIL WE WERE released from our morning rehearsals into the lunch hall. 'Morning rehearsals' was a bit of stretch, since very little actual rehearsing had happened. Instead, there had been quite a lot of performative crying, slightly less genuine crying, and a whole lot of first-year campers talking loudly about what a great friend Chloe had been.

So great that you didn't even notice when she disappeared and was drowned in a lake? I couldn't help thinking. *You barely even knew her.* Sure, friendships formed freakishly quickly at camp, like Sam had said, but even in this setting, even taking into account that people react in so many wild ways to death, their fawning felt a little fake to me.

None of the others were sitting at our regular table when I walked in – if a table we'd sat at exactly once could be called regular – and I looked around the room trying to find them. They were the closest thing I had to friends here now, even if that wasn't entirely by choice. Hanging out with them was definitely better than trying to get through this alone though. I noticed the light from the camera before I saw the pink hair peeking out from behind the lens.

Was. She. Joking?

We'd agreed to *keep our heads down* and *stay inconspicuous* and *see what we could find out* – and Juliet Stone was *vlogging*?!

VLOGGING?

JULIET STONE WAS VLOGGING.

I steeled myself and took a deep breath.

Then I started charging towards her.

Veering around tables and stray chairs, and any camper who wasn't quick enough to move out of my way, I had almost reached her, was almost within whisper-shouting distance and was *just* about to ask her what the hell she thought she was doing, when a strong hand landed on my upper arm and pulled me out of Juliet's path without her even looking up.

I knew who it was straight away.

I recognised his smell. Some sort of mahogany coconut concoction.

I hated that I recognised his smell.

So not the point.

'What the hell do you think you're doing, Sam?' I asked, finally looking up at him.

'I think that should be my line.'

His voice was calm. Measured. That only made it worse.

SAM drags LIVI to the edge of the dining hall. Her face looks like if she thought she could get away with kicking and screaming, she would be.

LIVI: She's vlogging.
SAM: I can see that.
LIVI: Don't you think that's weird?
SAM: I do.
LIVI: You're not acting like you think it's weird.
SAM: It's not weird for Juliet.

LIVI looks at SAM like . . . huh. Like she'd underestimated him. Like he has a point.

LIVI: I think I get it, but say more.
SAM: Of course she's vlogging. She's trying to pretend everything is normal. This, for Juliet, is normal.
LIVI: I don't think vlogging when someone has just died could ever be normal.

Well. Agree to disagree.

SAM: I know. I get it. But we agreed

> to stay under the radar, and if Juliet
> wasn't making content, that would make
> her stand out more. It's a clever move.
> **LIVI:** It's a vapid, self-obsessed move,
> and I hate it.
> **SAM:** Liv, why are you so angry?
>
> *LIVI stills. Considers it. He's good at
> making her do that. Better than she is
> herself. Not that she'd ever admit it.*

Why *was* I so angry?

Was it because she was using Chloe's death to further her own career? Well, *obviously*, but if I was honest, I wasn't really worried about that. I knew Celestia and Sophia would never let her post those videos if they mentioned a camper dying at all; knew the police would probably have something to say about it too, once they'd found out what really happened. Nothing Juliet filmed today would see the light of day until we got out of here, and who knew what would have happened by then, but still I couldn't let it go. In person, she was so easy to like, but the minute she had a camera in her hand, something about her screamed at me to back off. To keep my wits about me.

I couldn't say that to Sam, though. Not yet. Mainly because I knew he'd think exactly what I was thinking – that it probably wasn't about Juliet at all. That it was a Livi problem, all born from my own insecurity.

'Livi?' he said, and, oh yeah, I probably should say *something*.

'Forget it. You're right. Celestia will kick off if she posts it anyway.'

It was as if saying Celestia's name had summoned her. Say what you like about her, but she still knew how to put on a performance. The dining room went still as she walked in through the French doors, flanked by two police officers who seemed amused, I thought, by Celestia's display. Dark sunglasses, refusing to look straight at any of us, she floated silently right through the middle of the room to the counsellors table where Sophia and some of the others were waiting to gently place their hands on her shoulders and tell her how shocked and sorry they were.

'You didn't even find her!' I felt like screaming. 'You have no idea what's really going on here! Maybe if you were more focused on that and less on looking like the perfect grieving head counsellor, you'd realise Chloe was *murdered*!'

Obviously I didn't say any of that, and not only because Sam was looking at me with concern in his eyes, as if he thought I actually might.

I liked proving people wrong, OK?

'She looks *ruined*,' Daisy said as she came up behind us, and now I felt bad. Of *course* this had hit Celestia hard. She knew better than any of us that camp was supposed to be a safe space, and it was her job to make sure it was.

'The showcase should be a memorial,' I said. The idea was forming as the words were coming out of my mouth, but I knew straight away it was a good one by the way Sam looked at me, impressed. I carried on.

'We could do all of the songs we know Chloe loved. Well, we'll have to find out from her friends what they were. Then we could do songs about staying strong, finding a way through, because it's what she would have wanted.'

What we all need, I didn't say.

'That's a lovely idea,' Daisy said. 'I think you should tell Celestia.'

A quick glance over to where she was still being fussed by the other campers told me that now was not the moment.

'I will. Next time I get her alone.'

```
Dining hall. End of lunch. The bell rings
to mark the start of the next rehearsal,
but nobody moves. Nobody is quite sure
what they're supposed to do. Where they're
supposed to go. The usual chaos of campers
warming up their voices as they run to
their afternoon activities is replaced by
silence, as they collectively look towards
the counsellors table for . . . well,
counsel.

CELESTIA (sunglasses, still crying)
clearly isn't going to give it.
```

SOPHIA steps up.

SOPHIA: OK, listen up.

Once again, everyone is already 'listening up' when she says this.

SOPHIA: Thank you all for the way you've responded to . . . what happened this morning. To . . . The Incident.

Capitalised, because it's obvious that this is how they've decided to refer to it — officially.

SOPHIA: So that the police can do their work, we've re-jigged the schedules to keep you all inside and out of their way as they investigate. They'll want to talk to some of you in due course, and that'll be a lot easier if we know exactly where you all are.
LIVI *(quietly)*: And that nobody is messing with the evidence.

Nobody hears her, except the excellent microphone on this camera.

SOPHIA: For most of you, this will mean a slight deviation from your specialties while you wait for your next rehearsal to begin, but we've got some tasks for you all to do that'll hopefully pass the time quickly. So - Livi, you're on wigs.

The campers prick up their ears to find out what makeshift 'task' they've been given.

LIVI, we can see, is pissed.

CHAPTER 11

I WASN'T PETTY ENOUGH TO ADMIT THAT I WAS PISSED, or devoid of emotion enough to actually *be* pissed under the circumstances, but really? *Wigs?*

I don't know if you've ever found yourself in an entire room of them before – and I hope for your sake not – but when you look at wigs for long enough, especially on those faceless foam heads they use to keep the hair in shape, they become sinister quite quickly.

And I was supposed to spend the next hour alone with them. Excellent.

I was wrapped up in my own thoughts as I stomped down the corridor to meet my creepy fate, so the sound of footsteps rounding the corner almost made me jump out of my skin.

'Woah!' Juliet said, taking in my shocked expression. 'I didn't mean to startle you!'

'Are you . . . quoting *Wicked* on purpose?' I asked, and her face-splitting grin told me I was exactly right.

'Anyway,' I continued. 'I think *anything* would startle me right now. What the *actual hell* is this day?'

Juliet crowded closer, shaking her head.

'I know,' she said. 'I'm jumping out of my skin when my own hair brushes on my shoulder, let alone if anyone else comes near me. I can't help thinking, like...'

'Could it be you?' I supplied, and she nodded.

'Right. And wondering where they're watching from.'

I looked around, despite knowing there was no way anyone could be hiding in this completely open corridor. It was just the two of us, completely alone. I saw my opening.

'You didn't catch anything, did you?' I asked. 'In your vlog, I mean. From the night of the party?'

Juliet was shaking her head before I stopped talking.

'No. I wish my videos could be that helpful. I barely filmed at that party – just a few shots of the lights when we first got there. They're good for voiceover, when you really want the viewer to be focusing on what you're saying rather than what they're seeing. God, you don't care about the artistic direction of my videos. I'm sorry. No. Nothing of Chloe at all.'

I shook my head. *No need for an apology.* I'd thought as much.

'We're doing the right thing, aren't we? By keeping this quiet?' Juliet asked. 'I mean, I know we are, what choice do we have? But...'

'I know,' I said. 'I keep asking myself the same.'

Juliet nodded in recognition, and I was once again so glad that I wasn't in this alone.

'What are you doing here, anyway?' I asked. 'Didn't they put you with the stage managers?'

Juliet rolled her eyes. Apparently I wasn't the only one unhappy with my morning plans.

'Yeah, but nobody told me where to actually *go,* so I ended up in completely the wrong building looking like I'm trying to get out of it, when really I'm just lost, and new, and everyone assumed I'd just work it out!'

She had a point. There was a level of *working it out* expected here, not for any reason other than the fact that most of us had been coming for so long that we tended to forget some of our fellow campers might not know their way around for a while; forget to help them out. I pointed in the direction of the stage management office, where I assumed Oliver and co would be waiting for her.

'That way. Look for the yellow door and you're there.'

'Thanks,' Juliet said, looking much less frazzled now she was heading in the right direction, as if she'd caught the polished mask she wore in public just before it slipped completely, and pushed it back into place. 'Enjoy your wigs.'

'Ugh,' I said to her retreating back. 'Don't remind me.'

I had to admit though that a moment to myself was desperately needed, and when the door to the wig store closed with me on one side and the rest of camp on the other, I felt like I took a breath for the first time since breakfast.

Breathe, Livi.

It wasn't until I'd taken a few deep, deliberate inhales that I realised I was crying.

What the hell were we supposed to do?

It must be shock, I thought, that was making me react like this. It wasn't like I'd really known Chloe; wasn't like I had any right to be *sad*, not like Tasha and Kitty, who hadn't been seen since the body was found. I hoped someone was looking after them. In some ways, I thought I was crying more for Camp Chance. Crying at the thought that something – someone – had managed to penetrate our bubble. Had turned a dream into a nightmare, if we were going to be completely cliche about it. Had taken my safe space and sent a very clear message.

You are not safe here.

Well, screw that.

I was not about to let them win.

With more vigour than I probably should have, knowing how weirdly expensive they were, I picked up the first wig and straightened it on its creepy foam head, making sure the pins were all in place. It was a classic red *Annie* curls one. I had no idea why Camp Chance had so many of those, since *Annie* was outdated and obvious, and hadn't been featured in a showcase for as long as I'd been here.

Well, it's only fair to take it for a spin then.

I lifted the red curly mop from its no-face owner and carefully put it on, checking my reflection in the mirror. I looked ridiculous, but not in a way I hated. I almost always liked my reflection more when it was someone else I saw staring back. I could tell it hadn't been touched for a long time by how neat it still was, unlike the wild diamanté-encrusted Glinda beehive on the next stand, which was looking a little dishevelled after it's trip to the first-night party.

Should I be touching this? Could it be evidence?

I didn't think so but I pushed it to the back of the desk anyway, just in case.

Shame. I would have loved to try that one on.

I put Annie back on her perch and moved on to a pink shoulder-length number that I didn't recognise from any particular show. I shuddered as I looked at it, hanging half off its little foam head, like it had been jammed back on as an afterthought. These things were works of art! Creepy works of art, but still! What chance did we have if people weren't putting them back properly? If I didn't look too closely, it looked kind of like Juliet. Her hair was shinier, of course, and her pink a little less vibrant, less aggressive, but in a Juliet Stone costume, this wig would not look out of place.

I lifted it slowly from its stand. I just wanted to see if it would suit me before I straightened it out; if I could pull it off like she did. What it might feel like to be Juliet Stone. I slowly slipped it on.

Hang on – what?!

The note was pinned to the top of the foam head carelessly, as if it had been tacked there in a rush. I didn't even think before

I'd ripped out the pin and picked up the folded piece of paper; was already holding it before I stopped to consider whether I should have touched it at all.

Well, I thought, *you've done it now. Better get this over with.*

```
Costume store. LIVI, alone. She unfolds
the note, tentative at first, but then
quickly, like ripping off a plaster.
Hand to her mouth, she gasps.

We zoom, reading over her shoulder like
the ghost of danger yet to come.
```

Here's where the game really begins, and we all know that the best games come with rules, don't we? So, these are mine:

1. Tell no one. There are some things that should never be mentioned in a theatre, and, like Macbeth, I just joined that list. As far as anyone outside of the five of you is concerned, I don't exist. You know nothing. You say nothing.

All right, I thought, *you've said that already, we get it, we're clearly not going to tell.* I swallowed down a sick feeling. *Fine, Chloe's murderer is Macbeth, very clever, now tell us something we don't already know.* I read on.

2. Leave a light on. You know the superstition. You're theatre kids, of course you do. Like all professional theatres, Camp Chance leaves one light burning when the stage is vacated for the night. Somewhere for the ghosts to gather. A way for me to keep an eye on what is going on. And your light can't go out either. What do I mean by that? Act. Normal. Go to your rehearsals, your classes, your dinners. No hiding away, no skipping out on parties. No one can suspect a thing. Don't dim your light on my account. The moment anyone notices you acting suspiciously, sees that you're investigating, the game is up. All bets are off. No deal.

The rage I felt as I instinctively curled my free hand into a fist was white hot. How *dare* they dictate what we could and couldn't do – they seemed to be suggesting that they had eyes everywhere, that they'd *know* if we put one foot out of their made-up line. Every cell in my body wanted to defy them – wanted to kick, and scream, and say *what if I don't listen? What then?* Every cell, that is, except the ones that were terrified. That had no idea how far these threats might go, and did not want to find out. I looked back down at the piece of paper in my hand.

You get it, right? If you break these rules, there's

no knowing what I might do next. Remember, I'm watching.

Yeah, you've made that pretty clear.

I think tradition dictates that I'm meant to say break a leg here, but just this once . . . good luck.

```
LIVI screams. Quick, sharp, one moment
of frustration before we watch her steel
herself, make both hands into fists this
time, as if she's ready to fight, and
shove the note in her pocket.


Perfect timing from the girl who never
misses a cue. That's when CELESTIA enters.
```

Crap. I'd been so focused on the *completely unhinged* note that I hadn't heard her coming; had no idea Celestia had even walked into the wig store until she was standing right in front of me, looking at me like she'd said something and I'd missed it completely.

Too busy trying to stop my heart from beating clean out of my chest.

I forced my game face on; told myself it was just acting, and I was *great* at acting. Let's see if I could nail the part of 'girl who wasn't suddenly completely terrified'.

'Sorry, what?' I asked, trying to keep my voice light. 'I was daydreaming. Didn't even hear you come in!'

Celestia smirked. I couldn't tell whether I had pulled off the lie or not. 'Well, when you're quite ready,' she said, 'you're up. The police want to speak to you, then it's rehearsal time.'

I had never thought this before in my life, but the last thing I needed right now was a rehearsal – and a police interview ranked even lower on the list. I needed to talk to the others, and there was no way I could do that from the stage, in front of half of Camp Chance. *Crap*. I'd have to work it out on the way, because Celestia was looking at me like *why aren't you moving?*

I thought back to the note. *Don't draw suspicion.* I couldn't just stop acting like Livi; couldn't stop jumping at every chance to perform. Anyone who knew me would see that something was wrong straight away. I smiled at Celestia, turning Livi Campbell the Star back on.

'Let's go,' I said, my hand curling around the note in my pocket.

'Are you . . . all right?' Celestia asked as we walked down the corridor. 'After what happened, I mean. The Incident.'

As if there was any doubt in my mind about what she meant. As if I'd been able to think of anything else for a single second since it had happened.

You don't know the half of it, I wanted to say. *What you think you're asking me about and the reality are not the same thing at all.*

'I'm fine,' I said instead, my voice quiet. 'Are you?'

'Absolutely fine,' she said without looking at me, in a tone that suggested that she was not absolutely fine. Far from it.

'It's OK if you're not,' I said tentatively. It wasn't like I'd put her on a pedestal or anything, but it felt weird to be talking to Celestia like this. Like she was . . . just a human. Which was stupid, because obviously she *was* just a human, just not one who I'd ever seen look so . . . vulnerable. Defeated.

'It's just, we work so hard to keep this place . . . controlled,' she said. 'We work *so hard* to make sure everyone is safe, and thriving, and the investors are happy. And now it's day three of camp, and none of those things are true, and I just . . .'

She stopped, as if she had caught herself saying something she shouldn't.

'I'm sorry,' she said. 'I shouldn't be putting all of this on you. You should be *singing*. You should be spending time with your friends. Not worrying about . . . forget I said anything, Livi. I'm fine. It's all going to be fine.'

I felt quite sorry for her, if I was being honest. Celestia didn't make it easy to love her, but it couldn't have been easy to *be* her either – what with the pressure of her past career on her shoulders and the success of Camp Chance in her hands. Technically, there was a board of directors, investors, people in senior positions who knew nothing about what happened behind the rainbow gates because the only time they ever stepped through them was for the showcase at the end of the summer. Technically, Celestia had a boss, I was sure. Someone to guide her. We all knew, though, that everything that happened at camp was on her. That may have been the way she liked it, but it was a lot of pressure. Perhaps I should judge her weird reaction to Chloe's death less harshly, I thought. Give her more of a chance.

I didn't know why that line of thinking lead me straight back to Juliet.

OK, fine, obviously I did. Maybe I'd judged her too harshly too, as much as I couldn't understand *vlogging* in the aftermath of a *murder*. Maybe she was just doing her best. And Daisy, still pushing us to tell the counsellors about what was going on. Aaron, trying to turn our lives into a true crime podcast. Even Sam, clinging to Leah after three days like they'd been in love for ever. Maybe all of them were just trying their best.

All of *us*.

Just in case, though . . . 'There was one thing I wanted to mention,' I said to Celestia, and she turned, questioning, and gestured for me to go ahead.

'It's . . . Juliet,' I said. 'I don't want this to come across like I'm telling on her, but earlier, in the lunch hall, I saw her . . . vlogging?'

I made it sound like a question even though I wasn't a bit unsure. That was definitely what she'd been doing. Celestia raised an eyebrow.

'Really?'

Really was she vlogging, or *really* was I selling her out like this? I couldn't tell which Celestia meant, so I just nodded. The answer to both was technically yes, after all.

'Thanks for letting me know.' She smiled, but in a way that gave away nothing of how she felt about Juliet turning tragedy into entertainment. I felt better for having said it, anyway. Didn't I?

I almost laughed when I saw Oliver, the lead Stage Management counsellor, standing outside the door to Celestia's office like some sort of security guard, arms folded, stony expression on his usually sunny face. Even the non-actors were always putting on a show here. I supposed his sombre vibe was entirely appropriate though, especially if my hunch that the police interviews were taking place on the other side of the closed door was correct. He nodded when he saw us coming and raised a hand to stop me, as if I *wanted* to walk in there.

'One second,' he said, his face softening into a reassuring smile. 'They're just finishing up with Louis.'

Oliver had worked at Camp Chance for the past two summers, but I hadn't had much to do with him so far. I knew my strengths, and the methodical calm and always-one-step-ahead strategic brain needed to be a good stage manager were not among them. So I'd never got involved in any of his classes, preferring to go where I knew I wouldn't be laughed out of the room as soon as anyone saw what I was made of. That was entirely my own insecurity and nothing at all to do with Oliver, who was *lovely*, and always made the effort to stop and say hi anyway, like one day he might just convince me.

'No worries,' I said, right as the door swung open and Louis, pale, jaw tight, walked out. He stopped short when he saw me.

'Livi,' he said, as if breathing a sigh of relief. 'Are you all right? Why is your hair pink?'

'I'm fine,' I said, reaching up to touch the wig that was still sitting wonky on my head. 'Wig duty. But that's not important – why did they want to talk to you?'

'I chatted to Chloe at the end of the party,' Louis said. 'And the other two.'

'Tasha and Kitty,' I supplied, wondering again where they were.

'Right. It was two minutes – I'd had too much to drink and was feeling . . .'

'Chatty.' I smiled.

'Right. I never expected . . .'

'None of us did,' I said, hoping it would shut the conversation down and give him a way out of his floundering, and me a way out of having to talk about this in front of people; of worrying I'd say something I shouldn't. 'We couldn't have seen this coming. Don't . . . blame yourself, Lou. Don't give yourself a hard time.'

'Livi,' Oliver cut in, 'they're ready for you.'

Right. The police.

Louis stepped back to leave.

'Let's catch up later,' he said.

'Definitely.'

I didn't have my fingers crossed behind my back, but I might as well have if my intention to definitely *not* do that counted for anything. Louis was emotional; was prone to spilling his heart out to whoever was in the vicinity. We had to keep him as far away from this as possible.

The two people sitting behind Celestia's desk didn't look

like the police officers I'd seen on TV. Their faces were kind, open, smiling as I walked in and sat down on the opposite side of the desk. It was only the full uniforms that gave them away. Sophia was perched on the edge of a chair in the corner, looking as though she was pretending not to be there, trying to make herself small.

'This is Livi Campbell,' Celestia said from behind me, 'one of the campers who found Chloe.'

The female officer bowed her head slightly as she looked at me.

'I'm so sorry.'

'It's OK,' I said, which was my default response to any form of sorry, but in this situation was a *stupid* thing to say. Nothing about this was OK. I was practically vibrating with nervous energy. I hoped it wasn't visible to the naked eye.

Celestia left the room without another word, which the officers seemed to take as their cue to get started.

'All right, Livi,' the woman said, her blonde bob swishing in a way that made it look expensive as she sat back in her chair. 'I'm Inspector Laura Kidd, and this is my colleague, Officer Paul Wrighton, and we're here to ask you a few questions about any interactions you had with Chloe last night, and what happened this morning when you discovered the body. Sophia is here as an appropriate adult since you're under eighteen. Are you happy to go ahead?'

I nodded.

'We need you to say it, Livi,' the male officer said. Paul.

'Happy to go ahead,' I said, my hand curling around the note from the wig room where it was nestled in my pocket. What choice did I have?

Had I just *lied to the police?* I'd just *lied to the police.* My heart was pounding, hands shaking as I scuttled past Oliver with a wave and, as soon as I was out of his sight, started running towards the rehearsal barn. Their questions had been pretty gentle as far as I imagined these things went, but I was sure that any second now there would be a tap on my shoulder and they'd tell me they'd seen right through me.

You did what you had to.

I repeated it over and over in my head, like a mantra, like a line in a script I was trying to learn, drilling it until it sank in. Until it felt true, and not like I was playing a character.

They'd asked if I'd noticed anything out of the ordinary last night. An honest 'no'.

When I'd realised something was wrong. When Tasha and Kitty approached us, also honest.

If I'd seen anything 'off' at the crime scene. Presumably apart from the dead body. I said no. That was my first lie.

If I knew of anything else that might be relevant to their investigation. That was my second.

What I thought might have happened. From there, they kept on coming.

Sam could tell something was wrong as soon as I walked into the room, rushing over the moment he saw me, Daisy and Aaron hot on his heels.

'Livi, what is it? And why are you wearing a wig?'

I put a hand up to my hair, and a laugh burst out of me. I'd forgotten about that. I loved that Celestia hadn't even mentioned it. Neither had Sophia, or the police. Just another thing they all thought was Classic Camp Chance, I guess.

'Long story,' I said, 'and I can't tell you now. We don't have time, and if anyone hears, it's game over.'

'Has something happened?' Daisy asked, and I nodded quickly, hoping my face was giving 'please don't ask me what' vibes.

'Should we be worried?' Aaron asked, and I must have hesitated just long enough. 'That's a yes, then.'

'There's been another note,' I whispered. 'I can't show you here, but find Juliet and we'll meet . . .'.

Crap. Where were we going to meet? Our cabin was probably a safe bet, but I felt pretty exposed there, like if Louis, or Luke, or anyone else for that matter, looked through the window as they were walking past and saw us all there, they'd assume it was a party and invite themselves in. I knew from my secret meetings with Sam that the rehearsal barn was also quiet after dark, but midnight and 6 p.m. were very different times, and there was no telling who might come in looking for a space to practice earlier in the night. None of it felt quite safe enough.

We needed somewhere private.

Somewhere for the ghosts to gather.

'The main stage,' I said. 'After dinner. I'll tell you everything then, I promise.'

'Livi, are you ready?' Celestia called from the piano, where she was standing beside our musical director Tim like it was *her* who was going to put fingers to keys and play for me. 'Ready!' I called back, and in the walk from the back of the room to the stage, I made damn sure that was true.

Shoulders relaxed, chest open – I wouldn't get the sound I wanted if I was tensed, and I'd learnt a long time ago how, no matter what else was going on, to put everything out of my mind for as long as it took to get through a song. Besides, not *everything* had changed. As far as I was aware, there was still going to be a showcase. They were still going to need a lead. If the counsellors were pretending everything was business as usual then so must I. I wasn't going to let this out of my grasp because we were being stalked by a murderer, as good an excuse as that would have been.

I wasn't going to let the killer win.

Pulling my sheet music from my tote bag and handing it to Tim, I took my place centre stage and waited for him to start playing. It wasn't a performance – hardly anyone else even looked up, and almost nobody stopped talking to listen. That didn't matter. I was still going to use every opportunity like it was the real thing. Tim gave me my starting note, and I was off.

The rest of the room disappeared.

For the three minutes it took me to sing through 'Dyin'

Ain't So Bad' from *Bonnie and Clyde*, it was just me, my outlaw husband who in this fantasy looked a lot like Tom Holland, and our barn full of stolen cars and money. I'd never actually seen *Bonnie and Clyde* performed, but I got the gist, and that was what it was about. Basically. I didn't have to think about the words, or my breathing. I knew this song like the back of my hand, the rise and fall of the melody as easy as being strapped into a rollercoaster and somebody pressing go. I had no idea if I was killing it, completely unable to step outside of myself and imagine what I looked like from the audience, but I was *enjoying* it anyway, and wasn't that just as important?

I tried to convince myself that it was.

```
LIVI reaches the end of the song and
grins at TIM as she stands for a second
to get her breath back. She doesn't even
notice straight away that the whole room
has stopped. Is staring at her like 'what
just happened?'

She's good, anyone can see that. Just
like anyone can see that she has no idea
how hard she just nailed it.
```

CELESTIA: Livi, what the hell?
LIVI: What?
CELESTIA: That was . . .

```
She is lost for words, or pretending
to be. JULIET picks up the script
for her.


JULIET: That was out of this world, Livi.


It really was.
```

I could feel myself blushing as I thanked Juliet, thanked Tim, grabbed my music and got the hell off the stage. The moments straight after a performance were some of the most confusing to me. I *loved* the spotlight, really loved being told I was good, of course I did, but there was something lost in the transition from Bonnie back to Livi that made me feel so awkward about it at the same time. Like getting out of a warm pool and adjusting back to the cold air, and the way that, as your skin dried, it always felt colder than before somehow. That was the best way I could describe stepping *off* a stage, as opposed to on it. Crashing back to a reality that felt harsh knowing what the alternative was. If Bonnie was the sun, becoming Livi again was like the first days of winter.

Did I say already that it was awkward?

The others gathered around me as the next performer took their place.

'Where did you learn to *do that*?' Daisy asked.

'Here,' I said, because it was entirely true. Every practical skill I had was because of Camp Chance, at least at its foundation.

'It really was brilliant,' Aaron said, and I could feel myself blushing again.

Aaron Wilson thought I was brilliant. Even if he *was* just a normal person who was a little bit too obsessed with true crime stories, he was still a Hollywood star. I wondered for just a second if I could put that quote on my CV.

Sadly, I decided on *not*.

I caught Sam's eye where he was standing behind Aaron, and he gave me a small nod.

'Solid, Campbell.'

'Thanks.'

I knew what he *wasn't* saying. 'Keep up those late-night rehearsals, do a few more performances like that, and everything you wanted is yours.'

God, I hoped so. *Could it be?*

'Livi,' Celestia said as she walked towards me with a piece of paper in her outstretched hand. 'That was great. Really, well done.'

She handed me the report, but I didn't look at it straight away. I didn't want the others to see me react.

I had no idea where the camp tradition of written reports after each rehearsal came from, because it wasn't something I'd heard of happening in the actual industry, and believe me, I'd read everything I could get my hands on about professional auditions. I quite liked it though – it was something tangible to work on before the next time. As the others started talking about Daisy's song choice, I let my eyes drift down to what was written on the page.

'A truly brilliant performance, assured and technically excellent. In any other year, this would be a very easy decision. This year, you have your work cut out. So keep working.'

I scowled at the paper, as if it could see me.

Suddenly 'being more forgiving to Celestia' seemed a whole lot less appealing.

CHAPTER 12

SAM AND AARON WERE ALREADY WAITING WHEN Juliet, Daisy and I made it to the main stage after dinner. I could hear Sam pacing before we even opened the door, and the way he practically leapt towards us as we walked out onto the stage suggested he had a lot of nervous energy to burn.

'Where have you been? And why are you still wearing that wig?' he demanded. 'You're late.'

I looked down at my watch. *Technically true.*

'We're *two minutes* late, Sam. Relax.'

'*Relax?* You call us here to tell us there's another note but you won't tell us what it says, somehow we've found ourselves in charge of a murder investigation, and you, Livi Campbell, who I've never known to be late for anything in her life, is late. Forgive me if I can't *relax*.'

'What is *wrong* with you? Why are you being so—'

'I was *worried about you*, OK?' Sam shouted before I could finish my question.

He'd been worried? About me? A warmth bloomed in my chest, even though I knew it probably wasn't personal at all. There was, after all, a killer watching our every move. He'd have been worried about anyone, right? But still, I couldn't remember the last time someone had been worried about me – not that I made a habit of giving them reason to be, or letting them know when maybe they should. And now Sam Chambers was worried.

About me.

And I kind of liked it.

Even though I also, obviously, hated it.

'Sorry,' I said softly.

'It's all right. Now are you going to tell us about this note?'

I pulled the note from my pocket, where I'd been obsessively checking on its safety all day. I shuddered as I read it again, then handed it to Sam.

```
LIVI begins pacing as the others pass the
note around. At first, she doesn't speak
even though we can tell she wants to; can
see her opening her mouth to say something
and then stopping herself just in time,
because they haven't finished yet.


LIVI: I . . .


DAISY, JULIET, SAM and AARON look up at her.
```

LIVI: Doesn't matter.

They turn their attention back to the note. Livi turns hers back to pacing.

LIVI: I just . . .

This time only DAISY looks up. Smiles.

LIVI: Doesn't matter.

Pacing.

LIVI: But . . .
SAM: Livi, spit it out.
LIVI: OK! God! I'm just saying, this is bad. Really bad. Like . . . really really—
AARON: It's bad. Go on . . .
LIVI: But it also tells us a lot.
JULIET: Does it?

LIVI begins counting off on her fingers as she speaks.

LIVI: They're *actually* watching us. They know there are five of us. They knew I

would be in the wig store, they must
have. They're *here*. It tells us that
whoever it is . . .
DAISY: They're still here.

*Quiet. Nobody is quite sure how to
respond to that.*

SAM: So, what are we going to do about it?
AARON: If this were a true crime story—
JULIET: Which, by its very nature of
being both true and a crime, it is . . .
AARON: You know what I mean.
LIVI: If this were a true crime story . . .
AARON: Then we're due a first suspect.
We have to work out who had *motive*, and
opportunity. We need to—
JULIET: Are you just telling us we need
to solve it, Aaron, because I think we
know that.
SAM: Juliet, he's only trying to help.
LIVI: Guys . . .
JULIET: I know that, and I appreciate it,
I just think—
LIVI: Guys . . .
JULIET: that we need to be a little bit
more *realistic* than—

LIVI: GUYS!

JULIET: WHAT?

LIVI *(whispering now, like she wasn't just screaming)*: Someone's coming.

The others stop. Listen. She's right. Footsteps. LIVI pulls the group together in front of a large mirror and whips her phone out of her pocket, snapping the selfie just in time for SOPHIA to enter, looking confused.

SOPHIA: What are you doing?

LIVI: Taking selfies.

It was an excuse anyone would believe from a group of campers who, if you asked the counsellors, all loved the sound of our own voices and the image of our own faces. If you asked me, or any other camper I'd ever spoken to, it was a whole lot more complicated than that. It was *expected* that we had good body image. We were *meant* to believe in ourselves. A lot of the time, this was just another example of playing pretend. It worked though. Sophia gave me a disapproving look, as if I'd been the only one in the picture just because it was me that had spoken, and me that was holding the phone, but she didn't ask any more questions.

'You can't be out after dark,' she said. 'Not until the police have finished gathering their evidence. Get to your cabins.'

She didn't wait to see if we were going to follow her instruction, just flounced out as quickly as she'd arrived, confident that none of us were going to risk angering the police. Little did she know we were dealing with something a lot scarier than a couple of police officers, who weren't going to do anything worse than give a slight telling off to a bunch of scared kids who hadn't actually done anything wrong. Still, I thought we'd better comply. The last thing any of us needed was to draw Sophia's attention.

I trailed at the back as we made our way off the stage. I wanted to get Sam alone; to ask if we were still meeting later. I could tell he knew what I was trying to do by the way he stalled too – first to tie his shoelace, then to drink from his water bottle – but I wasn't the only one competing for Sam's attention. Aaron, too, seemed pretty enamoured with his new friend. There was no way I could say what I needed to without someone hearing. In the end I gave up, giving Sam a small smile as I stepped in front of him to leave the stage, hoping he read it as the 'see you later? Please?' that I meant it as.

```
The group leave the stage, heading for
their cabins. DAISY first, then AARON and
JULIET, LIVI and SAM.

Nobody notices the way SAM's hand lingers
on the bottom of LIVI's back as he
```

> *holds the door open for her; guides her through.*
>
> *Well. LIVI notices.*
>
> *I notice.*

I'd been staring at the ceiling in silence for what felt like for ever but what my watch promised had only been two minutes, when I finally decided to say it. Daisy was lying on her bed, scrolling through something on her phone, and the sound of the shower, as well as the steam escaping from under the bathroom door, suggested that Juliet would be in there for a while yet.

This was my moment.

'Hey, Daisy?' I said, and she put her phone down and sat up to look at me. I must have sounded serious.

'Yeah?'

'You know . . . Juliet?'

Now she looked like she might laugh, which hadn't been my intention. It was just an awkward kind of conversation to start.

'Pink hair, killer voice, currently in our bathroom?'

'Yeah, that one,' I said quickly, not giving her space to take the joke any further. This was serious. Daisy sat up straighter.

'Is she all right?'

God, Daisy was so *nice*. I was trying to gossip and her mind jumped straight to concern. I forced myself to soften a little as I leant closer to Daisy.

'Oh yeah, of course, she's fine. I was just wondering if you'd watched her videos?'

Daisy visibly relaxed, which made me feel even worse.

'Oh! Of course! I love them! I think what she's doing is so – wait, why are you looking at me like that?'

I could make my expression do a lot of the work when I was acting; could make anyone believe I was feeling something I wasn't with the twitch of an eyebrow, or a wry little smile, but when I *wasn't* performing? When I forgot to hide behind the mask? I couldn't remember the last time I had a feeling that wasn't immediately written all over my face.

'It's nothing,' I said. 'It's just . . . don't you think theatre should be experienced live? Isn't that a massive part of it?'

'Well, yeah,' Daisy said, like I was missing something obvious. 'But what about the people who never get to?'

'What do you mean?' I asked, now worried I actually *was* missing something obvious.

'Well, we didn't have any money – when I was growing up, I mean,' Daisy said. 'My parents never really took us to the theatre, because they didn't know it could be for people like us. That's why I'm coming to all of this so late. There wasn't anyone *like* Juliet then, or at least not that I knew about. If I'd have had someone like her to watch when I was eleven, maybe I would have been here with you for years by now.'

She was pulling on my heartstrings, but I'd heard this

argument for Juliet's work before. It was all over the internet, and of course it was *true*. It was *so* important for all kinds of people to have access to theatre. But weren't there better ways to do that? Wasn't that up to the producers, and the theatre companies, to find a way to these people and get them into the buildings? Shouldn't the goal be making theatre accessible, rather than redefining what theatre *was*?

I said as much.

'Sure,' Daisy came back quickly, 'but they *aren't* doing that. The way I see it, Juliet is helping. I see your side too, of course I do, and in an ideal world . . . well, we wouldn't be having this conversation if the world was ideal, would we? But it isn't. So . . .'

It was the most passionate I'd ever heard Daisy get about something. Sure, I'd only known her three days, but this was the first time she'd let the sweet, adorable girl I was coming to really like disappear, and brought out someone fierce in her place. I liked this Daisy just as much, I thought. Possibly even more.

'You're right,' I said, already regretting what I knew was about to come out of my mouth next. I couldn't help it, though. I hadn't been able to stop thinking about it, and something just was not sitting right. 'But earlier, in the dining room . . . I saw her vlogging.'

Daisy looked at me like she didn't *quite* see the problem; like she was trying to work out my angle here before she said anything. I got it. Even I didn't quite know my angle or know why it was bothering me so much. Even if she wanted to post those videos right now, which seemed so at odds with her personality that I was having trouble grasping it, Juliet wasn't going to be able to use Chloe's death to further her own career, at least not until camp was over, by which time surely we'd know what had happened? Maybe that was why I was struggling. The Juliet Stone – Jules – that I could hear singing in the shower was so *nice*. Not the type of person who would even think about exploiting a tragedy for clicks. So which one was real?

'That is . . . a little bit weird,' Daisy began. 'But I guess I'm not surprised? It's how she deals with things, isn't it? We all cope in different ways, we all have our things we fall back on. It's obvious she's at her most comfortable in front of a camera, isn't it?'

Well, it *hadn't been*.

Which made the crowning glory of this whole conversation – if I was honest, the reason I'd started it in the first place – even harder to come out with. But I'd gone this far. I'd be a coward if I didn't say it now, and I didn't want to be a coward. I was trying to be brave.

'There's one more thing,' I said, and Daisy was still looking at me with patience and not like I was just trying to find a reason to tear Juliet down. I *wasn't*, at all, there was just something about her presence which felt judgemental to me. Like she thought *her way* was better. In some ways, that was par for the course in a place where the whole point of being here was to perform; to watch the shows we were putting on for each other, and, if we were doing our jobs right, be unable to see the line between what was real and what was make believe, but it felt sharper with Juliet, somehow. Like I should be paying attention. I knew it was probably my own insecurity rather than anything Juliet had actually done intentionally, but something about her felt off.

'Go on...'

LIVI moves to sit on the edge of DAISY's bed. It's like she doesn't want to say this bit any louder than she has to. Like if it's quiet, she can get it out and then they can pretend it hasn't happened.

They don't know we're listening.

LIVI: I can't stop thinking about the night Chloe . . .
DAISY: Right.
LIVI: Juliet wasn't here. She came back late. We were both asleep, weren't we?

Well, no. DAISY was asleep, LIVI was halfway across camp, in the rehearsal barn with SAM.

DAISY: What are you saying?

LIVI: I don't know. Just - should we be taking notice of that?

DAISY: You think she knows something? Saw something?

LIVI: No! No, I don't . . . It's just . . . where was she? Why hasn't she told us?

DAISY: Livi, I don't know. Probably making first years take a part in her vlogs - she had her camera with her at the party, I remember. People were basically hanging off her for the chance to be filmed. She'd have told us if she'd seen anything, you know she would. You could ask her?

LIVI: I already have. She said she didn't see anything strange, and didn't film Chloe at all.

DAISY: And you think she's lying?

LIVI looks unsure.

LIVI: No, you're right. She definitely would have told us. She wouldn't pass up the opportunity to make a story out of it.

DAISY: Livi!

LIVI: Sorry! I get bitchy when I'm anxious.

DAISY: It's OK. I know you're just . . . you didn't mean it.

I sort of *had* though. I knew Daisy was probably right. Juliet had probably been filming the festoon lighting like she said, or taking selfies with other campers long after the party ended, and if we looked through their phones, or waited to see their social media feeds at the end of the summer, Daisy would be proven right and I'd look psychotic. Suspicious. Like a total bitch, if we're being honest. I decided to let it go, but there was still a tiny nag as I tried to put it out of my brain, telling me we didn't *really* have any idea where our roommate had been that night.

'Talking of sneaking around,' Daisy said, letting me off the hook with a swift subject change that I was grateful for, 'I heard Sam has been sneaking out every night since the beginning of camp to meet someone.'

I tensed my face muscles quickly, desperate not to give anything away.

Shut it down, Livi. Change the subject.

Except . . . I was intrigued. I wanted to know what people were saying – who they all thought he was sneaking out to meet.

'Go on . . .' I said, lounging across the bed in what I hoped looked like a totally casual way. Like I was just here for the tea.

'Well,' Daisy said, scooting closer, and *there she was*. I knew she had it in her to gossip. To her credit, I guess who was dating who was probably a more natural subject to whisper in the dark about than whether we thought our roommate knew something that she wasn't letting on about a murder.

'At first, people thought it was Leah, which makes sense because they've been all over each other since the coach, right?'

I nodded. Correct, they had been.

'But then Aaron said he didn't think Sam was that into her. She hasn't been to their cabin or anything...'

No, famously they were looking for a private space to hang out by the lake, I thought. *And besides, it's not like Aaron has been spending that much time in that cabin if the number of times I've seen him through Luke's window is anything to go by.*

I didn't know why I was genuinely trying to work out the answer, anyway. I *knew* who he was sneaking out to meet, by virtue of it being *literally me*.

'Who does Aaron think it is then?' I asked, trying to work out exactly how careful we had to be. If Aaron had any suspicion it was me, the game would be up pretty quickly.

'He thinks maybe Noah?' Daisy said, a question, like she wanted my opinion on the plausibility of that. I pretended to consider it, then actually *did* consider it.

Noah was a wannabe designer who had been coming to camp almost as long as Sam and I. He was very good looking and from the few conversations we'd had in years gone by seemed nice, but I didn't think I'd ever seen Sam say more than about two words to him.

'Really?' I asked, finding myself genuinely interested in why Aaron thought that, even though I knew it wasn't true.

Daisy shrugged.

'That's what he said. You'd have to ask him why. What do you think then? Not him? I'd feel bad for Leah if it was.'

'Don't feel bad for Leah,' I said. 'She's known him long enough to know he's Prince Charming personified. He can turn it on for almost anyone, and *does*. Sam doesn't do long term. He takes pleasure where he can find it, and we all know that. Leah definitely knows that. She's not jumping into this thinking it's for ever, I promise. Neither is Noah, or whoever else he might be meeting up with in the middle of the night. Sam is harmless, but he's not boyfriend material. Not yet.'

I hoped my make-up was hiding the blush I felt rising. Daisy didn't seem to notice.

'Have *you* and Sam ever . . .'

She trailed off, but it was pretty obvious where she'd been going. I shook my head quickly.

'Wouldn't work,' I said, careful not to let my expression slip for even a second, holding on tight to the *Why would you even ask that*? tone that I'd thankfully been able to pull out of thin air. At least I could say it with confidence because I was absolutely certain it was true, after all. I flashed back to last summer. Me leaning in. Him pushing me away. A definitive answer. Wouldn't work. Proven fact. Daisy visibly exhaled, which I hadn't been expecting. Did *she* like Sam? Was she asking for my permission?

'Why?' I asked. 'Are you—'

'Oh god, no.' Daisy cut me off. 'He's lovely, but . . . no. There was just . . . something I wanted to ask you about. Like how you just asked about Juliet?'

She had to be nervous if she thought she needed to explain the concept of asking a question. I was confused; had no idea where she was going with this.

'OK . . .'

'OK,' she said. 'I'm probably wrong, but if Sam has been sneaking out, and nobody is totally sure who with, could *he* have seen something? The night of the . . . the night with Chloe, I mean.'

Ah. No, she hadn't been explaining the concept of asking me a question at all, more telling me that in the exact same way I'd just questioned Juliet's innocence, she was questioning Sam. The thought was laughable to me. He'd been singing songs from *Hadestown* in the rehearsal barn! Not witnessing a murder! I could tell Daisy the truth right now, shut this line of questioning straight down, and take her suspicion off Sam. I *should* do that, I knew.

Something was stopping me though.

I wasn't ready to admit that every time Sam had snuck out of his cabin, he'd been coming to meet me.

Not Leah, not Noah.

Me.

I did not want that to be common knowledge.

I'd stopped putting on a show with Daisy, I realised, as I went to hide behind one of my usual defences and noticed it wasn't there. In here, with the door closed, I hadn't been acting since our first night. And now I needed Show-Livi to make a comeback, and fast.

I forced myself to laugh.

'You think *Sam* knows something?' I asked, my voice too loud in the otherwise quiet room. 'You think that if he did, he wouldn't tell us straight away to make sure he got even more attention? What you need to understand about Sam is that the thing he cares about most in the world *is Sam*. Is how people see him. That they love him. If he thought he knew something that would make him a hero, he'd be shouting it from the rooftops, I promise.'

'If he shouted it from the rooftops, he'd be breaking pretty much all of the killer's rules,' Daisy pointed out.

OK, true. I shrugged.

'Do you really think that?' Daisy carried on. 'About him wanting to be the hero, I mean? Just because . . . it didn't seem like that, when everyone found out he tried to save Chloe. It didn't feel like he was enjoying that attention at all.'

She had a point. I couldn't bring myself to argue it right now. Wasn't ready for the scrutiny it would rightly turn on to me. Besides, he didn't need me defending him. Didn't deserve it.

'Well, he'd at least tell us,' I promised. 'I've known Sam for years, remember? He wouldn't be able to resist.' Daisy visibly relaxed again, and sank back onto the bed.

'OK, thank god. I really needed to hear you say that. You're right. I know you are. I just had to . . .'

'You had to ask,' I said. 'I know. Same with me and Juliet.'

> *Awkward. The girls are silent for a second. Where are you supposed to go from there?*
>
> *JULIET enters from the bathroom, wet hair, bare face.*
>
> **JULIET:** What are you talking about?
> **LIVI:** Boys.
>
> *JULIET smiles, but makes no move to join in.*

The conversation ended pretty quickly after Juliet came back in, all of us exhausted by the day and I, at least, was jumpy – it felt like a risk to carry on, considering what I'd been saying about her just a few minutes before. I was tired enough that I was worried I might slip; might let out what I really felt. Feared. There would be no going back from that.

I couldn't sleep though. I couldn't switch my brain off even when the lights went out and the room fell silent. I laid there for the longest time after the others drifted off, just staring at the ceiling. Thinking.

Wondering why I was so adamant about keeping my meetings with Sam a secret.

Wondering why, when Daisy asked about the two of us being more than friends and I shook my head, it still, despite his very clear rejection that I knew we could never come back from, felt just a little like a lie.

CHAPTER 13

Rehearsal barn. Midnight.

Here we go again.

LIVI enters to find SAM already waiting. She's wearing make-up. (She's always wearing make-up, there are very few people she'll let see her with a completely bare face, and SAM is definitively not on that list.)

SAM: Hey.
LIVI: Hey.

He's sitting by the piano, flexing his fingers over the keys, and LIVI watches him for a moment before she speaks again.

He knows she's watching. He likes it.
We can tell by his face that he likes it.

LIVI: So, I just heard a rumour about you . . .
SAM: No comment. But go on.
LIVI: Rumour has it that you're sneaking out every night to meet someone.

She meets his eye.
Smiles.
Forces herself to stop meeting his eye.

SAM: Who do they think it is?
LIVI: Oh, you know. Leah. Noah. Anyone with a pulse.

SAM nods at the mention of LEAH'S name, raises an eyebrow at the mention of NOAH'S, grins at the final part of the sentence.

SAM: You told them it was all true, right?
LIVI: Of course I did. What do you take me for?
SAM: You jealous, Campbell?
LIVI: What? Me? Jealous? Of people being

linked with you? No! What are you talking about?!

If coming across as not jealous is the goal here, she's doing a terrible job.

SAM: I was joking. But if you say so.
LIVI: I do.
SAM: We'll see.
LIVI: We don't need to see, because I'm not jealous.
SAM: So you said. So you *keep* saying.
LIVI: Well why are we still talking about it then? When we should be rehearsing.
SAM: You wanna rehearse?
LIVI: It's why we're here, isn't it?
SAM: OK, then. Let's rehearse.

They do.

The whole two hours feel like they're building to something that never quite happens, though.

CHAPTER 14

I WAS *EXHAUSTED* WHEN I WALKED INTO THE WHOLE camp dance workshop the next morning, and not only from my late-night rehearsal. No, at least part of the blame for the dark circles under my eyes had to do with the hours I'd spent lying awake once I'd made it back to the cabin, wondering how Sam had found his way under my skin so easily. *Again*.

I hadn't even considered how weird it was that Celestia had called an entire camp dance workshop until I walked into the rehearsal barn to find *everyone* there. And I meant everyone - designers, lighting kids, sound crew. No matter who you were, it looked like you were spending the morning dancing. As an attempt to keep us all in one place, and away from the lake and the investigation, it was thinly veiled at best. The police had concluded their interviews and were following up on evidence at the station, but everyone was still walking on eggshells, as if anything we touched could be a piece of evidence and one wrong step from any of us might bring the whole case crashing down, and then we'd never find out what had happened to Chloe.

They don't know how right they are.

As if he had some sort of radar on us, Aaron, who was standing in the front row, which I guessed was the counsellors work and not his preference at all, turned to look as soon as we entered the room. His eyes were wide, his energy ... heightened, to put it mildly.

I knew straight away that something had happened.

'What?' I mouthed, and Aaron shook his head.

'Afterwards.'

So *that* did wonders for my concentration.

Dancing wasn't my strong suit at the best of times, and this was far from the best of times. Sure, I could pick up a routine and pull it off but I was not a natural mover, and among the campers who had been dancing since they were two, that was obvious. I hated the counsellors for putting us all together like this. Were they going to make the ballerinas belt next? Put the Shakespeare actors through their paces on a sound desk? I didn't think so – so what made it OK to humiliate us all like this?

Sweating, and honestly kind of seething, I was relieved when the music finally stopped and Sophia called time. My ankles were sore and my brain had spent the whole session working overtime, and not on the steps. Daisy had been surprisingly good and Juliet was predictably great, her petite body lending itself well to being flung in all directions, but it hadn't been my best work, I knew. Still, I was surprised when Sophia called me aside as I leapt in the direction of my water bottle, *so* ready to hydrate, get out of there, and find out what Aaron needed to tell us.

'Hey, Livi, two seconds?' she asked, and I didn't think it was the kind of question I was allowed to say no to.

'Of course,' I panted.

Sophia lowered her voice as she spoke again. 'Are you OK? I mean . . . are you struggling? With what happened to Chloe?'

Was I struggling . . . with what happened to Chloe? Was she being serious right now? Even discounting the bits that Sophia had no idea about, could she seriously be asking that question? Someone had died.

'I, um . . . guess?' I stuttered. 'Why do you ask?'

'I noticed that you missed a few steps there,' Sophia said. *Seriously?*

'I'm just tired,' I said. 'It's been a long few days, you know?'

Sophia nodded.

'Yeah, sure, I bet. Listen, Livi, you know we're seriously considering you for the female showcase lead this year, don't you?'

I had hoped. But hearing Sophia say it out loud felt like something slotting perfectly into place. Like a tiny, dislodged piece of my soul had found its way back to its rightful home. *Click.* I grinned.

'And I'm so thankful for that. You won't regret it; I'll work *so* hard—'

'Livi, don't get ahead of yourself,' Sophia said. 'I said *considering*.'

You said seriously *considering,* I thought, but it didn't feel worth splitting hairs over. For some reason, this didn't feel like an entirely positive conversation any more. I didn't think I liked where it was going.

'Right . . .' I said.

'But to pull this off, you need to be better,' Sophia said.

Ouch.

'Better?' I asked.

Sophia nodded, like there was nothing weird or hurtful about what she'd said at all.

'Livi. It's your senior year. Your last chance. You can't be missing steps at this point.'

'I-I . . . didn't realise this was an audition,' I stuttered.

'Everything that happens here is an audition,' Sophia said. 'It's OK – one bad workshop is not going to ruin your chances, Livi. You can take that worried look off your face. But make sure it *is* only one bad workshop. I want this for you. I want it for you almost as much as I wanted it for me, which, trust me, is a lot. But make it easier for me, Livi. Make it a no-brainer.'

She didn't give me a chance to say anything else before she was walking away.

What. The. Hell.

'What was that?' Daisy came up behind me, almost making me jump out of my skin. *God*, I was a mess today. Perhaps these late-night rehearsals, and the lack of sleep that came with them, were doing more harm than they were good?

No. I put the thought out of my head. Nailing our material was more important than sleep. Sophia's little display of concern just now was living proof of that.

'Nothing,' I said. 'Just . . . some performance notes. Where are the others?'

```
Clearing by the small lake. Daylight.
LIVI and DAISY enter, running, to find
AARON, SAM and JULIET already waiting.


SAM: Where have you been? We don't have
long; we're not supposed to be here.
LIVI: I know. Sorry, I got caught up.
What's happened?


AARON pulls a folded piece of paper from
his pocket and thrusts it in LIVI and
DAISY's direction. The way the others
look at them, expectant, makes it clear
they have already read whatever it says.
LIVI reads aloud.


LIVI: Against all odds, you've made it
this far. Nobody suspects a thing; not a
whisper that Chloe's death was anything
```

other than an accident. I'm impressed.
We know the truth though, don't we?
And so, your next clue.
Clue? Are these notes supposed to be *clues*? I don't think whoever is writing them knows what a clue *is*. Clues are meant to *actually help*. Where did you find this?
AARON: The lighting booth. But you haven't got to the best bit yet.

His eyes are sparkling. True crime come to life - AARON is in his element.

LIVI (reading aloud): You're still not looking hard enough. You accepted that Chloe met her end by drowning far too easily. Did none of you wonder how she made it out of the lake? Why she looked so peaceful, and not like she'd fallen foul to the water at all? If you'd looked a little deeper, dug a little further into the weeds, you'd know without me having to tell you that our poor little songbird didn't drown at all . . .
DAISY: What . . . the . . .
AARON: I know.

```
LIVI sinks to the ground, still clutching
the note.

LIVI: OK, Aaron. Start from the beginning.
```

He'd been hanging out in the lighting booth with Luke, he said. None of us asked what they'd been doing in there – none of our business. This note, though? That felt like our business.

'What does he mean?' Juliet asked, for what felt like the millionth time.

'How do you know it's a he?' Sam asked.

'Women don't kill women,' Daisy said, and she made it sound enough like a fact that both of the men looked sheepish, and made the very sensible decision not to continue that line of questioning. I looked up at the others from where I was still sitting on the grass.

'I think it's pretty clear what he *means*,' I said. 'Chloe didn't drown. Which we should have considered, right? She didn't *look* drowned. How did we not . . . Well, I guess we were in shock.' *Focus, Livi.* 'What I don't understand is, why put her in the lake at all? If she was already dead, what was the point?'

'Covering all their bases?' Juliet asked with a shudder.

'Or trying to get rid of the body?' Aaron added.

'Right,' I said, pointing at him, seizing on his point. 'But if *that's* the case, why get her out again?'

'Maybe he panicked,' Juliet said. 'Put her in the lake and realised too late that bodies float.'

'It's getting harder to pretend it wasn't murder, isn't it?' Sam asked, lowering himself to sit beside me on the grass. 'Harder to pretend that someone didn't *do this*, you know?'

I nodded. I knew exactly what he meant. It sounded awful, but in the panic of trying to find the killer, the fact that they had *already actually killed someone* had sort of become the least important part. I looked over at Aaron, who still looked wired by his discovery. I sort of got it – I wasn't proud, but there *was* something weirdly thrilling about all of this; about being a part of something *huge,* and literally life-or-death important. But on the flip side, somewhere along the road this had stopped being about Chloe, and I felt terrible about that. Sure, we had to find whoever had done this, and stop them from doing it again, but we couldn't forget the fact that they already had, either. We had to find them, to get justice for that too.

'So what happened?' I asked, knowing as I did that it was a pointless question; that none of us had the answer. 'How did she actually die? What do we do? Go back to the lake and look for clues?'

'There's no evidence left there,' Juliet said. 'The police will have made sure of that, and if we're not quick about it their autopsy reports are going to come back and let *everyone* know this was no accident.'

'So what?' Daisy asked, and Juliet threw up her hands in frustration.

'So I don't know! We have to work it out some other way!'

'Isn't it worth looking?' Aaron said, and I thought I saw a

flare of anger flash across Juliet's features before she quickly smoothed them out, smiled, and shrugged. She did not like being told she was wrong.

'We can try,' she said. 'I just don't want us to waste the already limited time we have. But whatever you think. You know best, Mr True Crime.'

Her tone was light, but I could tell there was something pointed behind it.

'Luke didn't see this, did he mate?' Sam asked, gently plucking the note from my hands, changing the subject before it turned into a full blown argument. Aaron shook his head as he joined us on the ground.

'No, course not. I feel like I'm becoming an expert in hiding things from him. Not the best way to start a relationship, is it?'

Aaron looked away as he called what he was doing with Luke 'a relationship', but he couldn't quite stop the small smile that played across his lips, the ghost of something good in a sentence that was anything but. I was pleased for him. He deserved that much, at least.

'It won't be for ever,' Daisy said, sitting down beside him. Sam and Juliet followed quickly.

'I know,' Aaron said, 'but I hate feeling like I have to put up a front with him, you know? I've spent my whole life trying to be more palatable – to be what people expect when they look at Aaron Wilson. I just wanted somewhere I could be *me*.'

'I know,' Juliet said, and I turned to her, surprised. For someone who put so much of her life online, she wasn't so forthcoming in reality. I felt like she kept huge parts of herself locked away, only ever revealing what she wanted us to see. Was she about to give us something that was actually real?

'I know it isn't the same,' she continued, 'but I came here hoping it would be easier to find the balance between who I am on camera and who I am in my real life, you know? I was looking for somewhere to learn where I wouldn't be watched. Ha! That was tempting fate, wasn't it? Now my every move is being watched, and if I do a single thing wrong...'

```
Silence.
She doesn't need to finish the sentence.
They all know.
```

DAISY: Can I see the note again? We must be missing something.

```
SAM hands it to her without a word, and she
begins to read in her head. Beside her,
LIVI pulls out her written report from
yesterday's rehearsal and does the same.
```

AARON: What's that?
LIVI: My report from Celestia, from rehearsal. There must be something in there I can actually work with, or what's the point? I have to work

out how to go from good to good *enough*.
SAM: Livi, you are *so* good enough.
LIVI: We don't know that.

JULIET, quiet, looks between LIVI and DAISY. Looks again. None of the others notice until she leans closer to DAISY, reading over her shoulder, then straight back to LIVI, doing the same. LIVI pulls the report close to her chest.

LIVI: Juliet, what are you doing?
JULIET: It's probably nothing.
LIVI: Spit it out.
JULIET: It's just . . .

She gestures for DAISY and LIVI to hand over the pieces of paper in their hands. DAISY does so easily, LIVI with suspicion. JULIET holds them up, showing the group.

JULIET: Like I said, it's probably nothing. But look at the tails on the Gs. Are they . . . Do you think . . . these could have been written by the same person?

> *The group lean in, as if scripted.*
> *Gulps. Hands to lips. Hands to eyes.*
> *Jaws dropped, mouths open.*

And just like that, all other half-formed theories forgotten, Celestia Sinclair has propelled herself to the top of the suspect list.

CHAPTER 15

WE WEREN'T EXACTLY AT THE TOP OF OUR GAME when we raced into showcase rehearsal, five minutes late and spooked as hell that the woman leading it might be the one behind all of this. She raised an eyebrow as we crashed into the back of the rehearsal barn but didn't miss a beat, carrying on seamlessly with her spiel about how things were going to work.

Was she too cool? I wondered. *Was all of this an act; a script that she wasn't going to deviate from to give us a lecture about how being late was unacceptable, especially when we shouldn't have been outside in the first place?* I didn't know, but I definitely didn't trust it. We'd keep a close eye on her, we'd promised on the speed walk over from the clearing.

'Hurry up,' she called now, without stopping the demonstration she was giving to some of the first years – and it was a small mercy that she didn't ask where we'd been, because I thought I was probably too on edge to think of a believable lie.

SOPHIA directs LIVI, DAISY and JULIET into a group with LEAH. A note about the way things work at Camp Chance – when it comes to the showcase, everyone learns everything. The team are very good at covering their backs. At making sure that if they change their mind at the last moment, there is someone else who can sing the solo; deliver the monologue; take the lead.

If they change their mind, or if their first choice can't take the pressure.

SOPHIA: We'll go from the top. Leah, I guess that means you're taking the first go, since you were the only one actually here to *learn* the top.

LIVI looks sheepish, DAISY stricken. JULIET just smiles.

LIVI: Sophia, we all know the top. We all know the whole song, it's a classic.
SOPHIA: That may well be true, but I can't be sure of it since you weren't at the beginning of the rehearsal. So listen

to Leah, because in three minutes you're up, and you'd better hope you do know it.

Clearly something has happened to piss off SOPHIA, and it feels bigger than a few campers being late.

LEAH begins the song from the beginning. She's . . . fine? Technically, there is nothing wrong with her performance, but it doesn't have the kiss of magic that any one of the other campers in this small group would bring to it without even having to try.

SOPHIA: Pay attention, girls. We're going to be drilling this until you get it right.

I was panting by the time Sophia finally called a two-minute break, my water bottle long since depleted, and I scrambled for the door so that I'd be the first to the water fountain in the backstage corridor, Juliet hot on my heels as soon as she saw where I was going.

'This is no joke,' she said as we made it into the hallway, the cool of the air conditioning drying the sweat on my skin so quickly that I knew I'd feel truly disgusting later.

'I know,' I said. 'It does get easier. I think they put us through our paces early so the rest of the summer feels like a breeze – and so they can see what we can do, obviously. Can see who they're going to pair with who. Who they're going to push, I guess.'

'Good to know,' Juliet said, twisting her pink hair into a knot at the back of her head and securing it with a hairband from her wrist. 'Although I'm not sure pushing me much harder will be productive for anyone!'

That's where we differ, I thought. I wanted to be pushed until I broke. To make sure I was getting the absolute best out of myself. I knew I worked best under pressure, and so I sought it out. Rest? That was for September to July. At camp, I would give *everything*, and at any second be ready to give just a little more.

'You're doing great,' I told Juliet, which was true. She was a natural performer, sure, but she could also turn it up to 1,000 like nobody else I'd ever seen. A normal human being one second and a supernova the next – it was easy to see why the camera loved her, why she'd found the success she had. I was going to watch her closely, I promised myself. I wanted to learn how to do that, but I wasn't quite ready to swallow my pride, my anxiety, and ask.

'You both are.'

I looked up at the sound of Celestia's voice, and saw her walking towards us from the direction of the star dressing room. I shuddered involuntarily. Everyone knew the superstition –

that if you set foot in the star dressing room before you'd been assigned it, before you'd been named the star, you'd jinx it. Game over. The dressing room would never be yours. I'd never stepped over the threshold. Celestia didn't seem to have the same qualms. I guessed when your career was already over you started caring a lot less about superstitions that didn't affect you anyway.

'Hey!' I said, forcing a brightness into my voice that I didn't feel as I switched from exhausted to hypervigilant. We'd promised to watch her every move, and it was like the universe had delivered her to us. I didn't want to waste a second.

'I'll go and grab the water,' Juliet said, prising my bottle from my hand and clearly not picking up on the 'what the hell are you doing, I need you' vibes I was trying to give her without looking like I'd lost my mind. Since I couldn't protest without drawing Celestia's attention to the fact that I was being really weird, I loosened my grip and hoped Juliet could feel the daggers I was mentally giving her as she walked in the direction Celestia had just come from.

'You seem to be getting on well with Juliet,' Celestia said, pointing to the little pink head bobbing down the hallway away from us. It felt like a test.

'She's really nice,' I said. 'I'm really happy with my cabin assignment. Daisy is great too.'

Celestia smiled like I'd given her the perfect in for what she wanted to say next.

'Yeah, I've noticed you've all been spending time together,' she said, a sweet smile playing across her lips that was very unlike Celestia. She usually made a point of not getting involved with our personal relationships; of taking her role as Head Counsellor very seriously and leaving the day-to-day bits, like making sure we were actually OK, with Sophia and the rest of her team.

'I guess it makes sense,' I said. 'Most of my friends from last year aged out, so I'm glad I've found a new group to hang around with.'

I was panicking. Why was I panicking? This was a perfectly normal thing for her to be asking me about, wasn't it? Celestia nodded, as if she'd heard me.

'Aaron and Sam, too? That's a nice little group. It looks like you're having a really nice time. I think it's really good for you, Livi. To let your guard down a bit. Remember you're supposed to be having fun.'

Why did nobody understand that, for me, working hard *was* having fun? I smiled, though all the while desperately trying to work out if Celestia was being sincere; if she really did think our friendship was good for me, or if this was all part of her psychological game. Was she trying to spook me? No need, I thought. I was spooked enough already.

'I am having fun,' I promised, hoping she couldn't hear the lump in my throat I had to push past to get the words out.

'Enjoy the rest of your rehearsal,' Celestia said, heading in the direction of the main entrance.

Crap. I had no idea why the conversation had made me so uneasy.

Because you seriously think she could be involved in this, I reminded myself. *You're jumpy, and anxious, and the last thing you need is Celestia's eyes on you – more than they already are, anyway.*

I needed to make sure we looked *real*.

Pulling out my phone, I scrolled to the photo we'd taken on stage – the selfie in the mirror. I hadn't looked at it closely at the time, more focused on making sure Sophia didn't suspect anything was afoot, but looking at it now, it was a really nice photo. We all looked *relaxed*, which was a miracle, and there was nothing in the shot that would identify our location, so Celestia couldn't say anything about me making it public. This would work perfectly.

I tapped out a quick caption before I pressed post: *To taking off the mask, and to new friends.* I set it as my wallpaper too, for good measure, even though the chances of Celestia seeing my phone were pretty slim.

A peace settled over me as I read the caption back, and I found that I meant it. They *were* my friends. Even Sam, sort of. Nothing like being thrown together with a bunch of near-strangers and dropped into the middle of a murder investigation to make people bond, right? *It's more than that though, isn't it?* the Livi in my head asked. *When you think of Sam, you're not thinking about how much you like working with him at all.*

No, I guess not.

I was thinking about how despite what had happened before, I felt safe with him now. How there was something real behind the Prince Charming persona, and that I regretted not being able to see past his rejection to find it. That I thought we could actually be friends and we were only finding that out now, when we had weeks instead of years left before this was over. What a waste that was. I tried to console myself that everything happened in its right time. That Sam and I hadn't missed our cues, we were too early. Looking for the wrong ones. That, when they came, we took them and ran with them.

That we *did* still have weeks.

The door at the end of the hallway opened and Juliet came back into the corridor holding our water bottles, condensation and overspill dripping down the sides.

Even she was a surprise to me. She was sweet. Genuine. Actually easy to like.

'What happened?' she asked now, as she handed my bottle to me and we started walking back towards rehearsal right as we heard Sophia call time.

'I'll tell you later,' I promised. 'She's watching us, I think. She said how good it is that we're all friends.'

'That . . . isn't good,' Juliet said. 'If what we suspect turns out to be true. We have to be at least a step ahead of her. Smarter than her. Less predictable.'

For some reason, I wanted to laugh. Did we *seriously* think Celestia was a killer? That she'd killed Chloe and was threatening to do the same to others if we didn't . . . what? Stop her? Did Celestia really have the brains to pull that off? The heart? The courage?

God, Livi, what is this, The Wizard of Oz*?*

I pushed the laugh back down. I wasn't sure Juliet and I were close enough yet that she'd get it if I just started cracking up.

We'd promised to meet on the main stage after dinner so I could fill the others in, and I was too nervous to eat more than a few bites. Not because I had anything scandalous to report – I mean, all Celestia had actually said was that she'd noticed us hanging out, which she was also doing in this dining hall right now, watching us eat our burgers and salads in plain sight. I felt hyper aware of *everything*. The feel of my jumper on my arms, my make-up on my face, every conversation at every table only amplifying all the things we *weren't* saying. Celestia's eyes on us from the counsellors' table. Sam's leg *just* stopping short of touching mine under the table.

Especially that one, which considering everything else that was going on just felt wrong. I tried to put it out of my mind, to change the subject from nothing, from silence, to something we could talk about for ever.

'What's everyone's favourite show?' I asked, and all four of them looked at me like I'd been possessed by aliens, which I guess the stilted question kind of made it sound like I had.

'Livi, shhh. Eat your burger,' Sam said with a knowing smile. His leg brushed against mine, and yeah, sure, that was one way to shut me up. *What the ... ?*

```
Dining hall. Dinner.
Not quite dark outside — the sun
```

teasing, lingering, as if it's watching for something; making sure all is well before it bows out for the night. LIVI, JULIET, DAISY, AARON and SAM sit at the table near the French doors. They're twitchy. Jumpy. Not saying more than they're saying, heads bowed together in a bubble nobody is trying to penetrate but couldn't if they wanted to. Every time they hear footsteps, they clam up.

It makes for a funny scene, watching these people, who are usually so poised, with their muscles tensed, their eyes darting back and forth as if they're wishing they could be looking in two completely different directions at once.

Doesn't seem like they are finding it that funny.

JULIET cracks first.

JULIET: God, I can't sit here any more! Not talking about it is worse than talking about it in front of everyone! I'm going back to the cabin for a jumper.

I'll meet you on stage in five.
SAM: I'll walk with you. I need to stop by my cabin too.

LIVI raises an eyebrow. It isn't meant for anyone to see, but I do. Noted.

DAISY: OK, we'll see you there.
AARON: Let me just tell Luke I'll see him later. I'll catch you up.

JULIET and SAM exit in the direction of the living area. AARON leaves to speak to LUKE. LIVI and DAISY, quiet, make their way to the main stage.

DAISY: What a weird day.
LIVI: Understatement.
DAISY: How are you feeling?

LIVI looks surprised. That someone has asked? That someone cares?

LIVI: I'm *pissed*.
DAISY: Oh. OK.
LIVI: Not at *you*. Not at any of you. Thank god for all of you. No, I'm pissed

at whoever did this. At whoever has
hijacked my last summer here and meant
I'm giving at least as much brain time to
whoever killed Chloe as I am to, like,
fixing my dancing so Sophia doesn't call
me out again. I've known how this summer
was meant to go for as long as I've been
coming to camp, and this . . . psycho has
ruined it. This was not how it was meant
to be.
DAISY: Livi, I'm sorry.

LIVI laughs.

LIVI: It's a good lesson in letting go, I
guess. My parents are always telling me to
do that - to forget how things are supposed
to be and embrace them for what they
actually are. They'd probably be pretty
proud of how we've had to pivot here.
DAISY: Proud you're chasing a murderer and
not telling anyone who could actually help?

*LIVI looks at DAISY. Her eyes are
sparkling. LIVI laughs, and pulls her
new friend into her side.*

LIVI: OK, maybe not. But they'd be proud
I've made friends. Proud I'm not doing it
alone.

*They step on to the main stage. The ghost
light is on, but otherwise, darkness.
LIVI flicks on the light.*

A beat.
She screams.

It was scrawled in bright red lipstick in the mirror, something I didn't think actually worked outside of movies. Clearly, I was wrong. Daisy's head snapped up at the sound of my scream, her gaze flying straight to where I was looking. The message was unambiguous.

DELETE THE
PHOTO.

I felt completely rooted to the spot, my brain whizzing through all the things this could possibly mean.

1. The killer followed me on social media and had seen the photo there.

1.5. (Celestia did follow me on social media.)

2. They were working with someone who followed me. Someone on the inside.

2.5. (Most of the veteran campers followed me, so that didn't really help.)

3. We were being watched. Not through our screens, but right now.

I pulled Daisy close, not trusting that we could speak in anything more than a whisper without being heard. Before I could say anything, the ancient Tannoy system at the side of the stage began to crackle. The voice that came out was distorted – run through a filter literally designed to serve as a disguise. I recognised it, though I couldn't put my finger on where from. I had heard this voice before.

'*Did nobody ever tell you that mirrors on stage are bad luck?*' the robotic stalker demanded. '*You're not taking this seriously enough, so let me make it very clear. I know who you are. You still don't know who I am. That means I am winning, and as long as I am winning . . . one of you could be next.*'

A crash from behind us almost made me jump out of my skin, and I spun, without thinking about how dangerous that could be, to find Aaron and Sam practically skidding to a halt at the edge of the stage, Juliet right behind them.

'What the hell was that?' she asked.

'You heard it?'

'Livi, everyone heard it,' Sam said. 'That Tannoy covers this whole building. We'd better hope nobody else is in here.'

I wasn't going to be the one to point out that since none of *us* had been the one making threats over the speaker, someone else was *clearly* in here.

'Let's get out of here.' Daisy's voice was shaky, and the others followed her lead immediately, shuffling off the stage as quickly as they could.

'We have to go back to the lake,' I said.

'But the police—'

'I know.' I cut Juliet off before she could protest again that it was pointless, that the police would have removed any trace of evidence, that being there might implicate *us* if they came back to search for more. That last one actually was a concern, but I thought we had more to lose by *not* going – that if there was anything left there to be found, it had to be us that found it. 'But we can't just do nothing. We all heard that voice. It's pretty clear we're being watched, and that means we're on the back foot here. It's like they said – as long as they can see us and we can't see them, we're losing. We have to get ahead. We have to—'

'She's right,' Aaron said. 'We should go to the lake.'

Nobody argued when *he* said it.

I couldn't resist one last look over my shoulder at the mirror as we left. I had my phone in my hand and knew the others would assume I was following orders, was deleting the photo to keep us safe.

I couldn't help it, though. I couldn't let go of this one last tiny bit of control.

So. I just let them believe that.

CHAPTER 16

IT WAS EERIE BEING BACK AT THE LAKE, NOT LEAST because there was no way of pretending we'd ended up there by accident once we'd carefully slipped under the police line still half-heartedly trying to keep us out.

'Are we sure about this?' Juliet asked, not for the first time – but even as she said it, she was limboing under the flapping blue and white tape, trying to keep her footing in the mud with a kind of balance I knew came from learning how to hold yourself in the type of dance training she professed to never have had. It was a practised kind of movement. I could tell, because I'd practised it myself.

'What are we even looking for?' Daisy asked, turning her attention to Aaron. 'Something to prove she wasn't here alone?'

'Or that tells us how she died,' he said. 'If she didn't drown, it means we've missed something big, right? Or something *small*, I guess. Something less obvious. They're telling us we need to look beyond the surface.'

Beyond the surface?

'Of the water,' I said, even though I knew that wasn't what he'd meant. 'What a hiding place. If there was a weapon, whoever did this could easily have just thrown it in there, knowing it would probably stay down there until someone drained the lake. Which, as far as I'm aware, they're not going to. If it's in there, they'll probably get away with this for ever.'

'Probably not for ever,' Juliet said. 'If the autopsy says she didn't drown, they'll be back here in a heartbeat, and then all bets are off.'

'Not if we get there first,' Sam said, crouching down beside the bush that Chloe's mask had been tangled in. I thought of it concealed in the box under my bed where I was certain nobody could find it without me knowing. I shuddered. The fact that it was there was creeping me out, but we couldn't let the police get their hands on it. Not if it might be evidence. Sam started pulling the weeds apart, running his fingers through the soil. Without any better plan, I joined him on the ground and Juliet followed my lead, kicking off her sandals and dipping her feet into the water.

In years gone by, campers used to swim in the lake on particularly hot days, wilfully ignoring how dirty we all knew it was for a few minutes of refreshing reprieve from the breezeless heat. But then, last summer, Noah had cut his foot on a sharp rock so badly that he still had the scar, and that somehow made it a lot harder to pretend we weren't swimming in a soup of algae, bugs, and now Noah's blood. I wasn't going to tell Juliet that, though. Not when she looked so chill, her eyes closed, head tilted back.

'*What* the hell was that?'

Her eyes flew open *right* as I was thinking how peaceful she looked, and she pulled her feet from the lake, scuttling backwards, a hand covering her mouth, the perfect picture of shock.

'What was what?' Daisy dropped down to join us on the grass as she spoke.

'Something touched my foot,' Juliet said quietly.

Well, you did have it in the water, I thought. *What did you expect?* The others, though, seemed as concerned as Juliet herself.

'Something like what?' Aaron asked, lowering himself on to his stomach on the ground, despite the mud, bringing his eyes level with the water.

'I don't know,' Juliet said. 'Something . . . scaly?'

Aaron raised an eyebrow.

'Like a fish?'

'Maybe?'

He rolled his eyes affectionately, smiling at Juliet.

'I thought you meant like *evidence*, not *wildlife*. God, Jules, don't excite me like that!'

I bit my lip at his use of the word 'excite' to stop me from saying anything, dipped my head so as not to meet his eye. He was right. It *was* quite exciting. I just hated thinking that way when Chloe had been *right here* just a few days ago.

Wait, what?

I leant closer to the lake, sure I was seeing what I thought I was but needing to confirm.

Why is there a whole cluster of tiny dead fish? It seemed unlikely that they'd all just exited this earthly realm at the same time completely by chance, right? Had something happened here? What would cause – I did a very quick count – upwards of fifteen fish to all die *at once*? It was like they'd been . . .

'Guys,' I said. 'What if the wildlife and the evidence are the same thing?'

They all turned to look at me, one smooth movement, like they'd planned it.

'What do you mean?' Juliet asked.

I didn't answer, pointing instead to where the fish were floating, drifting with the rhythm of the moving water, closer to us and then further away in a cycle they couldn't break, never quite reaching any fixed destination.

'The fish,' Sam said. 'They're – wait, Liv, what are you saying?'

'They're all dead,' Daisy supplied.

'Exactly. Doesn't it seem strange that they're *all* dead?' I thought what I was saying was obvious, but, Daisy aside, my friends were looking at me like I was speaking another language.

'Something happened here!' I said. 'It must have! Something that killed *all* of the fish and brought them floating to the surface. That probably was what touched your foot, Jules. Sorry,' I added, noting the way she grimaced at the thought.

'And you think maybe whatever killed them also has

something to do with what happened to Chloe?' Juliet asked, eyes closed, as if not being able to see the fish might help.

'It must have, right? Doesn't it seem like too much of a coincidence otherwise?'

'Massive fish kills usually means low oxygen in the lake,' Aaron said, and we all turned in his direction like *how on* earth *do you know that?*

'Google,' he said, interpreting our expressions correctly and holding up his phone. 'And not that helpful because that doesn't explain what happened to Chloe at all. The counsellors probably just don't look after the lake properly.'

Definitely also true, but a coincidence? I wasn't buying that. We were missing something; I knew we were.

'Google, again,' I said to Aaron. 'You said lack of oxygen or whatever is *usually* the cause. What are the others?' Before he had a chance to answer, I saw something catch Juliet's eye. Saw her decide to ignore it. Grapple with that decision. Change her mind – all in the time it took Aaron to lift his hand from his side to wake up the screen of his phone.

'There's something in the lake,' she said quietly, and the way she said *something* made it completely clear that it was a tangible thing. And there it was – not a lack of oxygen but a small glass bottle, floating towards the bank, tangling momentarily in algae and moss before it was freed again, and drifting right into Juliet's outstretched—

Wait. What the hell was she doing?

'Juliet, DON'T!' I shouted, but either I was too late or the shock of my voice made it worse, because her fingers curled around the bottle right at that moment and she pulled it out of the water.

'What?' she asked, looking between us and the bottle which had multiple chemical warnings on the still-intact label.

She hadn't realised yet what the rest of us had immediately known. That the tiny bottle *had* to be the murder weapon. And now it had her fingerprints all over it.

'Jules, put it down,' Aaron said calmly, as if he was trying not to spook her further. He was a very soothing presence, projecting confidence and a 'we can find a way out of this' vibe that I *definitely* wasn't feeling. I was glad someone else was taking control.

'It's fine,' Juliet said, sounding far from fine. 'As long as we have this, not the police . . . and as long as they don't know we've found it . . .' She trailed off. She had a point – it wasn't as if we were planning to hand the bottle over, or let anyone know it existed at all, but still. I thought pawing it over and over, like she was *still* doing, was inviting trouble we definitely couldn't afford.

'Of course it's fine,' Daisy said, jumping on Aaron's reassuring bandwagon. 'Just . . . put it down now. If whatever was in there *is* what killed the fish,' *and Chloe*, I mentally supplied, 'we don't need it getting on you too.'

That worked. Juliet dropped the bottle to the ground without ceremony, stopping it from rolling away with the toe of one of her pink sandals, and dropping to a crouch to get a closer look. I followed her lead.

'What is it?' I wondered aloud as I leant towards the bottle. The label, while still clinging on, was water damaged to say the least. Most of the writing had rubbed off, so I couldn't tell exactly what the contents had been, but my eye kept being pulled back to the chemical symbols along the bottom.

'Poison,' I said, answering my own question since nobody else was jumping to. 'Whatever was in this bottle was *definitely* poisonous to humans, and fish apparently. It showing up here can't be a coincidence. I'd be willing to bet that's our answer.'

'So what do we do with it?' Sam asked, reaching out as if to touch it.

'Not *that*,' I said, swatting his hand away. 'We don't want any more fingerprints on it than we already have, Sam!'

'Why implicate all of us when I'm already going to take the fall, she means.' Juliet's voice was droll, but I could tell she wasn't really joking.

'Juliet, that's not—'

'It's fine,' she cut me off. 'What's done is done, right? But Sam's question stands. What *are* we going to do?'

'Keep it hidden,' Aaron said. 'Jules, I'm sorry, but that has to be you. If anyone finds it, we tell them the truth.'

'WHAT?' I yelped, and Aaron put up his hand to show me he wasn't finished.

'Well, half of it at least. You *just* found the bottle and took it back to your room in case it was evidence. You were going to tell someone – in fact you were on your way to do just that. Of course your fingerprints are on the bottle. You picked it up.

You weren't thinking. *Yours* can be explained away. It's whoever else has touched it that we're interested in.'

```
They look at him, impressed.
He's good.
```

'But until that happens,' Aaron continues, 'we carry on as normal. In public, anyway. Behind the scenes we need to work out what was in that bottle, and where the hell it came from. Daisy, what time is it?'

Daisy pulled out her phone and held it up so Aaron could see.

'Right. So what we do *right now* is go to rehearsal.'

I'd spent my whole life wishing I could act every day. I'd never imagined it quite like this.

CHAPTER 17

THINGS THAT ARE ESSENTIAL FOR A SUCCESSFUL career in theatre, in no particular order:

1. Talent (actually one of the least important, if you look at the way some producers cast. Can be substituted with celebrity).

2. The right support.

3. Luck, in spades.

4. A whole lot of fighting spirit.

I had the talent, or I'd been told I did, but luck and support, at least from my family, didn't seem to be on my side right now, so there was no choice – I had to go into rehearsal with so much fighting spirit that the counsellors didn't have a choice but to pay attention. Sure, I'd been distracted – would I even be human if I *hadn't* been thrown by all the drama that was going on offstage? But today, I was going to be the most Livi version of Livi that I could muster. To sing, and throw my body around in some approximation of dancing, and show Celestia that she'd be a fool not to take me seriously. Not to give me a chance.

To show the killer that too.

Assuming they weren't the same person, that is.

From the moment I walked into the auditorium I knew my plan was going to work. Knew I'd be able to find the proper focus. I'd learnt a long time ago how to turn it on, but that didn't mean it always came easy.

Today it came easy.

I was *sparkling*. I was hitting every note, every mark. Everyone was watching, and so I put on a show. It was like every move I made was screaming 'if you don't pick me, it won't be because I wasn't the best you've got. Because I am.'

Funny how I could believe that so much more easily when I was playing a part.

When it came time to being matched with duet partners, the way I seamlessly slid into place next to Sam would not have looked out of place to anyone but the two of us. I made it look completely random, when really this moment had been days in the making. Unless something went spectacularly wrong, the people we were paired with today would be our partners until the final decisions were made. I couldn't think of a year when the leads hadn't been two performers who came together at this early stage.

'Livi and Sam,' Celestia called, and when I looked up to give her a grateful smile, the look she shot back in return seemed to be saying 'don't say I never give you anything'.

God, she was confusing.

I was buzzing when the rehearsal came to an end. I could have carried on for hours, my energy even higher than it had been at the beginning, and it was one of those sessions where it felt like we were all completely aligned – *everyone* had been on top form, stamina seemingly endless, hitting every mark not just technically but emotionally. Moments like this were why I did it. All of us, a part of something. It was my favourite feeling in the world.

'Seniors, I have a favour to ask,' Sophia said, once she'd finished telling us how great we'd all been today (true) and that if we kept it up, we were looking at Camp Chance's best showcase yet (which she said every year, but which this year *also* happened to be true). I watched as practically all of the seniors straightened our spines, keen to look helpful and to show that We Were Listening.

'I need someone to cover reception for an hour,' she said, and just like that the straightened spines were almost all slumped over again, campers more interested in looking invisible than helpful now. I got it – there was a party tonight, and losing an hour of getting ready time to sit on reception where it was almost guaranteed the phone wouldn't ring and not a single person would come in or out, did not seem like a fair trade-off. So I was surprised when Aaron's hand flew up.

'I'll do it.'

What?

All four of us looked at him like *have you forgotten we were meant to be going to a party tonight, to act like nothing out of the ordinary is going on, and to maybe, for just a few hours, pretend that's true?*

He looked back like *trust me, you're going to like this.*

At least that's what I think he was doing – the look lasted less than a second before Sophia said, 'Thank you, Aaron. It won't go unnoticed.'

As if Aaron Wilson needed to do *anything* around here for brownie points.

'No worries. I'll use the hour to watch Elphaba riff compilations on the internet.'

He was a good actor. His voice didn't falter at all, but I knew that whatever he *was* planning, it wasn't that. For one, he'd told me before he didn't really like *Wicked*. We'd decided that was an 'agree to disagree' situation.

'What are you doing?' Juliet asked under her breath as Sophia dismissed us, and Aaron waved her away with a smile.

'Don't worry. I have a plan. You all go to the party and I'll call when I'm done to see where you are.'

'You're not going to do that, are you?' Daisy asked. The way Aaron was fluttering his eyelashes completely gave him away, and he dipped his head as he smiled.

'Of course I am.'

I believed him. It was what he was going to do between now and then that I was more interested in. I could tell he had a plan.

NIGHT, THE CLEARING. (Not the one by the lake. Nobody hangs out there any more, and only partly because half of it is still cordoned off.)

A party. The first since . . . well, you know. The last one.

Low key. Subdued. Campers are trying to pretend everything is normal. Nothing feels normal.

DAISY, SAM and LIVI are keeping mostly to themselves. JULIET is close by, filming the lights strung through the trees, a whispered commentary about finding theatricality everywhere falling out of her mouth as if she's scripted it, which she might have.

LEAH walks past with two other girls and scowls in SAM's direction.

LIVI: What was that all about?
SAM: I don't think I'm her favourite person right now.
LIVI: What did you do?
SAM: What makes you think *I* did something?

LIVI: I know that look. That's how you look at someone when they've done something.
SAM: I didn't do anything. We just . . . weren't on the same page.

LIVI doesn't look like she believes him. DAISY'S phone beeps.

DAISY: Aaron. He wants us to meet him in reception.

CUT TO: Reception

AARON is sitting at the desk, leg bouncing in anticipation, tapping his fingers on the desk. We can see that He Is Waiting. He practically flies out of the chair as DAISY, LIVI, SAM and JULIET walk into the too-small cabin.

AARON: What took you so long?
SAM: Bro, we came as soon as you texted.

(Side note, Sam cannot pull off saying 'bro'. He doesn't sound cool.)

LIVI: What have you found?

AARON: Nothing yet. I haven't looked. I wanted us to do it together.

DAISY: Do *what*? What are we looking *at*?

Aaron gestures for them to gather as he drops back into the desk chair and clicks around on the screen.

AARON: CCTV.

SAM: Wait, the police didn't take it?

AARON: They looked at it on-site and didn't find anything. Didn't they tell you that, in your interview? Maybe they took copies too, I don't know. Doesn't matter. Point is, it's *here*, and these cameras have eyes on the gates twenty-four hours a day. If anyone came in or out, the cameras would know about it. Unless anyone has tampered with them, that is . . . If this was a murder podcast—

LIVI: Aaron, trust me, none of the counsellors know how to tamper with a CCTV camera.

AARON: I bet some of the stage crew kids do.

JULIET: It's hard and rarely worth it.

They all turn to look at Juliet. She shrugs, smiles, doesn't bother looking sheepish.

JULIET: What? Doctoring a video, at least in a way that'll look believable, takes a hell of a lot of skill. They're not that stupid — they'd have to have known the police would look at it at, right? It'd be a risk. Add in getting it out of the CCTV system in the first place, and you're far more likely to get caught than to get away with it.
LIVI: Do you know how to do it?
JULIET: Yes.

End of sentence.
Silence, verging on awkward.

AARON: Well that's a good thing, right? It'll make this a lot easier.
DAISY: Juliet knowing how to—
AARON: Not that. The fact that Celestia *won't* know how to do it. So if she has, we'll notice, and if she hasn't . . .
LIVI: We might just get our answer.

'Guys,' Daisy said, her voice serious, as if she was reasoning with a bunch of children. 'Do we really think it was Celestia? What reason did she have to kill Chloe?'

'Erm, she's a *murderer*?' Juliet said, as if it was completely obvious. 'Her "reason" doesn't have to make sense since *clearly* she's not in her right mind.'

'Maybe,' Aaron sounded calm as he stepped between them, holding up a hand in Juliet's direction. *Back off.* 'But Daisy is right. There's usually a motive. If we work out what Celestia's was – or might have been, we don't *know* yet that it was her – we'll be a step closer to cracking this. Jules, you first – motive. Doesn't have to make sense, like you said, just pull something out of the air. Go.'

'Um . . .' Juliet floundered for just a second. 'She was jealous of Chloe, as someone at the beginning of her career, when hers – Celestia's, that is – is all but over.'

I nodded, impressed. *Not outside the realms of possibility.*

'All right,' Aaron said, grinning – *god*, he loved this. 'Sam, you next.'

'Erm . . . what are they usually? Money, love . . .?'

'Lust, love, loathing and loot,' Aaron said. Of course he knew that.

'Right. Then I'm going . . . loot? Chloe's family owed the camp money and . . . I don't know?'

'I vote loathing,' I cut in. 'But you might be right about the family. Celestia and Chloe's . . . aunt? I don't know . . . anyway, they were rivals, and—'

'Guys, *please*,' Daisy said. 'I'm being serious! If we really think it's her, then *why*?'

'Fine,' Aaron said. 'Motive, we don't know. We can't know – we never learnt enough about Chloe while she was here to possibly be able to predict. But let's look instead at *why Celestia*. Obviously, there's the handwriting. The loops on her Gs.'

'Right,' I said, 'and she knew I'd be in the wig store, *obviously*, since it was her scheduling that put me there. She easily could have planted that note.'

Aaron nodded, like I'd said something right. 'Great! You see, Dais, it isn't about *wanting* it to be Celestia, it's about working out who even *could* have done it.'

'And she could,' Juliet cut in. 'She's one of the only people who has full access around here, right? Every key to every door, oversight on where everyone is the whole time.'

```
AARON: Precisely. So we need to look at
the CCTV. Catch up to her. Make sure we
know where everyone was too. Now, what
time window? Sam, what time were you and
Leah by the lake?
LIVI: Yeah Sam, what time were you
breaking Leah's heart by the lake?
SAM: Not helpful.
LIVI: Fine. Sorry. Carry on.
SAM: We were by the lake at like . . .
eleven? Or, quarter-past?
```

LIVI: Go earlier. Reception closes at nine, right? So any time after that, nobody would notice someone coming through the gate.
AARON: Good shout.

AARON clicks through the camera feed of the rainbow gates until he gets to 9.01 p.m., and watches SOPHIA on the screen leave the reception hut and lock the door.

AARON: OK. Showtime.

He speeds through the feed, but nobody comes or goes through the gates. Eventually, the screen shows morning, and one of the counsellors arriving at the reception hut for the morning shift.

DAISY: Does that mean?
AARON: No one came or went all night. Whoever killed Chloe, they were already here.
SAM: They were already here, and, after they did it, they *stayed*. We know they've been watching us . . .

DAISY: So that means . . .

AARON: That they're probably still here.

DAISY visibly shudders. LIVI, clearly in a more practical mood, swipes the signing-in log from a shelf above AARON'S head and starts flicking through it.

AARON: What are you doing?

LIVI: Looking at who has signed out since then. And it's like I thought. No one. Whoever killed Chloe is *definitely* still here.

JULIET: I mean, I doubt following proper visitor protocol is *that* high on a killer's to-do list. They could have just walked out, right?

SAM: Right. And without wanting to overstate the obvious, we *know* they're watching. They've literally told us.

LIVI: Fine! You're right! I was just checking nothing looked out of place!

DAISY: So what do we do now?

AARON *(already clicking through the camera feed at an impressive speed):* We find Celestia.

The CCTV system was janky as hell, and it took Aaron a minute to bring any of the screens into focus, what with cameras that had been knocked and so were giving us a live feed of the floor, and others that were out of action altogether. It was probably a safeguarding nightmare, but I doubted any of the counsellors even knew – nothing ever happened at Camp Chance that would mean they needed to check the CCTV. It had likely sat completely dormant as long as I'd been coming here.

'There,' Aaron said, satisfied, as he found Celestia on screen. I had to admit the camera loved her, even if the camera in question was just a CCTV system, and even if by loved her I just meant she was very easy to spot as she flounced from window to window in front of us like she owned the place, which she might as well have.

'Slow down,' I instructed Aaron as the images in front of us changed quicker than I could compute what we were looking at. 'Can we find a shot where she actually stands still for more than ten seconds and see how far we can track her from there?'

'Exactly what I was trying to do,' Aaron said as he paused on a shot of Celestia and Sophia, standing outside the rehearsal barn, vaping. The time said 10.52 p.m.

'Vaping!' I exclaimed. 'That's not exactly promoting healthy habits for a life in the theatre, is it? Shouldn't they be setting an example?'

'Livi,' Sam said, putting a hand on each of my shoulders, 'relax for once in your life. Nobody could see them. They're completely alone.'

'*We* can see them now,' I pointed out.

'*We* are not supposed to be doing this,' he reminded me with a squeeze.

He had a point. I shrugged him off anyway, pretended not to see how that made him roll his eyes and smile.

'Guys, she's moving,' Daisy said, and our focus flew back to the screen where Celestia was hugging Sophia and setting off in the direction of – I couldn't work it out.

'Where is she going?' I asked. 'Aaron, can you work it out? Can we follow her?'

'Livi, chill,' he said with a laugh.

I didn't like this new *Livi, chill* agenda that all my friends seemed to be pushing tonight. I was *so* chill.

'I've got this.'

To prove his point, he clicked once and the image on the screen switched, now showing the dining hall. Celestia walked into the shot seconds after we got there, like she'd been waiting for her cue. Without stopping, practically without looking up, she walked right through. In direct contrast to the *Livi, chill* instruction, my heart rate picked up. Where was she *going*? The time on the screen now said 11.03 p.m.

'Keep going,' I urged Aaron, pointlessly since he was already on to the next screen. The staff cabins. If she walked past here, there were only so many places she could have been going, and at 11 p.m. none of them made sense. I hated how excited I was getting. I could totally see where Aaron was coming from with the true crime obsession now.

'Wait, what?'

Celestia wasn't walking past at all. Instead, she unlocked her cabin and disappeared inside.

'It doesn't mean she's innocent,' Aaron insisted. 'Keep watching, she might be back out in a second and then we carry on.' He clicked through, as if to prove his point.

Celestia didn't leave the cabin.

'Speed run it,' Sam said, like it was some kind of video game and not a murder investigation. Aaron nodded and sped up the feed. I couldn't look at it for too long without feeling a little sick. Thankfully, Aaron was on hand with a running commentary.

'No movement. Still in there. Nothing yet. We're at 2 a.m . . . 4 a.m . . . 5 a.m . . . oh, wait, here she comes!'

My focus flew back to the screen.

'Wait,' I said. 'This is morning.'

That was when I looked at Aaron for the first time since he'd started the 'speed run'. It was written all over his face, but I had to hear him say it anyway.

'What does that mean?'

'It wasn't Celestia,' Juliet chimed in, and Aaron nodded a confirmation.

Crap.

'I thought clearing a suspect was meant to feel *good*,' Daisy said.

I knew exactly what she meant. This *was* a good thing, right? We'd cleared our top suspect! That was progress! Except Celestia had been our *only* suspect, so if it wasn't her . . .

we were completely in the dark. Back to square one. No idea what happened next.

Like I said, *crap*.

CHAPTER 18

RECEPTION HUT. NIGHT.

The mood is electric in a way that suggests SAM, LIVI, DAISY, JULIET and AARON, or any combination of, might be about to turn on each other. To suggest that they should have seen this coming, that of course it wasn't CELESTIA, that they were stupid to have gone down that line of investigation in the first place.

To be fair to them, it wasn't an awful theory. Basic, sure, and an insult to my intelligence, but a good first step. It would have been impressive if they'd got it right first time. Shocking, too. Hadn't AARON told them that in a true crime story it was hardly ever the first suspect? That they weren't looking hard enough? Apparently not.

Anyway.
Back to the action.

On the screen, the CCTV flickers, drawing their attention away from each other and back to whatever is happening elsewhere in the camp.

LIVI: Is that live?
AARON: Yeah. What is that? *Where* is that?

Where: The main stage.
What: A light flickering, then darkness. A person, in the shadows? It's not quite clear but . . .

SAM: It's the main stage. Who *was* that? We should—
DAISY: Should we?!
SAM: If we want to have any hope at all of finding whoever is doing this, *yes*. It could be them! They're *right there* and they don't know we're watching.

LIVI: Sam's right. I'll come with you.

JULIET: We'll stay here and keep watch on the screen.

SAM: Great idea. Call us if you see anything.

LIVI and SAM exit.

'What. The hell. Is that?'

The noise, which seemed to start the moment we stepped into the main building, was like something from a cheap horror movie – a crackling sound, slipping into a hiss every now and then just to keep us on our toes. And I was *on my toes*. We hadn't even reached the stage yet – whatever it was could be heard from halfway down the corridor. I stepped closer to Sam, and without missing a beat he wrapped an arm around my shoulders and pulled me into his side.

'I've got you.'

It was ridiculous – I didn't trust that Sam could save me from a psycho killer any more than I trusted the Tony Award voters who didn't give *Wicked* best musical. I rolled my eyes, but relaxed into him anyway.

'I don't need saving,' I said. I just hoped that was true.

The door to the stage-right wing was closed, a much-needed pause to gather ourselves and figure out if we were actually going to do this. Or so I thought. Without a word, Sam removed his arm from around me and flung the door open.

There goes being inconspicuous, then.

It was very dramatic. It was *very* Prince Charming.

Despite it being a *stupid* move, *why* was it so very hot?

Focus, Livi.

I scrambled on to the stage after him.

It was dark, and my eyes took a moment to adjust; to find the outline of Sam's body – *only* Sam's body – standing in front of one of the speakers. That was crackling and hissing like something from a cheap horror movie. I burst out laughing.

'Oh my god. It's just a broken speaker...' Sam spun round and looked at me, the brilliant white of his teeth still visible even in the dark.

'Livi, be quiet,' he hissed. That was rich, coming from the person who had almost taken the door off its hinges trying to get in here. 'It's dark enough that they could still be here.'

Why *was* it so dark? I looked around, trying to figure it out.

Gasped.

I couldn't believe it had taken me this long to realise what was wrong.

'Sam,' I said quietly, as if being quiet would make it better somehow; make it less true. 'The ghost light is off.' That must have been what was causing the flickering we saw on the CCTV. In the time it took us to walk over here, it had burnt out completely.

Leaving the ghost light burning was my favourite of all the theatrical superstitions. I thought there was something so romantic about the idea that when the theatre was closed for the night, a gathering of ghosts would come out to play; meeting on the stages where they'd once performed, fallen in love, become themselves – the place they chose to come back to in death. Where they wanted to spend their whole afterlife.

For me it was less about actual spooky dead people and more about the idea of memory. I *loved* going into theatres where I knew people I loved or admired had been before. Loved thinking of them there, loved feeling them in the corridors between the stage and the auditorium that most people walked through without a second thought. *That* was the ghost light to me. A physical manifestation of memory, or what felt like memory, because I'd heard it told so many times in stories that I felt like I was there.

So no, I did not like it that the ghost light was out.

We weren't in complete darkness, though – there was still a light source in the shape of three lit candles on a metal candle stick, placed as if it was an afterthought in the stage-right wing. *What?* Celestia was always going on about the ridiculous risk assessments needed to have 'a naked flame' on stage – I thought mostly because she liked theatrically saying 'a naked flame' instead of just calling it a candle like a normal person. There was no way these had been left lit by accident, right? Was it *them*? Chloe's killer, trying to entice us closer?

'Crap,' Sam said, snapping me back to the stage and apparently *not* jumping to that conclusion. 'Whatever blew the speaker probably tripped the light, too. I bet I can fix it.'

He stepped towards the lit candles.

'Sam, no!' I tried to stop him. Sometimes I wished I knew less about theatrical superstitions, because it turned out that as soon as you learnt them, you'd see bad luck everywhere, even without the very real possibility that they'd been lit by a murderer. He turned to me, the candlestick gripped tightly in his hand.

Too late.

'What?!'

'The superstition,' I whispered, like the candles could hear me or something. 'Whoever stands nearest to three lit candles on stage...'

'Will be the next to marry, right?' He preened; raised an eyebrow. 'Fine by me.'

I hoped it was dark enough that he couldn't see me blush; light enough that he *could* see me roll my eyes.

Why was I blushing, anyway?

'Or to *die*,' I hissed. 'Whoever stands nearest to three lit candles on stage will be the next to marry, or to die.'

I leant over and blew out the candle he was holding, but the breeze from my quick movement made the other two flames flicker too, then unceremoniously go out before I'd even fully stepped back. Crap. Now we *were* in complete darkness. I hoped to the gods of theatre that the figure we'd seen on the CCTV really had just been a trick of the light; that somehow the candles had just been forgotten at the end of a rehearsal. I stumbled, almost colliding with a wishing well that had been wheeled in as part of the showcase set as I turned back towards Sam.

Who was standing a lot closer than he had been just a second ago.

Who caught me.

Who gently put the candlestick on the ground, and then put his hands on my arms.

And then... did nothing for what felt like ages.

'Go on, then,' I whispered, inching *just* a little closer. Close enough to give him permission. To say *don't let me be the one girl you won't do this with. Not again. Not now. Not when we're already here.*

It seemed to work. He did this thing where he sort of dipped his mouth and came at me from underneath somehow, despite being significantly taller. It caught me off guard, which I think was probably the point – to give him back a little bit of control. To surprise me. So yeah, when it came to it, it might have been him that closed the final distance, but if you asked me, I kissed Sam Chambers. I was the one who started it.

Who in the world could have seen that coming?

```
The kiss, when it comes, is not
surprising. Not if you've been
paying attention.

SAM's hands on her arms, eyes on her
lips, LIVI's smile still growing as
she moves in. She'd tell you she
wasn't expecting it, even as it happened.
```

The look on her face doesn't say that.
The look on her face says 'finally'.

I guess the thing about practise is that it makes you good – I knew that better than most people, but I'd never thought to apply it to kissing before. Sam, though, was *good* at kissing, and I knew it was because he practised a lot. Somehow that didn't bother me. Somehow I was sort of grateful to those girls and guys who had taught him exactly which spot on my lower back he should rest his hand on to make me arch towards him at just the right angle, and how to tangle his other hand in my hair in a way that felt great instead of remotely hurting, and how to do that thing he was doing with his mouth. My legs felt like jelly by the time a crashing sound came from the direction of the corridor and had us springing apart so smoothly nobody ever would have known we'd been tangled up in each other just a second before, barely able to tell where Livi ended and Sam began.

Nobody ever would have known if they hadn't seen, I mean. Which, by the way Daisy was refusing to meet my eye when she ran on to the stage with her phone torch alight right as I sprang backwards, I thought she might have.

Crap.

She didn't say anything as she ran towards the ghost light and switched it back on, and *oh yeah*, that was why we'd come here. Five minutes ago suddenly felt like a different lifetime. I caught Sam's eye, and he grimaced. Clearly he was thinking the same thing. We'd been caught red-handed.

'Are you all right?' Aaron asked as he skidded on to the stage, Juliet right behind him. 'The screen got even darker once you guys turned up on the feed, so we thought we'd better come. Who was it? Were they still here?'

'We're fine,' Sam said, which I was grateful for since my lips were still tingling from the kissing and I wasn't sure how successful I would be if I tried to speak. 'It was just a broken speaker – I thought whatever happened to it must have tripped the light too, but Daisy just turned it right back on. There's nobody here, at least not that we saw.'

'Guys,' Daisy said from where she was still standing by the light. 'Look. It's a *puppet*.'

She was absolutely right. The figure in the shadows was just a puppet. When you looked at him up close, you could see he was just wooden limbs, hinged together with metal, a blank expression on his cloth face.

Juliet laughed. 'So the drama kids overreacted?'

I was glad she was making light of it – I could do that; could go down that route if it meant avoiding Daisy's gaze a little bit longer. If it meant avoiding thinking about what just happened with Sam.

'Wild, right?' I said, my voice coming out just a little too high-pitched to sound natural. 'And it was so dark when we got here that I stumbled and completely screwed my foot.'

I didn't dare look at Sam; hoped his face wasn't saying 'what on earth are you talking about?' in any way the others could translate. I was thinking on my feet – pun not intended.

I needed to buy myself some time alone with him. Just a second, to talk about what happened. To make sure we were still OK.

'Are you all right?' Daisy asked, still not looking at me, and I dipped my head to meet her eye. I didn't know why she was reacting so weirdly. She'd promised me she wasn't interested in Sam! But perhaps it was because I'd said I wasn't either? It wasn't like I'd lied! I'd been working with the information I had at the time. I *hadn't* been interested!

Had I?

'I'm fine,' I said. 'Are you?'

Are you going to make this weird? I was really asking, and I thought she knew, because she gave me a small, genuine smile before she said, 'Yes. I'm fine.'

'Should we get out of here?' Juliet asked, and Daisy and Aaron were quick to agree that we definitely should. Even with the ghost light back on, it *was* starting to feel pretty creepy being here all alone.

'I left my camera in the reception hut,' Juliet said. 'I should go back and get it before any of the counsellors find it and look through all my raw footage.'

'Do you want me to come?' Aaron asked, but she shook her head.

'No, I'll be fine. Thank you, though. Aren't you meant to be meeting Luke at the party?'

At the mention of Luke's name, all Aaron's chivalry flew out the window. He grinned. I loved this for him; was so glad he'd found someone he could trust when he'd become so used to hiding.

'Will I see you there?' he asked, already walking away.

'Maybe,' I said. 'Depends how my foot goes.'

At this, Daisy looked concerned again. 'Are you sure you're OK?' she asked.

'She's fine, aren't you Livi?' Juliet cut in before I could speak. *What was she doing?* 'Probably just needs to take her time?'

'Erm . . . yes?' It came out as a question, and Juliet gave me a look like *I'm trying here, you idiot. Help me to help you.* Quite what she was trying to help me *with* I hadn't worked out yet. Except then she said, 'Daisy, why don't you go with Aaron. Sam can help Livi sort her foot out – he'll be able to take her weight better than you can, because he's bigger – and then they can meet you there.'

Oh. *That* was what she was trying to do. I guessed that meant Daisy wasn't the only one who had seen us then. *Crap. The CCTV.* Had we inadvertently given Aaron and Juliet a show?

'Good idea,' I said, in what I hoped was a totally chill way. *Juliet Stone, a constant surprise.* 'We'll catch you up, I just need two seconds to stretch it.'

Daisy *didn't* raise an eyebrow, or say anything, but the way she pursed her lips told me exactly what she was thinking. That she was on to us. I guessed it was too late to worry about that now. She trailed after Aaron without another word and Juliet shot me a smile as she followed them, headed to rescue her poor abandoned camera from the counsellors who I was *sure* didn't care what she was filming. I would never say that though – especially not now I was supposed to be Being Grateful to her.

We stood in charged silence until I couldn't hear their footsteps any more, then it was as if I couldn't stop myself. 'What just happened?' I asked, sinking to a cross-legged position on the floor and rubbing my ankle even though there was absolutely nothing wrong with it and we didn't have to keep up the pretence any more. 'You *rejected* me. I thought you were . . . I don't know . . . repulsed by me or something. And now . . .'

'When did I reject you?'

Seriously? Had I really been playing this over and over in my head for a *year* when it had been so unimportant to him that he'd forgotten it had even happened?

'Last summer,' I said, and watched his mouth form a little 'o'.

'Livi, that was *for ever* ago. You weren't hanging on to that, were you?'

And now I felt completely stupid. Was I supposed to have just let it go? No big deal?

'No, but you were pretty clear it wasn't going to happen!'

'It was *a year ago*!' He sounded exasperated, like year and lifetime were interchangeable words here. 'And I was never repulsed by you!' His eyebrows were furrowed, forehead knotted with worry, like he had *no idea* that any of this had been living rent free in my head this whole time, which I guessed was fair enough. It wasn't like I'd told him.

'Then why did you—'

'Because I'm stupid,' Sam said, like it was a fact. And now I'd ruined it – this thing I hadn't even known I'd wanted any more until it happened. 'Do you really want to know why?'

I nodded. *Obviously*.

'It was because I didn't *know you*, Liv. It felt like it came out of nowhere. You'd barely spoken to me all summer and suddenly you were trying to kiss me? I mean . . .' He trailed off.

'That doesn't usually stop you,' I said.

'Ouch.'

'I don't mean that in a bad way!' I was scrambling to recover now, which didn't feel fair because *he'd* been in the wrong, hadn't he? 'I just mean . . . you kiss people casually all the time.'

'Yeah,' he said with a shrug. 'People I've had more than a two-second conversation with. It just felt like . . . you wanted Sam the performer and not Sam the person. It wasn't *like* you, Livi. I didn't get it.'

Well, fuck. Now I felt terrible.

'I just wanted to feel normal!' I said, going from *this is too vulnerable to talk about* to *making him understand is more important than that* in the space of a breath. 'I just wanted a first kiss, like everyone else had already had! I thought you were *nice* and, you know, not scary!'

So I'd jumped in with both feet, apparently never stopping to realise that Sam was a person too.

'I'm sorry,' I said. 'But . . . why now? What changed?'

Sam shrugged as he dropped on to the floor opposite me and mirrored my position.

'It just felt right? I don't know what you want me to say!'

I hid my face in my hands, smiling into my palm. I didn't know what I wanted him to say either, didn't know how I was supposed to feel about any of this, but 'it just felt right' was a very good start. I didn't think I'd ever made someone *feel right* before. 'You want to know why I kissed you?'

I nodded, and forced myself to look at him.

'Because with all those other people, or at least most of them, it was superficial. Physical. Something to do. And I'm not proud of that, but in the spirit of being honest with you . . . that is what it was. But it's different with you.'

'Different how?' I asked, uncrossing my legs and rising up on to my knees, like my body knew before I did that I'd want to move once he answered this.

'It feels real with you,' he said. 'You make me feel real. And I'm glad I rejected you last summer.' I must have looked wounded, because he held out a hand to beckon me to him. 'I'm glad because now we get to do it like this. The way it was supposed to be.'

It might just have been a line, but what can I say? It worked. Cancel me. I scooted a little closer, then a little closer still. *Your move, Chambers*, I thought, and as if I'd said it out loud . . . well, he made his move.

He pushed me up to standing, moved me slowly backwards until my legs hit the wishing well, then gently lifted me up so I was sitting on the edge. His lips met mine again – more softly this time, more subtle than the first kiss. It was like we knew we had time. Like there was more where this came from. I was only about a metre off the ground, not defying gravity at all, but that didn't matter. As act-one closers go, it felt like flying.

```
MAIN STAGE. Lit only by the ghost light.
SAM standing, LIVI sitting on the lip of
the wishing well.

We watch them uncurl.
We watch them drop the masks they
wear for the world.
We watch them move back towards
each other.
We watch them.

Meanwhile, oblivious to this, SAM and
LIVI share a small, lovely kiss.
```

CHAPTER 19

SO *THAT* HAPPENED.

I felt like a little girl when Sam finally pulled back with a grin – like I wanted to lie on the floor and kick my feet around in glee.

I didn't, though. I was still cooler than that. Just.

I was still cooler than that, and I was also still *confused*. If you'd asked me twenty minutes ago if this was ever in a million years going to happen, I would have said no. I almost would have meant it, too.

And yet.

I didn't think my brain was going to let it be as easy as 'this is a thing we do now.' I knew there were probably hours and days of overthinking in my immediate future, but I was delaying all of that as long as I could. Not letting myself think about it.

Basking in the good for once.

Because this *was* good, right?

Lying back on the stage, gesturing for him to mirror my

position, I stared up at the ceiling, trying to gather myself for a second before I headed back to the cabin, and inevitably to Daisy and Juliet's questions. I'd always been fascinated by the fly floor above this stage, where the tech crew put their lives in their hands (if you asked me. If you asked *them*, they'd say it was completely safe, I'm sure) to make theatre magic. Every year, Celestia and Sophia found some way to shoehorn flying into the showcase. It usually involved the leads hanging above the audience as they tried to belt a high note, all the while trying not to be sick, both from nerves and a mild fear of heights.

But maybe that was just me projecting.

It was sort of peaceful just staring up at the beams above my head. I could feel Sam next to me, but we weren't talking. It didn't feel like we needed to. There was nothing that needed to be said, at least not right now. I let my gaze drift across from left to right, my eyes blurring. The lighting rig looked kind of robotic like this, without any of the spotlights shining. I found it amazing that there were kids like Luke who could take what was essentially a massive lump of metal and twist it into magic; could make moonlight in the middle of the afternoon. I rubbed my tattoo absently. *There will be light*.

In so many ways, it was the most important part.

```
MAIN STAGE.
Two figures lying on the floor,
staring up.
Come on. Pay attention.
```

LIVI looks from right to left. Does it again, like she knows she's seen something but her brain hasn't quite caught up yet.
Once more.
Come on.
She spots the note.
Showtime.

It was probably nothing, I told myself as I scrambled quickly to my feet and reached for the harness that the small white piece of paper was dangling from. Probably a safety label or something, and I'd feel stupid for believing that the whole world revolved around what we were doing. That someone had left it for me.

Still, better safe than sorry.

'Livi, what?' Sam asked, a step behind but in a tone that suggested it wasn't the first time he'd spoken, and *oh yeah. Sam's here.*

'There's something there,' I said, pointing upwards. 'In the harness. It's probably nothing...'

'Yeah, but,' he said, scrambling to his feet.

I had no idea how to properly lower the harness and I felt bad for a moment that whatever I did here might break it – but not bad enough not to try. I'd ask for forgiveness, I thought, rather than permission. Anyway, I was sure Aaron could bribe Luke to fix it before the counsellors found out. He'd know what to do, right? Even if it wasn't *technically* lighting it was sort of connected to the same rig? I had no idea.

'Do you know how to operate it?' I asked Sam, hoping it didn't make me a bad feminist to be praying this was one of those things men just *knew*. Sam shook his head.

'Pull it?'

Well, in the absence of a better plan . . . I tugged at the black fabric, then tugged a little harder when it didn't move the first time.

Bingo. Sam whooped as it made a clunky sound that I was sure it wasn't supposed to, but the harness lowered enough that I could grab the piece of paper and then went flying up into the rafters as soon as I let go.

Which definitely was not supposed to happen.

Oops.

I'd worry about that later.

I unfolded the note quickly, reading it once without taking it in, then again with slightly more success, and a third time to really understand what it was telling me. Because it *was* for me. And Aaron, Juliet, Daisy and Sam, sure, but this note had not been left here by accident.

'Livi, you're not saying anything,' Sam pointed out completely obviously. 'It worries me when you're not saying anything.'

I read the note aloud, hoping that would bring it into even clearer focus.

This is not going so well, it it? Looks like you need another clue. Don't say I never give you anything. Chloe was killed at 00:13 a.m.

No pleasantries, no sign off, but a very unambiguous . . . clue? Could it even be called a clue if it was just a *fact*? Did this killer *still not know* how clues actually worked?

Sam laughed. I hadn't realised until he did that I'd said all of that out loud.

'God, Liv, if we spent as much time working this out as you are questioning their vocabulary, we'd probably have solved it by now. Come on. Why are we still standing here? Let's *go*.'

Good point. I stuffed the note into my pocket and started running.

What does this mean? I asked myself as I hotfooted it through the forest, leading us on a route that was definitely longer but wouldn't take us past the party where we might bump into people and be waylaid. *Chloe was killed at 00:13 a.m.* So it *had* been after the party. She had left the campfire alive. She'd still been alive when everyone was heading back to their cabins. *Or other people's*, I reminded myself. There had been a lot of misplaced campers as I'd run through the woods to the rehearsal barn that night; a lot of sightings through windows of people hanging out in rooms that were not their own. My radar for gossip would serve me well here. I'd been running pretty fast, but that didn't mean I hadn't spotted Luke and Aaron, hadn't noticed the three second-year girls filing into the cabin of the most popular second-year boys. Now that I ran back through it, I'd spotted almost everyone as I'd made my way across camp. I couldn't put my finger on anyone who had been conspicuously missing, aside from Sam, who had been waiting for me in the rehearsal barn.

Everyone else, I thought, was accounted for. I'd have to look properly through the list of campers and see if that shed any light. I couldn't deny, though, that this note cleared a lot of people from the suspect list. If I'd seen them in the living area as I passed, there was no way they could have left and made it back to the lake by the time Chloe died. Another thing that should have felt like an uncomplicated win but didn't. Who *was it* if it wasn't one of them?

I crashed through the door of the cabin, Sam hot on my heels, breathing heavily from running, and was surprised to find Daisy sitting there. She shot a pointed look at my foot.

Crap. Forgot about that. I winced as I lifted my foot and flexed it a bit, but I could tell she didn't buy it.

'What are you doing here?' I asked. 'What happened to the party?'

Daisy shrugged.

'I was tired. Didn't feel like it. Why do you look like that?'

'Like what?'

Like you just caught me kissing our friend who I said I wasn't interested in?

'Like something has happened,' she clarified. 'Spooked. You both look spooked.'

Oh, like that.

I whipped the note from my pocket and shoved it in her direction.

'Something has. Where's Juliet?'

'At the party,' Daisy said absentmindedly, her attention on the note. 'Livi, what does this mean? Where did you get this?'

'It was hanging from one of the harnesses on the stage,' Sam said. 'Whoever put it there must have known we'd come—'

'But Daisy,' I said, cutting him off, 'it clears *everyone*. We all left that party and went back to our cabins. I'd be willing to bet every one of us has an alibi. Nobody would have been alone, right?'

'I guess...' she said, considering it. 'It would be a pretty easy thing to prove...'

I couldn't tell her how sure I was, how I really knew that it cleared so many people, without admitting that I'd been out of the cabin myself – and since she seemed to have let the Sam thing drop for now and I definitely wasn't ready to talk about it, bringing it up felt like a very bad idea.

'So now what?' I asked. 'It wasn't Celestia and it wasn't a camper... so who *was* it?'

'Another counsellor?'

'But *why*?' I asked.

'Not everything has a why,' Daisy said with a shrug.

While that may have been true, I didn't think it applied to murder. We *must* be missing something.

Lust, love, loot or loathing, right?

'We should tell the others,' I said, pulling my phone out, and Daisy nodded.

'Should we ask them to meet us?'

I thought about it. Aaron was almost definitely with Luke, and I'd feel bad if I dragged him away, *again*, from this thing that I thought was really good for him. The party wouldn't go on that much longer, so Juliet would be back soon anyway. And Sam... I needed a minute away from him; some time to process, and to decide on my next move. He felt too close suddenly, now that he was in my cabin. I just... needed a minute.

'No,' I said. 'Let's just tell them what the note says. Aaron is with his boy, and Juliet is at a party, and they deserve that, you know? We can meet up first thing in the morning. Nothing is going to change between now and then, right?'

'Right,' Daisy said, and she was smiling, but she didn't sound sure. I fired off the text, then busied myself sorting out my pyjamas and gathering my stuff so that I could shower.

Hoping that Sam would take that as his cue to leave.

Never one to miss his line, Sam stood up from where he was perched on the edge of my bed.

'I'll leave you to it,' he said, barely looking at me as he opened the door to leave, which made it more conspicuous, not less. 'Text me if anything...'

'We will,' I said, waving him off, feeling like there was a beacon flashing above my head saying *Something just changed between these two.*

Closing the door behind him, I headed for the bathroom.

'Hey,' Daisy said, trying and not entirely succeeding to sound casual, and I turned to face her. 'What's going on with you and Louis now?'

I almost laughed. *Clever*. If she'd caught me just a little more off-guard that probably would have worked – ask about the guy you know I'm *not* seeing to try and get me to spill about the one I . . . am? Were Sam and I seeing each other now? I had no clue how this was supposed to work, and it would be embarrassing to ask him. Things were so much simpler when I was solely focused on acting.

'Nothing,' I said. 'We're just . . . hanging out.'

Daisy spent enough time with me to know that wasn't true; to know that I'd barely seen Louis, sort of by design, since Chloe had died. Part of that was because I *did* genuinely like him, and didn't want to drag him into this real-life murder mystery that we hadn't had a choice about. The other part was because I didn't like him *enough* to need him around while we solved it. It was confusing, especially on top of all the other confusing things going on, so I was mostly trying not to think about it.

'OK,' Daisy said, letting me off the hook and climbing under her duvet with a smile. My phone vibrated on my bed and I picked it up to see Sam's name on the screen.

'Are you OK? Should we rehearse tonight?'

Should we rehearse tonight? Part of me thought we needed all the time we could get – that missing a night when we were getting this good was basically throwing away our chances, that of *course* we should rehearse. Why wouldn't we? That weirdly felt like a past version of Livi having those thoughts, though. The version that had existed yesterday. Or an hour ago. The other part of me wasn't done processing yet – wanted some time with just my thoughts, was *really* tired. I hadn't slept a full night since getting here, after all. One night off wasn't going to ruin everything, right? I texted back to tell Sam I thought that we should get some sleep. Apparently a man of few words when it came to messaging, his thumbs-up emoji appeared on the screen almost immediately. Not the sweet nothings I'd hoped for. *Hoped for? Had I?*

God, my brain was fried.

Daisy was fast asleep by the time I came out of the shower, and for the first time since getting here I got into my actual pyjamas, laid down in my bed, and didn't have one eye on the clock waiting for the moment that I'd have to leave again. I was going to sleep *well* tonight, I thought.

I was still staring at the ceiling an hour later. Typical. My mind wouldn't stop racing, and my body was restless too. I'd spent ages running through what we knew about Chloe's death, and something just wasn't clicking. It felt within reach; like one piece of the puzzle was missing, and when we found that we'd be able to see the full picture.

You know what it is, Livi.

I closed my eyes, tried to think of *any* alternative. Anything I could say to the others without them thinking I was jealous, or just a straight-up bitch. Last time I'd tried to bring it up with Daisy, she'd shut me down so definitively that I felt like

I couldn't do it again; like no one would listen or take me seriously. Even knowing all of that, I couldn't get past the thought. I listed it all out in my head one more time.

1. The note had said that Chloe was killed at 00.13 a.m., after the end of the party.

2. Everyone had left the campfire and gone back to the living area.

3. I'd left the cabin to meet Sam and seen pretty much all of the other campers on my way, through windows, or walking in their doors.

4. By the time I'd passed, they wouldn't have had time to get back across camp and kill Chloe.

5. So they all had alibis, right?

Almost all.
It clears everyone, I'd said to Daisy.
But it didn't clear Juliet.

CHAPTER 20

THE CABIN WAS QUIET WHEN I WOKE UP SOMEWHERE close to 3 a.m., so I knew it was my own brain that had jolted me from sleep, rather than a light or a sound. I could hear Daisy breathing softly in her bunk, but other than that, silence.

Complete silence.

Juliet's bed was still empty.

Slowly, so as not to wake Daisy, I pulled myself up to sitting.

Think, Livi. How can we use this?

Usually, I wouldn't bat an eyelid at my roommate still being out at 3 a.m. Like I'd said to Kitty and Tasha, when it came to experimenting with *whatever* in a safe and supportive environment, there really was nowhere like Camp Chance, where we all knew we'd be back on stage with each other tomorrow, so we'd better not make it awkward. Usually, though, we weren't in the middle of a murder investigation. And Juliet not being here gave me an opportunity.

'Daisy,' I whispered. She didn't stir. 'Dais,' I tried a little louder, and this time she rolled towards me but didn't open her eyes.

'What?' she said, or at least I thought she said. It was hard to hear, since she turned her face into her pillow as she mumbled it, like she couldn't stay awake long enough to hear my answer.

'Juliet still isn't back,' I said, and Daisy waved a hand in my direction that I thought was meant to dismiss me; to tell me Juliet could do what she wanted and we should let her.

For this to work, I needed Daisy worried. I needed her to think that *I* was worried. Part of me *was* worried.

'Daisy, it's 3 a.m. She shouldn't be out there alone. What if something has happened to her . . . what if . . . it's like Chloe?'

I felt manipulative even as I said it, but needs must, right? If I could convince Daisy that I was worried, that Juliet wasn't safe and we should go and look for her, perhaps we could find out where she went when she disappeared. I was sure we'd find her filming a rock or something, waxing lyrical about the future of theatre to her camera screen, and I could finally get past this idea that she was hiding something; that something was off about her.

My manipulation worked a treat. Daisy opened her eyes fully this time, sat up, and looked at me.

'Do you really think something has happened to her?'

'I don't *know*,' I said, 'but I don't think we should leave it to chance. We know the killer is watching us. What if they saw Juliet alone in the middle of the night, and took an opportunity?'

Or what if she *did,* I didn't say.

Daisy was already flinging the duvet off and reaching for

her Ugg boots before she spoke again.

'You're right. We should look for her.'

She'll forgive you for exploiting her good nature if it works, I promised myself. *You can feel bad for it later. For now, we need to find Juliet before she turns up in the doorway and our chance is gone.*

'It's probably nothing,' I said to Daisy as I pulled on my own shoes. 'She's probably off somewhere having a lovely time.'

I genuinely hoped so.

```
THE WOODS. NIGHT VISION.


DAISY and LIVI leave the cabin, sticking
close to each other, neither admitting
it but both scared.


An almighty CRACK. The snapping of twigs
and the sound of running.


LIVI: Shit. WHAT WAS THAT?
DAISY: Livi, I don't know about this.
Should we call Celestia?
LIVI: What, wake her up and explain
everything? I wish, but we're so
far beyond that. We don't have time.
We can't give up on Juliet now.
Daisy, we've gotta go.
```

LIVI gulps. She's trying to be brave but when it comes to acting, she's better when she's pretending to be someone else, and not just another version of herself. She looks terrified. She starts to run in the direction of the sound anyway.

Good for her.

DAISY follows.

They reach the willow trees - the ones where people don't hang out rather than the ones where everyone does. The social rules in this place are weird.

LIVI sees it first. A light, from a camera screen, at the foot of one of the trees.

LIVI: What the . . .?
DAISY: Livi, what is that?
LIVI: It's her camera. Is it?
DAISY: It's a camera.
LIVI: Who else do you know who walks around filming everything?
DAISY: Good point.

They make no move towards the camera.

DAISY: So where is she?
LIVI: It's probably some elaborate shot setup, isn't it? We'll see it in a video about how the future of theatre is trees or something in a few months and it'll all make sense.
DAISY: Livi, don't be mean.
LIVI *(serious)*: I wasn't.

She kind of wasn't.

DAISY: So what do we do?
LIVI *(shouting)*: Juliet???

No answer. A breeze sweeps through the clearing, like it's daring the girls to move. LIVI takes the cue and walks towards the discarded camera.

LIVI: It's filming.
DAISY: What's the shot?
LIVI: The sky. Daisy . . . I don't know if she left it here intentionally.

Well done, detective LIVI.

Go on . . . just a little further.

DAISY: What are you saying?

But LIVI doesn't answer. Her eyes are trained on the figure in the trees, walking slowly towards them, hands held up, out into the clearing. Into the light of LIVI's torch beam.

LIVI: Louis! What are you doing here?
LOUIS: I think that's supposed to be my line. Start talking, Campbell.

Well, that wasn't supposed to happen.

OK, think faster than you've ever thought in your life. I ran quickly through every scenario. We could feign ignorance. Say we were just out for a walk. I dismissed that one quickly. He'd never believe it – a middle-of-the-night walk in the cold woods? Try harder, Liv. A half-truth *might* work. We could tell him we'd been rehearsing in secret; were headed back to our cabin... except our cabin was definitively in the other direction, and Louis knew it. I had to say something, and soon. Standing here dumbstruck definitely wasn't helping us *or* Juliet.

'Louis,' I said, 'this isn't what it looks like.'

'What does it look like?' His voice was steady. Too steady.

He was just *acting* chill, I realised. Doing something specific with his tone, with how slowly he was speaking, that meant he didn't sound like *Louis* at all. He was scared.

'Livi,' Daisy said, her voice a warning, 'we have to get out of here. Right now.'

I turned, my expression quizzical as I took in her face, which had paled to a ghostly white.

'What's wrong?'

'Livi,' she hissed, as if that might mean he couldn't hear us. 'It's him. It has to be.'

'*What* is me?' Louis asked, his voice still calm. Too calm? I couldn't tell any more what game he was playing. 'The person who's going to work out what's going on here? What sort of twisted scheme you and your whole crew of new best friends are in on? What you've been plotting since *day one*?'

His words barely registered as I took a step back to bring myself level with Daisy. *Think, Livi. Could she be right?*

'Why else would he be out here?' she whispered, as if she was reading my mind. Also as if he wasn't standing *right there*. I hoped my 'please shut up' eyes were translating for her.

'Why am *I* out here?' Louis asked, advancing towards us, although the expression on his face now was confused rather than threatening. 'I was looking for *you*. I was sitting on the steps of my cabin, minding my own business, messaging a girl from school since nobody *here* has given me a second look,' – he looked pointedly at me when he said that – 'and I heard you two coming from the other direction, sneaking around like you have been since we got here. Like you probably were when you all avoided the party tonight. Like *you* were, Livi, skulking around by the star dressing room in that stupid pink wig. Like you were in reception earlier – it doesn't take five of you to man a phone that never rings, how stupid do you think I am? I was going to wait in the clearing and confront you, but then I . . .'

All right, enough.

'Louis,' I said, holding up a hand and cutting him off mid-sentence, 'I'll tell you what's going on, but you *have* to trust me, OK?'

'Livi,' Daisy said, and I turned to smile at her.

'No, Daisy, it's OK. We're going to tell him. It's going to be OK.'

Game face on, Livi. This has got to work.

'We're filming,' I began, and Louis rolled his eyes like *you're going to have to try harder than that.* 'For one of Juliet's videos. See, that's why her camera is here.' I gestured to where it was still lying, discarded in the grass. 'She's directing, obviously, and Daisy and I are the stars.'

I looked to Daisy. *Jump in any time you like, Dais.*

'Right!' Daisy said. 'And when I was like *it's him*, I meant . . . you must be the third co-star Juliet told us about. I just sounded off because I was expecting Aaron. Except *you* just said you're only here because you were following us. So I must be wrong! I'm sure she'll set us straight when she gets here. Juliet, I mean. She'll be two minutes!'

God, she was floundering.

'She'll be two minutes?' Louis asked, jumping on the least weird bit of what Daisy had just said.

I nodded.

'Then this isn't real?'

```
LOUIS pulls a piece of folded paper
from behind his back.

DAISY: Louis, what is that?
LOUIS: I found it attached to the
camera.

DAISY and LIVI start to walk towards
LOUIS slowly.

DAISY: What does it say?

LOUIS reads aloud.

LOUIS: Too slow. You didn't find me, so
I had no choice but to up my game. Juliet
Stone . . . actual celebrity . . . lucky
me, although I imagine that means people
will be quick to realise she's gone.
Your mission? Find out how I made her
disappear. Make sure nobody else does.
```

```
And remember, I'm watching.
LIVI: Fuck.
LOUIS: Tell me the truth, Livi. Now.
```

I didn't tell him anything at all. Instead, I started running.

CHAPTER 21

WE WERE RUNNING AS IF OUR LIVES DEPENDED on it, which it was beginning to look like they might. We weren't speaking, our breathing too heavy to focus on anything but the next inhale, anything but how to take the next step. Daisy and I were holding hands. Hers was cold. Mine was sweating.

'We need to call Aaron and Sam,' she said as we flew up the steps of the cabin, banged open the door without even thinking about if it would wake the surrounding campers, and slammed it shut behind us. I leant on it with my whole body weight as I fumbled with the lock, trying to catch my breath.

'Do it,' I said. 'Get them here, *now*.'

Daisy wasn't waiting for my permission, the phone already to her ear.

'Aaron,' I heard her say, then I forced myself to block out the noise. To *think*. I couldn't listen to her tell them. Not when less than ten minutes ago I'd suspected Juliet herself. If I hadn't wasted so much time on that ridiculous train of thought, could we have seen this coming? Could we have helped her? I didn't notice I was shaking until Daisy reached over and stilled my hand with hers, still talking into her phone.

'Livi, what the hell is going on?' Louis asked, dropping down to join me as I sat on the edge of Juliet's bed. He'd seen way too much now for me to lie.

'Chloe was murdered,' I said, 'and whoever did it has been threatening more if we don't find them in time. I'm breaking their rules by telling you any of this – god, how are we going to hide that we've told you? Anyway, now they've got Juliet too. We've messed up, big time. I thought it might be *her* behind all this. I was so busy looking in the wrong direction and now . . . she's gone.'

'Are you joking?'

I spluttered an incredulous laugh. 'I wish I was joking!'

Crossing the room in one stride I reached under my bed for the box I'd been hiding Chloe's mask in, and pulled it out, thrusting it into his hands as I pulled off the lid. I noticed as I did that Juliet had also put the poison bottle in there, which I guessed made sense. Less chance of us touching it by accident if it was hidden in the one place we were categorically avoiding.

'We found the first note attached to this. By the lake. With . . . the body.'

Louis recoiled. Nodded like *fine, I believe you*. Closed his eyes. I got it. I didn't want to look at the mask either. I shoved it back under the bed.

'It's wild, I know,' I said softly, and Louis opened his eyes, speechless, staring at me as if he was waiting for a punchline that he knew deep down wasn't coming. We weren't performing any more. This was not a show.

'They're coming,' Daisy said when she hung up, and used her newly free hand to squeeze mine. I didn't realise that she was crying until I felt the tears hitting my skin. Crying seemed like an appropriate reaction. I wished I was crying. Instead, I just felt numb.

The banging on the door almost made me jump out of my skin, until I saw Sam's face at the window. I jumped up to let them in, and when Sam threw his arms around me and pulled me into his chest, I let him, not caring at all what the others would think. I felt safe with him. Still not like he could save us, we were in way too deep for that, but that if we were going down, at least we were doing it together.

'What is he doing here?' Aaron asked, pointing at Louis, and I pulled back from Sam in time to see Daisy shake her head.

'It's fine,' she said, locking the door behind the boys, 'I'll tell you later. But he knows. Everything.'

'Where is it?' Aaron asked, and Daisy picked up the note from where I'd left it on the floor and handed it to him.

'What do they mean by *disappear*?' Aaron asked. 'Is she dead? Are we looking for a body?'

'I'm going to be sick,' I said into Sam's chest.

'No, you're not.' He held me even tighter, which didn't help the nausea at all but I appreciated the gesture.

'This is all my fault,' I said. I had to say it out loud, to see their reactions. I needed to be honest, so they could decide if they wanted anything to do with me or if they wanted to cut me adrift.

'How on earth is it your fault?' Sam asked, pushing me back from his chest and holding me at arms' length, a look on his face that I thought was meant to be reassuring but just made me feel even worse. They all had so much trust in me, for some reason thought I was a good person, and now I had to tell them that I'd suspected our friend. I'd thought she was involved, and now she was *gone*. Disappeared.

I definitely was not a good person.

'I thought it was *her*,' I said, and if you could feel the weight of a look, I felt all of theirs. *Well, Liv, you've started now. The only way out is through.*

'She was the only person who's alibi we didn't know . . . from the night Chloe died, I mean. She wasn't *here*. And I was so dead set on proving her wrong about the stupid future of stupid theatre that I was looking for the worst in her. She was probably just out filming a frog or something for one of her videos, and I decided she was guilty, and now she's gone.'

It felt like I'd got the whole thing out in one breath, but it must have been vaguely coherent because Aaron was nodding, and Daisy had a look on her face that said 'Oh, *Livi*,' although in what tone I couldn't quite tell. Even Louis looked as if he was catching up fast. I didn't dare look at Sam.

'Livi, this is not your fault,' he said, and pulled me back in to him. I couldn't help but notice his grip was looser this time.

'But if I'd realised sooner—'

'Any one of us could have realised sooner,' Daisy said, her voice fierce.

'But I got you out there under false pretences,' I protested. 'I thought if we could find out where she was, we'd be able to prove that she was innocent. I wasn't *worried* about her. If I'd actually been worried—'

'Livi, you got us out there,' Daisy cut me off. 'If it weren't for you, anyone could have found that note!'

'Anyone *did*,' Sam said quietly, looking at Louis out of the corner of his eye. Daisy gave him a *stop talking* look.

'It doesn't matter why you took us out, not now. What matters is that you did.'

'She's right,' Aaron said. 'If anything, you've helped Juliet. If she can still be saved, you might have saved her.'

Daisy choked out a sob, and I felt bad all over again because I still hadn't cried. Sam's arms around me were stopping the shaking though, and I could feel the curtain that had come down in my brain when Louis had shown us the note beginning to clear. Aaron was right. We might still be able to save Juliet. I pulled back from Sam.

'What do we do?' I asked.

'We need to decide if we tell the counsellors,' Aaron said gently, like he expected one of us (read, me) to fly off the handle at that suggestion in true Elphaba-just-before-Defying-Gravity fashion. I didn't, though. For the first time I thought he might be right.

'I have no idea,' I said. 'What do you think?'

'I think it's up to you and Daisy,' Aaron said, 'since you found the note.'

'Did they?' Louis asked. Nobody paid him much attention.

Sam nodded in Aaron's direction. 'Makes sense to me. Your decision, ladies.'

I knew they were trying to be kind, but the pressure felt like too much. I had *no idea* what the right thing to do was. If we told Celestia and Sophia, at least we wouldn't be in this alone any more. It was starting to feel like we *really* needed an adult around; someone who was actually in charge and could tell us what to do. The counsellors knowing would take some of the weight off us, right? So surely, we should tell?

But then there was the note. The direct instruction to make sure no one else found out what had happened to Juliet, and to Chloe too. We didn't know the full extent of what this person was capable of, but one thing was for sure – they weren't afraid to take bold swings. They had *Juliet*. I knew she wouldn't have gone with them without a fight. So surely we should take their threats seriously?

'What do you think?' I asked Daisy, who had gone white but had at least stopped crying.

'I don't have a clue,' she said, and I nodded.

'Neither do I.'

'How do you feel,' Aaron asked, *very* gently, like we were feral cats he was trying not to spook, 'about sleeping on it? There's not much we can do tonight in any case, and I don't think we should be out there in the dark.'

'He's right,' Sam said, his tone just as soothing. 'Some sleep will do you good, then we can meet up before breakfast and make a proper decision.'

I liked the idea of taking the pressure off for the (very) few hours left until breakfast, and as much as I hated the idea of leaving Juliet out there with that psycho, I knew they were right. We definitely shouldn't be running around in the dark. It wasn't safe. We were no help to her if we 'disappeared' too.

'OK,' I said, looking at Daisy for confirmation. She nodded, like she'd been waiting for me to say it first. 'But we need a plan – what are we going to do about Louis?'

'I'm *right here*,' he said. 'Not some abstract *thing* to be dealt with!'

I wriggled out of Sam's grip and positioned myself in front of Louis.

'I know. I'm sorry. But we have to be careful here. They said tell no one, and you're very much someone. So we need to think.'

Sam stepped up behind me.

'Louis, bro, you're not going to like it, but whoever is doing this *can't* know you know. It puts all of us in danger, including you. *Mostly* you, probably.'

'So what?' Louis asked, stopping just short of squaring

up to Sam. 'You want me to just walk out of here and pretend tonight never happened?'

Sam shrugged. 'Sort of.'

'Not happening,' Louis said, stepping just an inch closer.

What was wrong with boys?

'Guys,' I said, 'this is stupid! Louis, don't take it personally – Sam's right. We're not asking you to pretend it didn't happen, but you do have to pretend you don't know.'

'Act!' Daisy cut in. 'It's just acting!'

'Right! Think of it as a role! I'm really sorry, but you can't suddenly be seen with us. It will draw way too much attention. We know they're watching us.'

At the mention of actual danger, Louis seemed to be softening a bit. Withdrawing. Regretting ever following Daisy and me into the woods. Or maybe I was just projecting again.

'But you'll keep me updated?' he asked, appealing directly to me.

I didn't look at the others before I answered, because I knew they'd try to talk me out of it, but what choice did we have?

'We'll keep you updated, I promise,' I said, placing my hand on his arm. 'Louis, thank you for being so . . . I don't know, normal, about this.'

Louis rolled his eyes.

'Not like you've given me an option. Not like whoever wrote that note has either. Be normal about it or die? I know which one I'm choosing.'

I supposed he had a point.

'We should go,' Sam said to Aaron. 'Let Liv and Daisy get some rest and clear their heads before the morning.'

It was technically already the morning and my head was the opposite of clear, but even thinking that made me anxious so I definitely wasn't going to voice it. Instead, I hugged Aaron and Louis goodnight and unlocked the door to let them out, turned to Sam as Daisy said goodbye to the others.

'Thank you,' I whispered, and he shook his head.

'Nothing to thank me for.'

He leant in quickly and planted a kiss on my forehead right before Daisy turned back to hug him goodbye. I felt terrible about how good the warmth of his lips on my skin made me feel. Juliet was missing, we'd been caught by Louis, and I was swooning over a boy? I really had to get my priorities straight. *God*, Sam Chambers had my mind completely scrambled.

'What are we supposed to do?' Daisy asked when we were alone again, and I closed my eyes and didn't say anything for a second.

'Daisy, I have no idea. I feel like I'm losing my grip on reality. Like everything I thought was true when I came here has turned out to be a lie.'

She didn't ask what I meant by that, which I was grateful for. I wasn't sure how I'd properly articulate that I was starting to think acting wasn't the be all and end all I'd spent my whole life thinking it was, that Sam Chambers had looked in my direction for five seconds and drawn my attention away from all the things I thought were fundamentals of my personality, that trying to catch a killer was starting to feel a lot more normal than I ever in a million years thought it would, and that I didn't know what it meant that I *still* hadn't cried about Juliet.

'We'll sleep on it though, right?' Daisy said, and I knew she was desperate for someone to tell her that we'd wake up in the morning with all the answers, because I felt exactly the same.

'We'll sleep on it,' I promised.

I don't think I slept a wink.

CHAPTER 22

I FELT A TINY BIT BETTER BY THE TIME AARON KNOCKED on our door in the morning, thankful for a warm shower and a disgusting but necessary instant coffee from the stash Juliet had left on her dresser.

Juliet.

It had been hours, and there was still no sign. Not that I'd expected there would be. That hadn't stopped me from spending most of the night staring at the ceiling fantasising that she'd walk back in when the sun came up and ask what all the fuss was about. No such luck, obviously.

This was very much happening.

'Where's Sam?' Daisy asked.

Good. I'd been wondering the same but didn't want them to question why I was asking, so I was glad Daisy had done it for me.

'He's catching up,' Aaron said. 'He'll be here in a minute. I think he finally fell asleep at about 5 a.m., so getting up was hard.'

I knew the feeling.

'Yeah, none of us slept,' I said, harsher than I intended since the person I was aiming it at was the one who wasn't even there. 'Doesn't mean we have time for a slow morning! We have to hit the ground running! Find out what happened to Juliet, and who killed Chloe, and end this once and for all so we can put the drama back on the stage! I'd even take *dancing* right now. In front of *Sophia*, and we all know how crap she thinks I am, and how much she loves to tell me about it. If Sam isn't here, we'll just have to start without him!'

Daisy and Aaron were looking at me like I had two heads or something.

'You're in a . . . strange mood,' Daisy said.

Strange? No, I wasn't, I was just *over it*. I wanted this *done*.

'No, I'm not.'

'No,' Aaron said, 'you are . . . what aren't you telling us?'

'Nothing!' I protested.

'Thinking about it,' Daisy said, her tone somewhere between light and faking light pretty badly, '*you* had reason to want Juliet gone. With your competition out of the picture you're definitely going to get the lead.'

I heard Aaron whisper 'oh shit' under his breath right as the room went cold. I knew Daisy had been joking, but it wasn't funny. I tried to brush it off quickly. I didn't want this to turn into an argument, but I didn't want her to take the joke any further either.

'How could it have been me?' I said. 'I was right here, asleep next to you the entire time.'

Daisy raised an eyebrow. Aaron wouldn't meet my gaze.

'Do you think we're stupid?' Daisy asked.

Wait, what was happening here?

'No?' I said.

'Livi,' she said, 'everyone knows you've been sneaking out since night one. Who *knows* what you've been doing, but who's to say that whatever it is you weren't doing it last night too.'

Oh. Crap.

'I...'

'Don't say you haven't,' Aaron said, sounding resigned. 'Please just... don't do that.'

I'd been caught. That much was obvious. Now I had to decide what I was ready to tell them.

'OK,' I said, holding my hands up in surrender. 'You're right that I've been sneaking out. And I'm going to tell you everything. But I promise you, I didn't go anywhere last night. I was right here until I woke you up, Daisy. *Please* believe me on that.'

'I do,' she said quietly, and that was my decision made. If she could give me her trust, I owed them both the truth. I only regretted that Sam wasn't here to tell it with me. I could have used him in my corner, to steady my nerves. Perform in front of hundreds of strangers? Easy. Tell my friends something *real* about my life? My hands were shaking.

'I've been meeting up with Sam,' I said.

'Knew it!' Aaron sounded triumphant, and I couldn't help matching his grin before I tried to calm him down.

'Aaron, no, it's not like that!' I said. Another raised eyebrow from Daisy. 'Well, maybe it's a little bit like that now, but it *wasn't*. Not until last night, I promise. We've been sneaking out to rehearse, that's all.'

I could have sworn I saw Daisy swallow down an actual laugh before she said, 'That is the most Livi thing I've ever heard in my life.'

'I don't know how to take that,' I said, and that time Daisy did laugh.

'Take it as a fact!'

'But hang on,' Aaron said. 'Maybe it's a little bit like that now?'

I could feel my cheeks reddening.

'Last night, before you guys found us on the stage . . . we kissed.' I looked at Daisy. The lack of shock on her face confirmed that she'd already known that. 'Twice,' I added. She didn't look shocked at that bit either. She smiled when she saw me looking.

'Livi, you're not subtle.'

That was fair.

'It really wasn't anything,' I protested. 'When you asked me before? I meant it when I said it would never work. Something happened . . . last summer, I made a move and he rejected me. Big misunderstanding, and a weird move from me – we've talked about it and it's all good. Obviously. But believe me when I say I was the last person who saw any of this coming.'

'Livi, this is good news,' Aaron assured me as I put my face in my hands, shy suddenly. 'We love the idea of you with Sam.'

Obviously that was the moment Sam chose to walk through the door.

'Sam's doing what?' he asked, and I guessed the way I bit my lip and tried not to smile gave the game away. 'Oh,' he said. 'We're talking about that.'

'Happy for you, mate,' Aaron said, clapping Sam on the shoulder in the most laddish move I'd ever seen from him. Boys were weird.

'If we're quite finished with Livi's love life,' Daisy said, 'What are we going to do about Juliet?'

Sam came to sit beside me on the bed and wrapped an arm around my shoulders. And yeah . . . now I was ready to fight. I felt *powerful*. Like there was no way we didn't win this. Like we were going to find the answers, and it was going to happen *today*.

'Let's start with the note,' I said, pulling it out from under my pillow where I'd hidden it for safekeeping. 'Start with the note, and go from there.'

```
All four of them read the note again
in silence.


AARON: I think we need to go back
even further. I think to work out what's
happened to Juliet, we need to start
with what happened to Chloe.
```

LIVI: I've got a note for that crime somewhere too . . .

SAM laughs half-heartedly, but it isn't very funny. LIVI pulls out the wad of earlier notes from under her pillow too, and hands over the one she'd found on stage. The one telling them Chloe's time of death.

DAISY: You're right that it clears a lot of people. We *must* be missing someone though.
SAM: Unless it isn't a camper. We have no idea where the rest of the counsellors were.
LIVI: We didn't see any of them all night. They know the drill on party nights - they stay out of our way. They were probably in the staff bar or hanging out in their cabins. I just don't think they'd be out roaming the woods.
AARON: They might if they had murder on the mind.
DAISY: Aaron, this is still not a true crime podcast.
AARON: Sorry.
SAM: So it clears a lot of people,

but it doesn't answer the question of
what's happened to Juliet.
DAISY: Or what we're going to do about
it. I know we were meant to sleep on it,
but I still don't have a clue.
LIVI: Me neither. I think what we need to
do right now is buy ourselves some time.
AARON: What do you mean?
LIVI: Obviously Celestia and Sophia are
going to notice that Juliet is missing.
We can't lie that she's sick in the
cabin - look where that got us with
Chloe, it won't work again.
DAISY: It didn't work the first time.
LIVI: Yes exactly, and there's even less
chance of them letting it slide if one
of their celebrities doesn't turn up.
So, like I said. Buying some time.
SAM: What did you have in mind?

What I had in mind was risky. If Celestia and Sophia decided to be good at the pastoral care part of their job for, like, a single second, we'd be caught straight away. One phone call to Juliet's parents and we were done for. For want of a better plan, though, I told them.

'Let's tell the counsellors she's had to go home suddenly,' I said. 'We can come up with a reason – something that meant she had to leave straight away and couldn't wait to see them.'

'Why wouldn't she just tell them herself?' Daisy asked. 'Not saying it's a bad idea, just covering all our bases.'

'Because it was an emergency. It was the middle of the night. They were asleep and her parents sent a car. She was embarrassed to be quitting before the finish line. She was . . . throwing up. Someone stop me at any time, guys!'

'I don't know,' Daisy said. 'I just don't think they'd buy that she'd leave without a word. They're going to call her parents.'

I thought she was probably right, since that had been exactly my fear too.

'Hang on,' Sam said, his eyes sparkling. 'Why *wouldn't* she just tell them herself?'

I peered at him, wondering if the lack of sleep had made him lose his mind.

'Because we don't know where she is, Sam. And it hasn't really happened? Remember?'

'No need to snap, I haven't lost it,' he said before I could even get the whole sentence out. 'I'm saying . . . there is a way she can tell them herself.'

Daisy gasped. 'Oh my god. The videos.'

Sam looked very pleased with himself.

'The videos.'

I had to admit it was clever. We could almost definitely edit something together using Juliet's actual voice and play that down the phone to convince the counsellors of our story. If we had editing software and *time*, that is.

'It's a good idea,' I said, 'but how are we going to pull it off with the minus twelve hours we have to do this?'

It hadn't been quite twelve hours since we'd found out Juliet was gone, but the point still stood.

'We take it a step further,' Aaron said, looking a little nervous about whatever it was he was about to say. 'We have the videos, right?'

'Right . . .' I said.

'And we have the best actor in camp.'

'It *could* just work,' Sam said, apparently catching on to whatever the hell Aaron was talking about quicker than I had. 'She'll have to be really brave, but . . . it could just work.'

And then they were both looking at me?

Was I the *she* they were talking about?

'Guys, what are you saying?' Daisy asked. I was glad it wasn't just me in the dark. Except then she said, 'I think I get it, but I need you to just confirm.'

'Livi pretends to be Juliet,' Aaron said, looking to me for an answer.

What??

It was a crazy idea. There was no way it was going to work. We sounded nothing alike and the counsellors knew my voice well enough to recognise it anywhere, I was sure.

'No way,' I said. 'That's throwing ourselves *straight* under the bus, I promise you.' I looked to Daisy for back up.

'I mean . . . I think you could do it,' she said with an apologetic shrug. *So much for loyalty.* 'Think about it. You've watched enough of her videos and spent enough time with her to know exactly how she speaks, and Aaron is right. You are the best actor in camp. If anyone can do this, you can.'

It was the 'if anyone can do this' part that worried me, since I didn't think anyone *could*, but I had to admit I was flattered that they believed in me that much. If this blew up in our faces, it would be all of us going down. They had skin in the game too.

'You know if we get caught it's over, right?' I asked, and Sam took one of my hands in his. It still felt weird to be doing this in front of the others, weird to be doing it at *all,* but not so weird that I didn't squeeze it and relax into the touch.

'Livi, it's over if we don't do it too. They'll notice Juliet is gone within minutes, and they'll call her family, and it all comes crashing down. We have no idea what the killer will do if we let that happen . . . so don't you think we have to try?'

I thought about it for just a second, but I already knew what I would do. He was right. We had to try. We'd come this far without telling the counsellors what was going on so I knew that when they finally found out, we'd be in a whole world of trouble. Holding that at bay for just a little longer; trying just a little harder to find the answer so that at least we'd done *something* good in amongst all the lying . . . it felt like the only option, really.

'Fine,' I said. 'Hand me a phone.'

CHAPTER 23

LIVI, DAISY and JULIET'S cabin. Morning.

LIVI reaches the end of the video she's watching on her phone - one from JULIET's channel. It's the third one she's watched, and every now and then she repeats a word after the JULIET on the screen has said it, making sure she's getting the inflection right. She's pretty good.

AARON: Where do you get the worst reception in this cabin?
DAISY: Why?
AARON: The less clear the line, the less Celestia will be able to hear her.

LIVI looks wounded.

LIVI: You don't think I can do it?
AARON: I *know* you can. I just think we need all the help we can get, don't you? You'd usually rehearse a part for weeks and you were only cast in this one ten minutes ago.
DAISY: It's the corner by the bathroom. My headphones are always cutting out over there anyway.

Without another word, LIVI goes to stand in the corner by the bathroom.

SAM: Ready?
LIVI: Ready.

LIVI reaches for the pink wig she never returned to the wig store and places it haphazardly on her head. Transformation complete.

She dials.

To give them their due, it's a clever plan. Cleverer than I thought they'd go, what with the sleep deprivation and the stress. I'm not as confident as they are that it's actually going to work, but it's a valiant effort. Whatever happens, we have to give them that.

CELESTIA answers.

LIVI *(as Juliet)*: Celestia! Hey! It's Jules. Stone.
CELESTIA: Oh hi, Juliet! Is everything OK?
LIVI *(Juliet)*: Yeah, all good. Listen, I've had to leave camp - just a small emergency, everything is fine. I'll be back before the showcase, promise.
CELESTIA: You have to leave?
LIVI *(Juliet)*: No, I've had to leave. I'm already gone. So sorry not to have told you in person, it was all really last minute so my parents sent a car straight away. I barely had time to pack.

LIVI is twirling her hair in an absent-minded, very Juliet fashion. She's getting into this.

CELESTIA: Oh . . . well, OK, I guess. If you're sure everything is OK?

LIVI *(still Juliet)*: All good, I'm sure. Listen, I have to go, but I'll see you really soon, OK?
CELSTIA: OK . . . keep us updated.
LIVI: I will.

She hangs up. The others are looking at her in awe as she puts the phone down, shakes out her body, smiles. LIVI again.

LIVI: Was that OK?
DAISY: Who *are* you?
AARON: Livi, it was perfect.
SAM: Perfect.
LIVI: She seemed a bit confused, but I think she bought it, right?
AARON: She totally bought it.
SAM: You're really good, you know?
LIVI: I know.

*She smiles. Flips her hair.
Allows herself that.*

I was on a complete high after the phone call. I couldn't believe it had worked, but also . . . sort of could? Maybe I *was* as good at this; at playing a part as I'd hoped. I had a new fire in me. We were going to crack this and it was going to be *soon*.

'What's next?' I asked, sinking back on to the bed beside Sam.

'Right,' Aaron said. 'What else do we know?'

'Chloe was poisoned,' Daisy said. 'Had to be, right?' Somehow because of the red herring that she'd drowned, and in all the Juliet drama, I'd mostly forgotten that until I'd seen the little bottle again, nestled in my box. *Poisoned*. Where would someone find poison at Camp Chance?

'The dangerous chemicals cupboard,' I said aloud, forgetting that they weren't privy to my inner monologue so it probably sounded like I was just saying random words. 'Surely that's where they got the bottle, I mean. Where else would they find something so toxic that it could actually kill someone?'

The dangerous chemicals cupboard was what gave Camp Chance it's fireworks. Literally. All the special effects that our showcases were famous for were born behind that locked yellow door – I'd seen things set on fire, blown up, the works, and known that the stage crew, who were as skilled in alchemy as they were making us fly, had mixed together acids and dry ice (I have no idea how you make fire, leave me alone) and come up with magic.

'We need to go back to reception and look at the CCTV,' Daisy said. 'See who went in.' Aaron was shaking his head before she'd finished speaking.

'The camera that's meant to be trained on that door is actually pointing at the floor, so unless you want to match our suspect to their shoes . . .'

Crap.

'Fine, then we need to get in there ourselves,' I said.

'It's always locked,' Sam said, like I didn't know that. All these years and I'd never seen the door open even a crack. I hadn't even realised my confidence had been wavering the last few days until the phone call brought it crashing back, but right now I felt like I could do anything, if I was in performance mode at least.

'I can get in there,' I said, a promise. 'I'll tell the stage management counsellors that I'm *considering my options* if performing doesn't work out, and ask them to show me.'

'Livi, no one would ever believe you'd have a back up,' Sam said.

I grinned.

'Sam,' I said, 'Keep up. I'm a *very* good actor.'

I hadn't had much to do with the stage management counsellors before, not this year or any other, so I guess that explained the look of surprise on Oliver's face when I turned up in the doorway to their office with a grin on my lips and a sparkle in my eye.

'Livi,' he said, and I took that as an invitation to come in and sit down, which only intensified the surprised expression. Good. If I could blindside him with charm and confuse him into helping me, this would be easy.

God, I hoped this would be easy.

'How's it going?' I asked, my elbows on the desk, leaning towards him. He shifted back in his seat, just a little bit, like he was scared of this force of nature who had barged into his office for apparently no reason. I could make that work.

'Good,' he said, in a tone that sounded more bemused than good. 'Is everything . . . OK? How can I help you?'

I looked around the cramped office, walls lined with safety information and schedules, and had to surpress a shudder. I thought stage management was a *miracle*; a skill more precise and specific than most others in theatre, and one I knew I would never, ever have. This really was going to test my acting skills.

'Stage management,' I said. 'I want to know more. I know I'm all about performing, and that hasn't changed, but . . .' *Gulp. Deep breath. Remember you're playing a role . . .* 'it's good to have a back up, isn't it?' I choked out.

I felt awful when I saw how Oliver's eyes lit up. He loved stage management the same way I loved nailing a solo. I should have known anyone else showing an interest would have him fired up. I was also just a little smug, though. From the look on his face, I could tell that this was working.

'What do you want to know?' he asked, less suspicious now, mirroring me as he leant towards me over the desk like he was about to tell me a secret, pushing his coffee aside to shift his elbows closer.

'How to set things alight,' I said. 'Literally.'

I probably could have timed that better, since Oliver had

just taken a sip and was now threatening to spit it back out in shock. *Oops!*

Dial it back, Livi.

'Joking,' I said quickly, but I knew the seed had been planted. If he wanted to impress, wanted me to take stage management seriously, he'd want to show me something cool. I had a feeling he was going to give me *exactly* what I'd asked for.

```
STAGE MANAGEMENT OFFICE.


LIVI leans into OLIVER, somewhere between
acting and straight up flirting. How does
he not see through this? She is so obvious.
```

I was so subtle.

Oliver didn't even *try* to resist. I knew it was nothing to do with me – it was entirely his love for his job that made him push back from the desk, stand up, and say, 'Come on, then'. All he wanted was for me to see how cool stage management was, so that if I ever really *was* looking for a back up, it would be the first place I went. I got it. It was exactly the way I felt about performing, except if performing was your back up you'd already lost. Nobody got away with having performing as their *back up*. I imagined that was how Oliver felt about managing stages though, to be fair to him.

'Where are we going?' I asked as he led me down the hallway, innocent as anything.

I knew exactly where we were going.

'You said you wanted fireworks...'

I actually hadn't said that, although I had been thinking it. Could Oliver read minds now?

'To see how you set things alight,' I clarified, and he nodded.

'Same thing when it comes to the process. Well, sort of.'

I put on my best 'this is very cool' face as we reached the tall yellow door and he tapped in the code. Cupboard was hugely playing down what the dangerous chemicals cupboard actually *was*. It was more like a whole, admittedly small, room – shelves from floor to ceiling filled with substances considered so dangerous that you were supposed to declare them on the clipboard dangling from a string by the door before you left with them. If whatever had killed Chloe *had* come from here, I was willing to bet it hadn't been properly signed out, but there were so many small glass bottles on the shelves that spotting the gap where ours had come from would be almost impossible. *All right. Plan B.*

'What's the most dangerous thing in here?' I asked, making sure to punctuate it with a grin so Oliver thought I was being quirky and funny rather than that I was a dangerous psychopath. I had always rolled my eyes at people who pretended to be 'weird' or 'not like other girls' to get what they wanted, and I silently apologised to all the girls I'd judged before... it turned out that in situations like this, their method actually worked. Oliver set off talking about some sort of flammable liquid that ... made things flammable? I wasn't really listening as I flicked through the sign-out sheet, hoping I was dropping my 'hmm's at the right time to make him think I was really interested. It was as I thought – nothing had been signed out the day Chloe died. We were going to need a closer look at the contents of this cupboard, and I couldn't do that with Oliver around.

Feigning a time check, I gasped.

'Oh my god, I'm late for a rehearsal!'

Please god let Oliver not know our rehearsal schedule in any detail.

He laughed.

'Never thought I'd see the day that Livi Campbell got so into a conversation about stage management that she'd forget about performing for five minutes.'

'You make it sound so compelling!' I said as I got out of the cupboard so he could close the door, making sure there was no way anyone was getting back in without him. 'Thank you so much for everything, Oliver.'

'Any time,' he said. 'Just let me know if there's ever anything else you want to see.'

'You've given me everything I need for now,' I said sweetly.

True.

```
DANGEROUS CHEMICALS CUPBOARD.
A FEW HOURS LATER.
```

LIVI, SAM, AARON and DAISY in the hallway. The 'no access' flashing across the keypad seems aggressive, like it's taunting them. It doesn't even have a handle they can try to force, or a keyhole they can try to pick. This door is Very Locked.

AARON: So what's the plan?
LIVI: The code is 3714.

Very well played, Campbell.

AARON: How do you know that?
LIVI: I've been carrying it around in my head all day, ever since I saw Oliver type it in this morning. Now, hurry up - someone could walk round that corner at any second and we're caught red-handed.
SAM: Are we sure it's not alarmed?
LIVI: Well, it might be if you type in the wrong code, but that isn't the wrong code. I watched him do it! No alarms! Can someone just . . .

AARON types in the code. The door swings open to reveal . . .

LIVI: What. The . . .
DAISY: What does this . . .
LIVI: Someone knew we were coming.

Pull back. Zoom out. Look at the cupboard and not the campers standing jaws-to-the-floor in the doorway.
Those floor-to-ceiling shelves?
Completely empty.

CHAPTER 24

I DIDN'T THINK THERE WAS A SINGLE MILLIMETRE of the ceiling above my head that I hadn't studied in forensic detail by the time I had to leave for my not-secret-any-more rehearsal with Sam that night. I lay there in silence long after Daisy fell asleep, going over and over everything we knew in my mind. I was missing something, I knew I was. It felt close enough to touch, but when I tried to focus in on it all I saw was a blur. The vague shadow of an answer, but nothing I could actually work with.

Why couldn't I work this out?

Why had the cupboard been emptied? And by who?

My phone buzzed beside me, telling me it was time to leave, and I peeled myself off of the bed and slipped my shoes on. I was *tired*. Tired of all of this. I tapped my cheeks, hard, trying to bring a little bit of life back into them, and a little bit of energy back into me. I had to be alert. Sam and I had promised to keep a close eye on our way to the barn tonight – to notice who we saw. Who we didn't. I hoped that it would bring back a memory I'd let slip from the night Chloe died. I really needed it to, because right now I was coming up empty.

Walking through the forest slowly enough to actually observe things, when I knew that the killer was probably watching, tested every single one of my nerves. Sam had offered to come and get me, so that we could walk together, but I'd been so fired up after a day of successes that I'd forgotten to be afraid. Said no. Was now hugely regretting my choice.

One foot in front of the other, Livi. Eyes up. Show them you're not scared. That they wouldn't dare *touch you right now.*

Except I *was* scared and they probably would, so using that as a mantra wasn't going so well.

Should I try to make as much noise as I could, so the other campers heard me and would know I'd been out here if something happened? Or should I try my very best to be silent? Hope the killer hadn't seen me leave and *wasn't* watching me right now, even though they somehow seemed to *always* be watching me? Seemed to see *everything;* be *everywhere*?

In the end the forest made the decision for me, since I was so distracted trying to decide what to do that I didn't even notice I was stepping on the branch until the almighty crack echoed through the trees as it snapped under my foot and I tripped on thin air at the shock.

Jesus.

That did it. I was running.

It was only as I reached the steps of the rehearsal barn that

I realised I was scared of a sound that *I'd* created. That I was running away from myself.

That felt like a metaphor.

Sam was nowhere to be seen yet, so I turned on the lights, sat down at the piano stool and tried to catch my breath using the deep breathing techniques I couldn't really remember from the meditation app I used when I couldn't sleep back home. That was never usually a problem here – the long days of intense rehearsals and fresh forest air knocked me straight out when my head hit the pillow. I missed that; looked forward to all of this being over so I could get back to the real reason I came here.

I was still kidding myself that there was a way back from this.

I checked the time on my phone. 12.05 a.m. Just as I was hoping Sam hadn't stood me up, or fallen asleep (admittedly more likely), the motion sensor lights outside the door cut a beam across the floor and in he sauntered, a happy-to-see-me grin on his face.

My heart dropped to the pit of my stomach.

Click.

The thing that had been making me uneasy fell into place, somewhere right between my ribs, where it really hurt.

Sam.

The one person I hadn't seen between leaving the party and arriving here on the night Chloe died.

The one person whose alibi I didn't know for 12.13 a.m.

The last person I ever would have suspected – had all of

this, everything we'd been through together, been a clever ruse to throw me off the scent?

Because that night, he'd been even later than he was now. That night I had no idea where he'd gone when everyone else went back to their cabins.

Had he been freshening up? Saying goodnight to friends like he'd said?

Or had he been with Chloe, by the lake?

I speed ran through everything that had happened since that night. Had he been acting strangely since we found out the time of death? He'd seemed *different*, sure, but I'd assumed that was . . . the other thing. I'd assumed that was the kiss, that now I thought about it felt more and more like it had come out of nowhere.

Typical Livi, making it all about yourself. Forgetting why you were supposed to be wary of this man. Forgetting that he literally rejected you. Look what you've missed because you were so desperate to be wanted.

I opened my mouth, gaping at him, seemingly unable to say any of this out loud. Unable to speak at all. Whatever my face was doing obviously tipped him off that Something Was Wrong. He started to walk towards me. I stumbled backwards, my brain moving faster than my body could keep up with. *Get away from him.*

I weighed up my options quickly. I could get myself out of this. Game face on, keep calm as I told him I was sick. That I got my period. That Daisy needed me.

I'd get out of here fast, find Aaron and Daisy, and raise the alarm.

I could *do this*. Possibly the most important role of my life, but I'd trained for it, hadn't I? I had all the skills.

'Livi, what's wrong?' he asked.

He spoke, I broke. The plan went out of the window as soon as I heard his voice, confused, pleading. *Sam*.

'You know what!' I screamed.

Screamed? I thought I was screaming, but the voice that came out was tiny. Scared. *Sam*. How could I have been so stupid? Let my guard down so entirely? This was why it was good to be guarded; to focus only on yourself and your goals. The minute you let someone else in, they might turn out to be a murderer. I choked out a little sob.

'Livi...'

He was advancing slowly now, and I was pressed up against the back wall, nowhere else to go. Daisy knew where I'd gone, right? This was where she'd look if I didn't come back? I was shaking violently, terrified. I couldn't look him in the eye. If I looked him in the eye, I'd crumble, and none of us could afford that. But if I didn't look him in the eye, I couldn't be sure.

And I had to be sure.

I raised my gaze, ready to ... well, not fight, but ready to pretend I could. To show him I wasn't scared (I was) and that I was not prepared to lose (true, but I still expected to). I locked eyes with him.

'Livi,' he said, confused. 'What the hell is going on?'

What? I *knew.* Why was he pretending, when he could see that I'd worked him out? Was he trying to throw me off the scent? Buy himself some time? He was a very good actor, I reminded myself. That was the whole point, wasn't it? How I'd ended up in this room alone with him in the first place? The look in his eyes went from amused to concerned, like he thought I might have lost it.

Wait... was I wrong?

No! That was what he wanted me to think. Stupid little Livi, so focused on getting the lead that she won't notice what's going on under her own nose. Well, not any more. I was poised. Calm. Ready.

```
LIVI is shaking. Terrified.
```

'Sam,' I said, 'I know it's you.'

He looked at me like that couldn't be the end of the sentence. Like he was waiting to hear *what* was him. It felt like a dare. *You want me to say it? Fine, I'll say it.*

'I know you killed Chloe,' I said.

There was a moment of true silence – like even the air was waiting with baited breath to see what his next move was going to be.

Then Sam began to laugh.

```
LIVI is thrown as SAM stands there, his
laugh booming around the optimised-for-
```

*projection rehearsal barn. It's like he's
finally cracked.*

*He looks at LIVI like 'why are you
not laughing?'*

She recoils.

*He must see something on her face,
because he stops.*

Holds up his hands as he steps back.

SAM: Wait, you're not joking, are you?

*The movement is small, but impossible to
miss – LIVI shakes her head.*

'Livi, what are you talking about?'

He was the one who sounded scared now, but not because he knew he'd been caught out. No, this was fear that something was really wrong with me. He was looking at me with so much confusion, so much *care*, that I knew I'd got it very, very wrong.

Right? This was genuine?

The thing about Sam was that he was a brilliant actor.

The thing about me was that over the course of our late-night rehearsals, I'd made him even better.

I thought I could tell when he took the mask off, when he was just Sam instead of a performer playing a role, and I thought this was real, but I didn't trust anything any more.

'You don't have an alibi,' I said. 'I saw everyone else, but you were late. Where were you? Between leaving the party and meeting me here, where did you go?'

I meant it to sound like a challenge, but it came out as a plea. *Please don't let it be you. Please have an answer that makes sense.*

'Livi, I can't tell you that.'

Another sob bubbled in my chest, but I pushed it down. No. He did not get to see me cry here.

'But you have to believe me,' he said. 'I had nothing to do with what happened to Chloe. I promise you.'

'Then what could possibly be so bad that you can't tell me? What could have you so spooked that you'd rather me think you were involved?'

'It isn't me that's spooked,' he said, and that made absolutely no sense. 'I think . . . you would be. If I told you where I really was that night.'

Why were men so stupid? What could he possibly have been doing that would have me more spooked than thinking he was a murderer? I had only just managed to peel myself off the back wall of the barn, that was how spooked I *already was*. What could he possibly say that would make this worse?

'Sam,' I said, 'there is very little that could spook me more than thinking the guy I'm falling for – or *was* falling for – has killed someone. So, try me.'

'You're . . . falling for me?'

Of course that's what he took from that.

'Is that the important part?'

'I think it might be,' he said, slowly walking towards me. I tried to stand my ground, but I flinched just a little. I thought I believed him, but I still wasn't convinced this wasn't all about to blow up in my face; that he actually might be about to tell me something even worse.

'No, Livi, trust me.'

'OK,' I said quietly, planting my feet. *Let him say his piece. Let him get it out, and then you can decide whether to be scared.* 'Go on.'

'I was late because I was with Juliet,' he said, and yes, OK, he was right. That was worse.

'Livi,' he said, clocking the way my expression had changed, 'let me finish.'

I nodded.

'I lied, when I told you I was with Leah by the lake. Or, I *was* with Leah, briefly, but she left at the end of the party, when everyone else did. I was with Juliet. She asked me to be in one of her videos and I couldn't resist. She left me with her camera while she went to the bathroom, asked me to film a piece while I was there.'

'Why didn't you just tell me that?!' I screamed. Screamed? No, still barely more than a whisper.

'Because I knew how you'd react! I knew how you felt about Juliet's videos—'

'How?' I cut him off. 'I never told you that.'

'You were hollering about it on the coach,' he said, as if it was obvious. 'Your voice projects, Livi. Besides, you told Louis. He's the biggest gossip going, you know that.'

Not untrue. *Way to stress me out further, Sam, since he's also the only other person who knows what's really going on.*

'It was before we knew her,' he continued. 'Before she became one of us. I knew if I told you, this good thing we had going would be over before it really started, and then she went missing and that seemed more important than any of this . . .' Sam trailed off.

'Wait,' I said. 'Back up. She asked you to be in one of her videos – what did she have you doing?'

Sam huffed with frustration, a short sound that I thought was trying to say *Why do you care? Can't you just forgive me already?* Apparently not. I'd made that mistake with him once before, and now look where we were.

'She asked me to talk about why camp is so special to me. It was . . . weird. It didn't feel like her usual stuff at all. It was like—'

'You've watched her usual stuff?'

'Are you jealous?'

Yes.

'Obviously not,' I said. 'Carry on.'

'It was like someone had fed her the lines and I was her puppet – like she was making some sort of camp propaganda. She told me exactly what the talking points were . . . Livi, it doesn't *matter*. I just need you to believe that I wasn't late because I had anything to do with what happened to Chloe. That as soon as I realised I was late, I left. I put the camera down and I left, because I would rather be with you.'

'*Why?*' I asked, incredulous. Sam shook his head, the stupid affectionate look on his face making me want to avert my eyes. It was too much. I couldn't trust any of it.

'How do you not see how great you are?'

Ah. That made sense.

'All of this is because I'm talented? Because you think doing this with me is how you win?'

'Livi Campbell, are you being deliberately obtuse?' he asked, walking towards me as he ran a hand through his own hair, frustrated.

OK, that was hot. I didn't move back this time.

'No,' I said. 'I mean it. Why would you want to be with me? I know I put on a good show, but everyone knows I'm annoyingly single-minded about performing. *I* know it doesn't make me a good friend, so I'm sure everyone else does. And that it wouldn't make me a good . . .' I could hardly even get the word out, 'girlfriend.'

'I don't think that's true,' Sam said, entirely matter-of-fact. 'Maybe it was once, but I think you've changed this summer. I don't think you *are* single-minded any more. Not at all.'

'What gives you that idea?' I asked, cringing at how desperate I sounded. I *so* wanted it to be true; so wanted to be the kind of person who could be a *whole* person, and not completely fixated on an industry that might never love me back, no matter how hard I worked or how good I got.

'Well, look at us,' he said with a shrug. 'You were all about our relationship staying strictly professional, and I'm pretty sure you were there when we kissed, Liv. Both times. That doesn't sound like staying single-minded.'

'I was ambushed,' I said, and he laughed.

'You were the one doing the ambushing in at least half the cases, if I remember rightly,' he said with a smile. 'But that isn't the point. The point is that I think you've realised there's more to life than acting. That you weren't *living*. But now you are, Livi C. And so ... here we are.'

Here we are.

It was embarrassing how good I felt about what he'd said.

I don't think I'll tell you what happened next.

```
What happens next is that she kisses him.
She kisses him, no ambiguity.


I wish we could fade to black, but that
isn't how these cameras work, so instead
we watch them.


We watch them, and think about stepping
up the plan.
```

CHAPTER 25

THE FOREST. NIGHT VISION.

Exterior shot of the door as LIVI and SAM leave the rehearsal barn, his arm around her waist, her tucked into his side. Not the easiest way to walk down stairs, but they're making a valiant effort, bless them. Young love.
Disgusting.

They stop at the bottom of the stairs. This is where they diverge - where SAM goes one way back to his cabin, and LIVI goes the other back to hers. They're taking their time, reluctant to let each other go.

Enjoying it while they can.

Eventually:

LIVI: So I'll see you in the morning?
SAM: Already looking forward to it.
LIVI: Sam - I'm sorry. For the . . . for what I accused you of.

SAM waves a hand. It's already forgotten.

SAM: Don't be. It was some good detective work. Aaron would have been proud.
LIVI: Let's not tell them I thought it was you.
SAM: But it's hilarious.
LIVI: Not for me!
SAM: OK, I won't say a word. Not until we find out who actually did it, and this is all just a really good story.

He leans in. Kisses her.

SAM: Goodnight, Livi.
LIVI: Night, Sam.

A crossroads. SAM walks one way,

LIVI another. We see them from above as they drift away from each other, both trying really hard not to look back. They've both seen Hadestown. They know how dangerous that is.

A sound. SAM's voice?
LIVI spins.

LIVI: Sam? Did you say something?

But SAM is not there. She's hearing things. She pulls her hoodie tighter, walks a little faster.

It must have just been wishful thinking.

CHAPTER 26

'YOU'RE IN A GOOD MOOD,' DAISY SAID, BUMPING my shoulder as we walked into the dining hall, and of course with everything going on it was a lot more complicated than that, but it was also *true*. I had woken up smiling after my conversation with Sam; was going into the day feeling positive – like all we had to do was work out what had happened, find Juliet, and we could start the rest of our lives. All of us.

Not hard at all, right?

Sure, I was struggling to have more than about three thoughts in a row that weren't about Juliet, about how we were failing her right now, but we were trying our best and I hoped the killer could see that. Besides, they were going to slip – it was only a matter of time, it had to be. And when they did, *we'd* be watching *them* for once. It felt, for the first time since Juliet had gone missing at least, that everything might just be OK.

'I just slept well,' I said to Daisy with a smile and a little shimmy of my shoulders to let her know that while that was true – I *had* slept like a log for the few hours after coming back from rehearsal – it also wasn't the whole story.

'I'm glad you're happy,' she said.

I caught Louis' eye and waved as we walked towards the table where Aaron was already waiting, Luke excusing himself as Daisy and I sat down. I wanted to show him that I'd meant it – that he may not officially be one of us, but I was going to keep Louis updated the best I could.

'He can stay, you know,' I said as I watched Luke's retreating back heading to the table he shared with the other lighting kids, and Aaron smiled.

'I know. But he likes talking about gels and rigging over breakfast – those are lighting words, Livi . . . he's very good at keeping things separate.'

I gave him the middle finger. I knew what rigging was, thanks.

(Gels?!)

'Still going well, then?' Daisy asked, and Aaron looked bashful as he nodded, and took a sip of his black coffee to try and hide his smile.

'Really well. I like him a lot. I guess we'll see what happens once we're back in the real world – my real world is not the same as most people's, and I know it can be a lot . . . he'd have to be sure he was ready for that. But if he wanted to . . . I think I'd wanna try.'

I knew what a big deal that was for Aaron. Having a relationship wasn't just introducing them to his family –

whether he wanted to or not, it would eventually mean introducing them to the world. Could Luke handle it? I had no idea. But if this summer had taught me anything so far, it was that we were all capable of things we'd never dreamt of. I wished them luck, truly.

'Where's Sam?' Daisy asked, and it was like the room came into hyperfocus – I'd been dully aware of the fact he hadn't arrived yet, but now Daisy had asked it was like there was a physical hole in the room where he should have been. Like I could *feel* that he was missing.

Nobody had ever told me the beginning of falling in love felt so much like an overture; like a taste of what came next, and how good it might be. If they had, maybe I would have tried it earlier.

'Probably struggling to get out of bed again,' I said, trying to sound nonchalant; trying not to let on how excited I was to see him. 'You know what he's like.'

'Do you think he's OK?' Daisy asked, her voice low. 'You don't think . . .'

And suddenly I felt sick. Aaron could clearly see me spiralling, my mouth opening and closing like an overactive goldfish, because he put his hand on mine. Stilled me.

'Livi, I'm sure he's fine.'

'What if he isn't, though?'

Neither of them even pretended to have an answer to that.

'Celestia incoming,' Daisy said quietly, and I tried so hard to ignore the parallels to the morning Chloe hadn't turned up to breakfast but couldn't stop the rising sick feeling. I pasted on an unconvincing smile.

'Where's Sam?' Celestia asked, no time for pleasantries, and I could not be that person any longer. Couldn't be the one with the answers, the one who never fell apart. I'd been putting on a show my whole life, and I simply ... couldn't do it any more.

Shouting or crying, Livi? Which way is this going to go?

Unfortunately, I chose shouting.

'Celestia, we *don't know*.'

She physically recoiled. *Oops. That was loud, wasn't it?* Aaron tightened his grip where he was still holding my hand.

'Why does everyone expect us to have all the answers? He's his own person! I can't know where he is at every second, none of us can! So *please* just *stop asking*!'

I pushed back from the table, cringing at the sound of my chair scraping on the floor, and ran out of the dining hall. *People are looking, aren't they?* I didn't have to glance back to know that yes, they were. I could hear Daisy and Aaron's footsteps behind me, following me, but I didn't stop, just kept running. I tried not to think about the fact that running out on Celestia would have ruined *their* showcase chances, too. I was messing everything up, for everyone. I didn't think Aaron would care, but *Daisy*! Poor, sweet Daisy who deserved everything good. I hated that this had been her Camp Chance experience; hated that now she'd never get a fair chance at a good part.

I hated it all.

I was so tired.

I finally stopped running as Sam's cabin came into view.

'Did he come back last night?' I asked, not looking at Aaron, who I knew was right behind me.

'I don't know,' Aaron admitted. 'I was with Luke. When did you last see him?'

'After rehearsal,' I said. 'We went separate ways outside the barn. I . . .'

I trailed off, but Daisy could tell there was something I wasn't saying.

'Livi, what?'

'I thought I heard him calling something, after I walked away. I thought I heard his voice . . . but when I turned around, he wasn't there.'

None of us said anything for a second. We just stared at the cabin.

No lights were on.

'Should we . . .?' Aaron asked, and I was glad he was taking control. He hadn't mentioned true crime once, I noticed. I couldn't decide if that was comforting or made me feel worse. Except now he seemed to be looking to me for an answer, waiting for me to tell him what to do. I had no *idea* what we were supposed to do, but I didn't have time to think about it either. If Sam was in danger, we needed to work with every second we had.

'Let's go,' I said, and was up the stairs of the cabin, was pounding on the locked door, was trying to break the lock before Aaron caught up to me with the key and opened the door in a frankly impressively swift motion.

It was obvious straight away that Sam wasn't there. The cabin was quiet. Cold, even though it was thirty-two degrees outside. We stepped over the threshold.

It was Daisy who saw it first. Pinned to Sam's pillow, like whoever had left it there wanted to make absolutely sure it wasn't going anywhere – a small white envelope. She leant towards it. Turned back to me with a grimace.

'It's addressed to you.'

Crap. Whether it was from Sam or someone else, being left a note when he was nowhere to be found couldn't be a good sign, could it? I pulled out the pin, picked up the envelope, slid out the small piece of card inside.

Dear Livi, it began. Without even reading any further, I knew it wasn't from Sam. He would never say *Dear Livi.* He'd say *Hey.* Or *Hi, bro* – god, it made me cringe when he said 'bro', but what I wouldn't have given to hear it, or read it, now. I carried on.

> Dear Livi,
> I really hoped it wouldn't come to this, but you've been putting your attention in all the wrong places. From theatre to Sam . . . haven't you realised yet that neither is going to save you? You've not been concentrating, so let me spell it out: you should have been giving all that focus to how Chloe ended up dead by the lake. To what happened to Juliet. I warned you that if you didn't find out who killed Chloe, she wouldn't be the only one, and I make

good on my promises. Do better. Time is running out. For all of you.

```
The scream that comes out of LIVI
is guttural, but she is not scared.
She's furious. One thing I'll say for
performers - excellent lung capacity.
Every time it sounds like she's reaching
the end of her breath, she finds more
from somewhere.

She screams, and screams, and screams,
and screams.

AARON and DAISY let her. Nothing that
they can say is going to make this
better. Finally, DAISY steps towards her.
Places a hand on LIVI's arm.

Contact.

And then - collapse.
```

Daisy's hand on my arm broke something in me; the kind of snap you can never come back the same from. I felt something deflate. People are not supposed to go from screaming to the kind of crying I was doing so quickly – or possibly even slowly.

It was like a physical wrenching as my body tried to get the pain of everything that had happened out, not realising that wasn't a physical thing – that it was too widespread, too nebulous, not something you could touch, or expel that easily. Still, my poor little body was trying. I felt like I was going to throw up. I couldn't breathe, but I couldn't stop. Daisy just stood there, kept her hand firmly on my arm, and didn't say a word. She just let me cry.

I had no idea how to process any of this – my emotions surfacing, tangling, crashing into each other and retreating, just to surface again a second later in a way that was too much for me to handle; too fast for me to keep up with.

Was I scared? Of course – and then . . . no. Not scared, defeated. So tired I wanted to curl in on myself and not wake up until it was over. Except that was replaced by a surge of energy so strong it took me by surprise. Tired? I'd never felt more alert. I could *do this*. Could find Sam, find Juliet, save us all. Except I had *no idea* how to do this. I wanted my mum; wanted a real adult involved who would have some answers, or at least know how to get them. But if we *told someone* . . .

All of that, on repeat, over and over and over.

Right back round to terrified.

It felt like it was going to go on for ever, but I eventually ran out of steam, and in the second between gasping out the end of one breath and pausing to take another, I decided . . . no. I was too tired. I couldn't do this any more. I couldn't even *cry* – they'd somehow taken even that. I planted my feet more firmly on the ground, closed my eyes.

One huge breath in.

One huge breath out.

I opened them.

'Thank you,' I said.

'It's nothing,' Daisy replied, and she was so genuinely *good* that I knew she meant it. She was wrong, though. It was not nothing. I looked over her shoulder to where Aaron was standing with a worried expression on his face.

'Sorry,' I said, and he shook his head.

'You have nothing to be sorry for.'

'Say something about true crime,' I pleaded. 'Make this feel a bit more normal.'

They both laughed at that.

'If this was a true crime story, we'd probably be close,' he said. 'I know it's the way podcasts are edited and all of that, but the dark night of the soul always seems to come right before the investigators remember something they'd been missing.'

'That helped,' I said with a small smile. It was true.

'What are you thinking?' Daisy asked.

'That I can't do this any more.'

I sank to sit on Sam's bed and inched backwards until I was leaning against the wall, my legs dangling off the edge.

'Everything is falling apart. I tried focusing on theatre, and I probably still won't get the showcase lead because theatre can never love me back. What a waste of my time! The minute I start focusing on Sam, he *dies*. Probably. I'm the problem. I'm cursed. Every time something good is within reaching distance it shatters right in front of me. I just can't. I can't do it any more.'

Daisy came to sit beside me on the bed.

'Livi, can I say something?'

'Yes,' I said.

'It isn't about you.'

She looked so sincere. So *earnest*. I choked out a sound that was somewhere between a sob and a laugh, and Daisy took that as her cue to carry on.

'Yes,' she said, 'you're powerful, but you can't control the world with your thoughts! You didn't *do* any of this. And Sam is not dead.'

'You don't know that.'

'Well you don't know that he is.'

True, but it somehow didn't make me feel better.

'Do you think this has gone too far?' Aaron asked, perching on the end of the mattress.

'Yes,' I said. 'Ages ago.'

Aaron laughed. I wasn't even slightly joking.

'I mean . . . has the time come to tell the counsellors? We tried really hard to do this on our own, but there's no shame in admitting we need help.'

'It isn't that,' I said. 'I just can't escape the feeling that telling puts more people in danger.'

'We can't know that,' Aaron said. It was like that, or variations of it, was the only line in their script.

'Livi, I think it's time,' Daisy said gently. 'Telling might help Sam and Juliet.'

I knew she didn't mean it to, but that felt like emotional blackmail. Like of *course* there was a right answer, if one might help our friends. But what if it meant more people got hurt? I had no idea what I was supposed to do.

'It's your choice,' Aaron said, like I wasn't already about to collapse under that particular pressure.

'I have *no* idea,' I said, holding my hands up.

Don't look to me. Everything I touch shatters.

What I *did* know was that rehearsal was about to start. Whatever we decided, not being there would look suspicious. Would take the choice away.

I was done with my choices being taken away.

'We have to go to rehearsal,' I said, propelling myself up and off of the bed before either of them had a chance to argue with me. 'You asked what I want to do, and what I want to do is that. I want to go to rehearsal, and I want to absolutely smash my song, and I want to leave everyone in the room with no doubt that I am a *great* performer, even if I'm a questionable person. That'll clear my head. Then I'll be able to make my decision.'

Neither of them moved.

'Daisy, Aaron, I'm not joking,' I said. 'Let's *move*.'

I guess they had no choice but to follow me, one on either side, like we were walking into a lion's den.

Which felt accurate.

Maybe we were.

CHAPTER 27

Main Stage. Rehearsal.

Campers, including LIVI, AARON and DAISY sit cross-legged on the ground waiting for CELESTIA to begin.

She sweeps towards them, a face like thunder.

CELESTIA: Why are all my best performers skipping out on me, and why are they all friends with *you*?
LIVI *(not in the mood)*: What are you talking about?
CELESTIA: Sam Chambers. Left a note at reception saying he had to leave urgently, which throws *all* my plans

```
    into disarray. Are none of you thinking
    of anyone but yourselves?
```

That didn't feel fair, but I was too tired to argue with her. I had to decide quickly which direction I was going to go in here.

```
    LIVI: Celestia, he didn't tell me he was
    going either, so we're all in the same
    boat here. Sam disappearing doesn't help
    my plans either.
    CELESTIA: I guess that's true.
    LIVI: I guess I didn't mean as much to
    him as he said I did.
```

Blind her with information. Make sure she had no reason to suspect anything.

```
    CELESTIA: Sorry. I . . . I didn't know.
    LIVI: Yeah, well, nothing to lose now,
    is there. No reason to keep it secret
    if it isn't happening any more.
    CELESTIA: Sorry.
```

She goes to walk away. What LIVI does next is masterful. You wouldn't even notice if you weren't looking closely. But I am looking closely.

Silence . . . silence . . . she watches CELESTIA leave. And then:

LIVI: Celestia?

CELESTIA turns.

CELESTIA: Yeah?
LIVI: Can I have the note?
CELESTIA: The note?
LIVI: The one Sam left. It's just . . . he's taken all his things. And I'd really like something to remember him by.

CELESTIA looks at LIVI like she's grown a second head.

CELESTIA: You want the note? That he wrote to *me*? Telling me he was leaving?
LIVI: Leaving me behind, yeah. I think it'll help with the closure.

I hated the way she was looking at me like I was someone to pity, but it was the only way to make sure she gave me what I wanted. What we all needed.

'Of course,' Celestia said, her face softening. 'I'll get it for you after rehearsal.'

'Thank you,' I said. I knew I was a good actress, but that had been easier than I'd expected. Celestia walked away, muttering under her breath about how this *really did ruin everything*. I guessed that was confirmation that the showcase leads *had* been mine and Sam's, at least at one stage. Even if they weren't now. It was a small consolation, I supposed.

'What is she so wound up about?' Aaron asked as soon as Celestia was out of earshot. 'As far as she's concerned, both Sam and Juliet are safe and sound back home, and if she's thinking about the showcase there are any number of campers chomping at the bit for those parts.'

'I bet it's the police sniffing around,' Daisy said. 'It's not a very good look, is it? And they still haven't figured out what actually happened to Chloe. I think that would put most people a little bit on edge, especially if they were meant to be in charge of keeping everyone safe.'

```
LIVI is conspicuously quiet.
```

'Liv, that was really good work putting her off the scent,' Aaron said. 'She thinks we're even more in the dark than she is.'

'There is one problem,' I said, smiling. 'We have to hide all Sam's stuff now since I told her he took it.'

It wasn't that funny. You might argue that it wasn't funny at all. In either case, that was all it took to tip the three of us over the edge, until we were all laughing so hard we could barely breathe. It felt good to open my chest and let it all out, felt good to get all of those laughing chemicals in my brain, even if the thing we were laughing at was so tragic that we probably should really have been crying. *God*, I was so over not being able to keep up with myself.

'Liv,' Daisy asked, when we finally managed to calm down, 'did you really want that note to remember him by?'

Of course I didn't. But this wasn't one of our cover-ups. None of us had written it.

Which meant whoever had taken Sam had.

'All right,' Sophia called from the front of the room once we were done warming up 'We're going to do some partner work. Numbers are odd since Sam had to leave, so Aaron, you're the lucky man who gets two ladies.'

Aaron grimaced. I leant forwards in my seat. It felt weird to still want this so much now I was actually friends with him, and considering everything else that was going on, but if I was about to get my chance to act with actual Hollywood royalty – whether he wanted to be or not – I was damn well going to be present for it.

Sophia saw me move, and smiled.

'Livi and Daisy,' she said, jerking a thumb in Aaron's direction.

Well, she didn't need to tell me twice.

The exercise was a scene that had been sent to us to learn

before camp even started – one of those that by this point we should all know like the back of our hand, and despite the fact that I hadn't thought *at all* about the lines, the context or the blocking since I'd been here, it was all still there. Buried somewhere in my brain for when I needed it.

The scene was from *Waitress*, somewhere near the end of the show, and included my favourite lines of musical theatre script of all time, probably. I'd been so excited to take this one out for a spin when our material packs had arrived – I hadn't even noticed when it had dropped out of my mind; stopped being important.

You said you wanted to come here, smash this rehearsal and clear your head, I reminded myself. *So do it.*

So I did.

As soon as I stood opposite Aaron and became Jenna rather than Livi, all her words came flying back. I remembered exactly where I'd wanted to stand, exactly what I'd planned to do with my hands on that one line, exactly how excited I'd been for all of it.

And *Aaron*.

My god, when he stood on a stage, he stopped being Aaron and became Aaron Wilson. Of course, I respected his decision – he didn't want to do this with his life, and that was fine – but wow . . . the world was missing out. The family business would have been lucky to have him.

I hated Hollywood, in that moment, for ever making him question whether he had a place in the industry that was more than just a token. Screw any industry that made someone who was *this good* ever feel like that.

We made it through the scene.

I'd known we had an audience, obviously, since the shape of this rehearsal meant that we all watched each other, but it really felt like it was just Aaron and me in the whole world, until we reached the last line of the script, and he smiled at me, and I was back to Livi, and the rest of the room was clapping.

'Excellent work, both,' Celestia said, stepping between us, slow clapping like a weird villain in a movie. I think she thought it was encouraging, but it felt patronising. Ever since we'd genuinely thought she might be capable of murder, Celestia had lost some of her shine for me. Even once we knew she was innocent, I couldn't completely escape the fact that it could have gone very differently, and I wouldn't have been entirely surprised.

```
MAIN STAGE. REHEARSAL.
CELESTIA stands between LIVI and AARON
and takes their hands, lifting them up as
if in victory.

CELESTIA: Well, it's unconventional to
announce it like this, but I think we
all need a boost and I think it's pretty
clear we have our showcase leads.
```

*AARON looks like he saw this coming. LIVI
looks shocked. Pleased, yes, but also . . .
kind of numb. Like she isn't sure how this
happened.*

*Everyone knows that part wasn't meant to
be hers.*

*Everyone else knows she only got it
because she's the one still here.
But they also know she deserved it.*

Well played, LIVI.

I concede that you earnt this one.

*But remember, just because you've won
the battle, it doesn't mean I'm not
still winning the war.*

What the hell?

Never before in the history of Camp Chance had the showcase leads been announced this early, or this informally – at least, not as long as I'd been coming here. At first, it felt almost like an anti-climax, like even though I was getting exactly what I wanted, I was missing out on The Moment I'd been hoping for since the first time I realised the leads always go to the seniors, and worked out exactly when my time would come. I'd wanted the build-up, the nervous energy. I'd wanted people to look at me walking down the corridor towards the cast board – I'd wanted to be able to tell from their faces which way it had gone.

I'd wanted it to be an uncomplicated joy.

Don't get me wrong, I wasn't ungrateful.

It just didn't feel like I'd always thought it would.

As everyone clapped and swarmed towards Aaron and me for hugs and congratulations, I was thinking of a lyric I had always loved from *Wicked*. 'Happy is what happens when all your dreams come true' . . . *isn't it?*

As she sings it, Glinda is realising that, no. Not always. Dreams-come-true doesn't account for the fact that dreams change as we do. It doesn't account for realising a dream is not a whole life, it's just a tiny part of it. It doesn't account for someone going round picking off your friends. It doesn't account for starting to fall in love, then losing them.

Specific, I know, but those were the things that were clouding *my* dream-come-true.

Well, that and the fact that it was coming true with the wrong person standing beside me.

CHAPTER 28

THE REHEARSAL FELT CHARGED AFTER CELESTIA'S announcement, most of us ready to start staging the showcase and getting it as good as we could now that we knew who would be leading, some of us – looking at you, Leah – going absolutely feral trying to prove that Celestia had made a mistake, and it should have been them.

I went through the motions – you could never accuse me of not being 'on' when I was on stage, but my head was spinning.

Step, kick, spin – I'm supposed to be doing this with Sam.

Find your light – I know that if she was here, it would have gone to Juliet.

Hit the high note, full out – We still don't know who killed Chloe. The note said we had to find out by the end of camp. Time is running out.

End up centre stage, breathing heavily, Aaron's arm around your waist, the ensemble at your back.

Music ends.

Take a bow.

Try to stave off complete emotional collapse until you're alone, or at least more alone than 'in front of the entire camp'.

All in a day's work.

```
CELESTIA gestures for the campers to
sit, and everyone sinks exhausted to the
ground right where they already are.
Scattered all over the stage, sweating
and on the brink of exhaustion, but all
of them grinning.

It makes a beautiful shot.

I'm almost sad I'm not there to capture
it in person.
```

CELESTIA: All right - that was some great progress! Really good work everyone. Now get out of here!

```
The campers look at her like they must be
missing something. CELESTIA's notes never
come without constructive (or plain brutal)
criticism - she must be testing them.

Nobody moves.
```

CELESTIA: I mean it! You're done! You gave it everything! If you did *exactly that* in the showcase, I'd be happy. Knowing how you all get in front of a proper audience . . . well, you might just save us all.

A weird thing to say.

If anyone notices, they keep quiet, all more focused on getting out before she changes her mind.

LIVI doesn't move.

LIVI: I'm just soaking it all in.

CELESTIA looks at her like she gets it.

CELESTIA: Just don't spend so long soaking it in that you miss dinner.

She leaves, and in clusters the rest of the campers drift out, until just DAISY, LIVI and AARON are left on stage. They look small, just the three of them up there in that vast space. It really feels like JULIET and SAM are missing.

'Well,' Daisy said, after we'd been sitting there in silence for a minute, not even having to talk about it, all knowing we were waiting to make sure everyone else was gone. 'You did it. Congratulations. How do you feel?'

Crap. Did her voice sound flat? Was she upset? What with everything else going on, I hadn't even thought about *Daisy* wanting the lead. She'd never said anything; had been so supportive of my efforts. And now . . .

'Livi, I can literally see you spiralling,' she said with a laugh. 'What's wrong? I thought that was a simple enough question!'

'Wait . . . are you upset?'

She didn't sound it any more. Had I read this completely wrong?

'Why would I be upset?'

'I don't know!' I said. 'You sounded a bit flat when you asked, and I realised I hadn't asked *you* how you felt about the showcase, and if you were trying for the lead, and—'

'I don't care about the showcase,' Daisy cut me off.

Aaron gasped exaggeratedly, and she looked at him with an expression so full of affection that it kind of took my breath away. I knew then that I'd been completely wrong – Daisy wasn't upset at all. She'd *won*. She'd made proper friends here, and found her place. The way they looked at each other . . . a proper friendship, forged in fire. I knew they'd love each other for a long time.

'I was never going to get a lead, Livi! In my first year? Are you joking? I came here to *learn*, and to see if this thing I've *just discovered* that you've all been doing since you were like, two, could actually be a part of my life! We love you, and we're proud of you! Don't overthink that!'

I put a hand to my heart. I had no words.

'How about you?' I asked, turning the attention on to Aaron. 'Is getting the lead everything you hoped and dreamt it would be?'

He laughed at my sarcastic tone.

'Doesn't exactly help with the fact that I still haven't worked out how to tell my parents that I'm not sure I want to be in this industry. And that even if I did, I have no idea if there's a place for me. The arts are hardly the place for Black kids with no interest in being the diversity hire.'

I opened my mouth to reassure him that he would figure it out, but he held up a hand, stopping me.

'I just did it again,' he said. 'I told you I don't know if I want to be in this industry. I'm softening it. But I do know. And I don't want to.'

He exhaled after he said it, and it looked like an exorcism. I didn't think he'd ever said that out loud before.

'What *do* you want to do?' Daisy asked, leaning closer.

I knew before he even spoke.

'True crime,' we said at the same time.

'Not actually *doing* crimes,' he clarified, and I knew he was playing for laughs because he felt vulnerable, so I gave him one, 'and not even the entertainment side of it. I get it, Dais – what you said before. These are people's lives. But the psychology behind why people do what they do? That I could research for ever.'

'People come to Camp Chance to find themselves,' I said. I'd always believed that, and here Aaron was, tipping it on its head, but proving it to be absolutely true.

He smiled.

'And aren't you just the living proof of that.'

'But I haven't been brave either,' I said. 'You couldn't figure out how to tell your family you don't want to perform. I can't work out how to tell them I *do*. That I'm not going to accept what they've chosen for me. Not any more. I'm good enough to do this, and I *want to*. And yes, this summer has changed a lot of how I feel about theatre, and I'm sure I'll be unpacking that for a long while yet, but I do still want it.'

'It's like we've all been playing a part,' Daisy said.

'Exactly. And I'm not going to do that any more. Screw them telling me that I'm not helping anyone with my acting. Or that it's useless, which makes *me* feel useless. If I could tell them anything about what's happened this summer, it would be that I've learnt acting *is* a useful skill to have. It *can* help. Without my acting, we never would have got the combination to the chemical cupboard, even if that turned out to be nothing. We couldn't have explained Juliet being gone *or* got the counsellors off our back when Chloe first went missing. Acting being useless is just a story my family tell themselves to make themselves feel better than none of them ever followed *their* dreams, and I've never known any better. I've always believed them. But not any more. I'm the only person who can control the stories I tell myself about myself, so I'm switching it up. I'm telling myself I'm going to make it, whatever that means. I'm changing the narrative. And yeah, I might be scared, but if there's one thing I'm good at, it's making things sound believable. Being convincing. It's all just a story after all, isn't it? It's all its own form of theatre.'

I stopped.

Oh my god.

It's all its *own form of theatre.*

It's *theatre.*

It was like a light came on.

CHAPTER 29

OF *COURSE* IT WAS THEATRE. IT WAS ALL AN ELABORATE show. Look at where we were! In a place where theatre always wins! I couldn't believe it had taken me this long – *how* was I only just seeing this for what it was? A performance! What we were being told wasn't *real*, even if it really felt like it was.

Whoever was behind this understood theatre.

Really got it.

I leapt up, and even though it felt like there were limbs flailing all over the place I landed firmly on my feet, which felt like a good omen. It was the most clear-eyed, the most grounded, I'd felt since Chloe went missing.

'It's theatre,' I said to Aaron and Daisy, for either the millionth time or the first, I couldn't be quite sure.

'What is?' Aaron asked, and *OK. Let me explain*.

'All of this,' I said, gesturing around the room, although even my biggest gesture could not possibly have encapsulated just how big this thing was. This show was happening *everywhere*.

In every inch of the camp. 'Not Chloe – she really has died, and that's the bit I haven't worked out yet. But Juliet? Sam? The notes? Someone is pulling the strings here, and it isn't because they're a psycho murderer, although they might well be that too. But no – focus, Livi. Someone is pulling the strings, because they're putting on a hell of a performance, just for the three of us. It isn't *real*. And if it isn't real . . .'

'Sam and Juliet might be alive,' Daisy caught on, hand to her mouth, scrambling to her feet to join me.

'Whoever did this is playing a game,' I said. 'I don't think they ever intended to kill anyone. And if that's the case . . . *was* Chloe's death an accident that they decided to exploit after the fact?'

'Livi, how does your brain do that?' Aaron asked, incredulous.

It doesn't. Not in any other area of my life. But I'd seen enough stories translated to enough stages that I could recognise one. That once I did, I could see all the elements clearly for what they were.

'They needed to get our attention, and Chloe was an easy target. She was so excited, so up for getting involved in anything, that if someone presented her with "a cool opportunity" she probably would have jumped at the chance.'

'How could anyone convince her that dying was a cool opportunity?' Daisy asked, incredulous.

'That's the point. They didn't, because she was *never meant to die*. Nobody was!'

Daisy looked like she couldn't decide between getting excited and being physically sick. I knew the feeling but I needed to keep the momentum up, needed to work through this, to work it out.

So I went with excited. I kicked my feet around in a little dance, trying to generate even more energy, and accidentally kicked my tote bag where it was still lying on the ground. Half my possessions flew across the floor, but I didn't have time for that right now.

'So,' I said, 'Chloe was to get our attention, but she's not our protagonist. *Juliet* is the real main character. The celebrity. The one they really wanted. But before she could disappear, they had to make sure that we knew the rules. Otherwise, what would stop us from just telling the counsellors straight away? If we did that, their game was up.'

'But they couldn't have known what we'd do about Chloe,' Aaron pointed out, Mr True Crime focused in on the details as I'd hoped he would. 'That we wouldn't go straight to Celestia. Or the police.'

'No,' I said, 'they couldn't. But that's another reason they *needed Chloe*. They needed to see how we'd react before the main event, so they could write this messed up play around us. Every step is based on how we deal with the last one, and Chloe was the first test. If we'd told the counsellors when we found the first note it might have been game over, but I think they knew we wouldn't. They had us in the palm of their hand by telling us that others might be in danger.'

'Why us?' Daisy asked.

'I think that might have been a coincidence,' I admitted. 'The first time, at least. There's no denying the later notes have been written specifically for us, but that first one... I think they were waiting to see who would find it and letting that inform the rest of the script. They've been writing as they go along, I know it.'

'And Sam?' Aaron asked. 'How does he fit into all this?'

I smiled. That was obvious.

'Taking away our secret weapon; our strongest member,' I said. 'It's classic dark night of the soul stuff. They need us at our lowest point, where we're going to either give up or get stronger.'

'But why would they want us to get stronger?'

They really weren't getting this.

'For the *story*,' I said. 'It makes for a better ending. They don't want us to lose, they want us to make it. That's why they've been feeding us clues! Telling us where to look! Nobody wants to watch a show where the bad guys win, do they?'

'So they took Sam to make us question our faith?' Aaron asked, his face doing something that I thought was Working It Out. 'And they hoped it would make us fight back?'

'Exactly,' I said. 'But they got one thing wrong.'

'What's that?' Aaron asked.

'Sam wasn't our secret weapon,' I said. 'I am.'

Because there was nothing that said we couldn't improvise, nothing that said we couldn't rewrite, and Sam wasn't here.

Sam wasn't the one who'd worked it out. That was always going to be me – the one who recognises theatre in all its forms the moment the curtain goes up. *Me*. For the first time in a long time, not playing a part. This was all Livi Campbell.

'Yes, girl,' Daisy whispered. Aaron gave me a grin.

'One more question,' Daisy asked, and I raised my eyebrows like, *go on*.

'*Why?*'

'That's the part I haven't worked out yet,' I said.

But that wasn't the whole truth. If I was being honest, that was the part that maybe I *had* worked out but was begging the universe for any conclusion that wasn't the one I'd jumped to.

```
MAIN STAGE


LIVI and DAISY, visibly excited about
what they think they've worked out.


AARON is gathering the things that flew
out of LIVI's bag when she kicked it.
This girl has got them all wrapped
around her little finger.


I don't get it, personally, but there's
no denying — she was right when she said
Chloe wasn't the main character, but not
quite right with her alternative theory.
```

It was never JULIET, either.

Look back over the shots in this video. LIVI CAMPBELL is in every single one.

AARON goes to put something back in the bag.

LIVI: Wait, what is that?
AARON: Juliet's camera. It fell out when you—
LIVI: I completely forgot we had that. How have we not looked at the photos yet?! Gimme!

LIVI sinks back to the floor and AARON hands her the camera, joining her. DAISY follows. LIVI turns the camera on and begins to click through.

Think fast.

Quicker than they can look at them, the photos on the screen begin to disappear, a 'this photo has been deleted' notification popping up in their place.

DAISY: What the . . .
LIVI: Someone has access to it!
The photos are backed up somewhere
and whoever it is, is deleting them!
Right now!
AARON: Who would have access to
Juliet's camera?

That was when I stopped asking for the universe for another answer. Because . . . well . . . who indeed?

She doesn't say anything. Not yet. Instead, she jumps to her feet again. As she does, she kicks her phone which is still on the floor and it lights up, the mirror selfie still her wallpaper.

Cute.

DAISY picks it up.
Hesitates.

DAISY: Um . . . guys?
AARON: What?
DAISY: I think I just worked out why the killer was so angry when Livi posted the photo.

AARON: Can we still call them the killer?
LIVI: Yes, because they still killed Chloe. *So* not the point — Daisy, what are you talking about?

She thrusts the phone out so LIVI and AARON can see.

DAISY: Look. Underneath the door. There's a light coming from the star dressing room.
LIVI: Was someone *in there*? Is that why they wanted it gone? In case we saw they'd left the light on and worked out where they were hiding?

My mind flew back to something Louis said, when he'd found us in the woods.

When you were skulking around the star dressing room in that stupid pink wig.

LIVI: We have to go.
DAISY: But what about the superstition? If we go in, we could ruin your chance at actually playing the lead. What if it's real?
AARON: It isn't real.

'It might be,' I said with a shrug, and I could tell he was

going to argue with me, tell me it was an old camp legend born from the need to tell a good story rather than the truth, so I put up my hand to stop him before he started. He hadn't worked out where I was going with this yet.

'It might be, but even if it is, it doesn't matter. How can we still be worried about that? I mean, I *am*, I'm done with feeling cursed, thanks, but I'm trying really hard not to be, because it doesn't *matter*. None of it does. Only finding Sam and Juliet. We have to go, guys.'

I took the phone out of Daisy's hand for a closer look, and as I did, my thumb accidentally opened the gallery app to another photo. It stopped me in my tracks.

'It's from the party,' I said quietly. 'Chloe is there. We all are.'

I remembered it being taken. It was a group shot, from right before we all dispersed, and we're all grinning, crouching and crowding to make sure we're all in shot of the lineup of phones on the floor, all set to self-timer so nobody had to miss out by playing photographer. I looked again, scanning all of the faces, trying to work out if anyone at all was missing.

'We have to go,' I said again, and handed the phone back to Daisy to put back in my bag. Instead, she slid it into her pocket without locking it.

'*Hi, everyone, and welcome back to my channel!*'

Wait, why was Juliet's voice coming out of Daisy's jeans? It threw me for a half a second before Daisy pulled the phone back out and I realised it was one of Juliet's old videos.

'Must have been the last thing I watched,' I said. 'Before the phone call.' She paused the video right as the sound changed. Right as Juliet's voice switched from the one we all knew to something twisted. Menacing. Horrific.

She's using a voice changer.

'I recognise that,' Aaron said, at exactly the same time I thought it.

'That's the voice!' Daisy said. 'The one that threatened us over the Tannoy! I knew I recognised it from somewhere! It's a voice changer – Juliet uses in her videos all the time! But . . . how did the killer get it?'

OK. Time to say it.

The old me would have been scared of being wrong. The new me *wished* I was. Knew I was not.

'We're not all there,' I said. 'In the photo from the party. Juliet isn't.'

They look at me like . . . so?

'And this voice, the one from her video, threatened us over the Tannoy . . .'

'But Juliet was *there* when that happened,' Daisy said, the penny finally beginning to drop.

'She wasn't,' I reminded her. 'She rocked up *seconds* later. She must have run.'

'Run from where?' Aaron asked. 'Where is the Tannoy?'

I gently took the phone from Daisy's hand once more and scrolled back to the photo I'd taken in the mirror. I pointed at the light coming from under the door on the right-hand side of the shot.

'There are a few,' I said. 'But there's definitely one in the star dressing room.'

'Livi, what are you saying?' Aaron asked, and *OK, I'll spell it out.*

'I think Juliet did all of this herself,' I said. 'She'll say it's pushing the boundaries of what theatre can be, or something, but I say it's all a massive game. Except she's been playing with our lives, and I'm done with it. No more.'

'And you think she's in the star dressing room?' Aaron asked.

'Louis said he saw me, skulking around there in that pink wig. I was so . . . I don't know, overwhelmed with everything else that was going on that I thought nothing of it. But I never went anywhere *near* the star dressing room in that wig. Not once. So yeah, I think she's there. I'd be willing to bet her life on it.'

'How would that even work?'

'If she's not there, I'll kill her. And if she is . . . I might just do it anyway.'

Daisy laughed.

'That doesn't make sense.'

'Does any of this?' Aaron asked.

But actually? Yes. Juliet Stone – so desperate to prove her point that theatre doesn't have to happen on a stage that she's created a show all of her own.

Except it isn't theatre if the actors don't know they're a part of it. It's puppeteering. Exploitation.

Over. It's about to be over.

'Let's go,' I said, instead of answering his question.

Imagine a slow-motion walking-towards-the-camera montage, like in a movie.

In my head, I was wearing a gold cape, killer heels, my hair flowing behind me as if there were wind machines tracking our walk. In reality, I was still wearing tracksuit bottoms, a T-shirt, rehearsal clothes. Doesn't matter. It was all in the stance.

I looked powerful.

`She looks scared.`

Aaron and Daisy were beside me, my army, small but perfectly formed, waving our metaphorical red flag for revolution, like this was a production of *Les Misérables* rather than our actual lives. One moment more, then it would be done. I knew before I tried the door that it was going to be locked, but I tried anyway.

It's locked.

'Is she in there?' Daisy asked.

'Stand back,' I said, and then I backed up and braced myself, and ran at the door, throwing my full weight at it. It hurt me more than it hurt the door, but these things never work first time, so I backed up again, and this time Aaron got the hint and joined me, both of us throwing ourselves at the wood, again and again and again, until it splintered. Finally, the area around the lock began to look damaged.

'Out of the way,' Daisy said, and I stood aside, exhausted, as she slipped her hand through and started jangling it. I could hear movement on the other side of the door, and breathing, but whoever was in there didn't speak.

Not even when the *clunk* of the lock pulled my attention back to Daisy.

Not even when one last yank from her pulled it clean off.

Not even when she flung the door open, Aaron and I at her back, and we were faced with a scene from a nightmare.

Juliet, looking like she'd won.

Sam, restrained.

I tried to tell Daisy to stop screaming, but the words wouldn't come out, and only when Aaron put his hand on my back and pulled my focus, did I realise that the screams were actually coming from me.

CHAPTER 30

JULIET HAD TURNED THE ROOM INTO SOMETHING FROM a horror show. The whole dressing table was taken up by monitors, and on them . . . I had to look twice before I could believe what I was seeing. They were all us. Our whole summer, playing on a loop, captured on camera and beamed back to these screens, an edit suite from hell.

There's Chloe, singing on the coach, right back at the beginning, Phantom mask in hand.

There's me and Sam, the first night we met in the rehearsal barn. Never as secret as we thought. A few screens over, Daisy meeting Aaron for the first time. In the row below, the first time Sam and I kissed.

She's captured it all. It's . . .

```
It's my masterpiece.
```

It *isn't* impressive. Not at all.

Protest too much, Livi?

I need her voice out of my head. I silenced her, turned my full attention back to the screens. What I noticed next made me feel sick.

There's Chloe, singing on the coach, and when we drive through the gates and we all get off, Juliet, one of the last, looks straight up at the camera and grins.

There's Daisy meeting Aaron. Two seconds later, there's Juliet, smiling straight down the lens.

There's Sam and I kissing. The moment we leave?

Juliet.

She'd somehow planted cameras *everywhere*.

It felt like a complete violation.

Which I guess was the point.

This whole time, she'd been the only one who knew she was starring in this twisted movie. Of course Juliet didn't care about being cast as the lead. She knew she already was.

'Why?' I asked.

A complete question. She knew exactly what I meant. She stepped away from Sam before she answered me, and I could see it wasn't just her hands holding him in place. He was shackled to the chair, restraints at both wrists and feet, but he looked defiant. Like he knew we would come. As Juliet moved towards me, Aaron drifted in Sam's direction without her noticing.

Good. He's got this.

I turned back to Juliet.

'I had a point to prove,' she said. 'Against people like *you*. I wanted to create a piece of theatre the likes of which had never been seen before. I wanted to see what would happen if the other players in my murder mystery didn't know they were supposed to be acting. Isn't that more interesting than parroting off lines and standing where you're told to?'

You want to know about character growth? I just let that wash over me. I didn't *care* what she thought of the kind of theatre I loved. We had gone so far beyond that.

'So you *killed Chloe*?'

Juliet shook her head, like I was missing the point. Maybe I *was*, since none of this felt like the innovative art piece she was trying to make it sound like.

'Chloe was collateral damage,' she said.

'She was a human being,' I countered.

'The drink wasn't supposed to kill her! Just sedate her long enough to be part of the video so I could get her where I needed her to really kick things off. She drank it by choice! It wasn't hard to convince her – I thought it would just send her to sleep for a little while, so she could play her part authentically. It took a little convincing, but *she* picked up the bottle, and *she* drank. That girl had what it takes to get wherever she wanted to go. But when she didn't wake up . . . I thought that really gave the project a kiss of magic. Took it down an even more realistic path.'

'So that's why you picked it up,' I realised. 'The bottle, in the lake. You knew your prints, and hers, were already on it, and if the police got their hands on it and found them...'

'Right,' she said. 'I needed you to see me touch it, so you'd tell them there was a good reason for my DNA to be all over it.'

Clever.

'Weren't you scared?' I asked.

'Of course I was,' Juliet said, the first thing even close to the truth she'd given me. 'I was terrified. That's why I put her in the lake. Tried to make it look like a complete accident. But then I changed my mind! I pulled her back out! I *really tried* to save her. So, when I realised it was too late, well, that was fate,' she said dreamily.

'It was *murder*!' I shouted. She'd clearly forgotten how good I was at projecting, since she jumped back, startled, then tried to pretend she hadn't.

Out of the corner of my eye I saw Aaron finally free Sam of the last restraint. Juliet didn't notice. She was too busy looking at me like she didn't understand why I was reacting like this.

God, why didn't we tell Louis where we were going?

'It's nearly ready,' she said, instead of anything proportionate or appropriate to the situation – that she had killed someone and kidnapped someone else and was pretending we should be ... what? Impressed? 'I have all the footage I need. That was why I had to go missing myself – to start editing it together for my channels. You have all played your parts *perfectly*.'

She gestured to all of us in turn and began to slow clap.

Enough.

'Now it's time for the grand finale,' she said, picking up

a small camera that I hadn't noticed from the desk. 'Your reactions.'

'Haven't you been filming this whole scene anyway?' Daisy demanded, and Juliet turned, like she'd forgotten Daisy was here.

'Ah, she speaks. Of course I have. As I think we've established, I know what I'm doing here. There are just a few more shots I need. Close-ups of my stars.'

'How?' I asked. A smile. I'd asked the right question.

'They let me in before the season started. For a private tour. To see if Camp Chance and I could work together. They wanted me to make some sort of promo video – boring things like 'what camp means to me', and I said I couldn't give them an answer until I'd seen the place for myself. None of the counsellors were even here, just an uninterested guy with the keys to the gates. I had the run of the place for *hours*. It was perfect.'

So *that* was why Celestia hadn't seemed surprised that Juliet kept vlogging.

'This is *fucked*,' Sam said, and when Juliet turned to look at him, she seemed surprised. That he was free? Or by his reaction?

'Did you actually think we'd be OK with this?' Suddenly I had to know. I tried not to care, but she seemed to have expected we'd be . . . *happy*? I had to understand it.

'I thought you, of all people, would get it,' she said. 'We all came here to create interesting work, right? And isn't this the most interesting thing that's ever happened at Camp Chance?'

'That isn't the point *at all*,' I said. My voice was measured.

I cannot lose this one, she is so unambiguously wrong. 'The point of us being here is to find out who we are, and maybe become better performers as we do it.'

'Oh, well look who's deviating from her script. Well done, Livi. What do you want – for us to congratulate you on your eleventh-hour plot twist? Well, I've got news for you – it's only happened because of the theatre *I* created. *I* did this to you.'

'How can it be theatre if none of us were performing?' I asked.

'Oh come on, Livi. You were *all* performing, *the whole time*. The show you were all putting on for each other was at least as dramatic as what was happening on stage!'

```
LIVI has no idea how to react to that.
She runs at JULIET.

At me.

Right before she can reach out, I grab
her by the hair.

Still her.

Whisper something in her ear.

LIVI loosens her grip.
```

I had a feeling that would do it.

That's when CELESTIA bursts into the room — dramatic, because those idiots have closed the door behind them.

CELESTIA *(into her phone)*: I found them. The star dressing room. They're all here.

Well, crap.

I had never been so happy to see Celestia Sinclair. She was breathing heavily as she looked straight at Juliet, and then at the four of us where we'd all scrambled to Sam's side. I put out a hand to lightly graze his – just to let him know that I was here. He grabbed it and squeezed, hard. It felt so good to touch him again; to know that he was really real.

'I knew it,' Celestia said, pointing at Juliet. 'I worked it out! I knew you were all up to something!' She turned back to the rest of us. None of us spoke. None of us moved. We barely even breathed. She hadn't seen it yet, we all knew. She was acting far too calmly for someone who . . .

Oh wait, she's spotted the hell suite. She's leaning into one of the screens. She's watching Chloe slip into the lake, Juliet holding her arms, once, again, again, on a horrific loop.

That was when Celestia started screaming.

A much more understandable reaction.

'What the hell have I walked in to? Oh my god, this is so much bigger than I thought.'

She wasn't speaking to any of us, more monologuing to try and process what was going on, but I was going to be the one to reply. Before Juliet could.

'How did you work it out?' I asked. 'What's that in your hand?'

She passed it to me. I knew what it was straight away – the note 'Sam' left at reception when he 'left'. The one she'd promised me.

'I matched the handwriting to Juliet's personnel form,' she said. 'Or . . . Louis did, I suppose.'

That's clever.

'I was trying to find a number for your parents,' she continued, looking at Juliet. 'I just wanted to check in. Check . . . we still had a deal.'

'That I hadn't skipped out without delivering the video that was supposed to save you,' Juliet said dryly. Celestia nodded, just once.

'Sam's note was beside me on the desk. Enter Louis, frantic because he can't find Livi, Chloe's mask and an *empty chemical bottle* in his hand. He found it in your cabin,' she said, turning her attention to me. 'Which almost had me dialling 999 to turn you in immediately, but Louis unplugged the phone before I could get there. Told me to give him two minutes and to just *listen.* Once I realised he wasn't just trying to shoot his shot with Sam out of the picture again, I thought I'd better pay attention – which was difficult because he point-blank refused to tell me anything tangible. It was him who made the connection between the handwriting, in the end. But . . . what the hell am I looking at here? This is not just where you've been hiding, is it? It's so much more . . .' She directed the last bit to Juliet.

No. I would not let her be the one to control this narrative.

'She's been filming everything,' I said. 'Right from the moment we got here. She's had cameras all over the place, running all the time. And she's been sending us threats – oh, backtrack, we knew Chloe was murdered right from the start. Sorry. I can explain later. Anyway, Juliet has been leaving notes where she knew we'd find them, telling us that if we spilled, Chloe wouldn't be the only one. When she went missing herself, it was because she almost had everything she needed and wanted to start editing it into whatever horror this is. Sam was an afterthought, I think. Something to throw us and make us doubt what I think she thought we were working out.'

'Jesus Christ,' Celestia said. 'I thought it was all of *you* who were acting suspiciously.'

'Us?' Aaron asked.

'I see now that I was wrong,' she said. 'But you've been sneaking around all summer. Whispering. Lingering after rehearsals have finished. I thought you'd done something to Juliet. Driven her out, somehow. But it was the other way round, of course it was. *God.* When Oli told me he'd taken you into the chemical cupboard, Livi, I knew I had to do something. I thought you were planning something stupid. And then when Louis burst in, with the mask he'd found in *your* cabin... well, I was sure I'd solved it. But I never could have imagined—'

'So *you* emptied the cupboard,' I said. That was one more puzzle solved.

'Nobody puts my campers in danger,' Celestia said. 'Or my camp... although it might be too late for that now. Wait, what? Emptied...?'

'What do you mean?' Sam cut her off, the first time he'd spoken. His voice was hoarse. I squeezed his hand tighter. I already knew what she meant – at least I had suspected. Her words were the final puzzle piece, because I had seen this, or something like it, coming. I knew something strange was going on with her from the way she'd been behaving – snapping at campers, stressing Sophia out so much that she'd been snapping at *me*, casting the leads so early. That had worked in my favour, but it was so out of character that I'd been worried about it ever since. And now, I was sure.

'It's over, isn't it?' I said.

'This might be the last year for everyone, not just you seniors,' she said, looking straight at me. 'The investors are threatening to pull the funding. It's been a few years since we had a real success story – it was always meant to be Soph, but we all know how that went. If we didn't find one this year, it was all but over. That's why you two were offered places at all,' she said, pointing at Juliet and Aaron. 'We needed at least one star name in a leading role so they'd keep the money coming. That's why we asked you to make the promo video.'

Even after everything that had happened, even though I *knew*, or at least thought I did, I felt like I'd been gut-punched. No matter what I did, that part was never supposed to be mine. It had been decided before we even got on the coach. How had I given so much of my life to an industry that repaid me like that?

'You used me,' Juliet said quietly. It was the most wounded I'd ever heard her sound. She was so good at taking everything in her stride, or at least pretending to, but this? She sounded shaken.

I felt unsettled suddenly. More than I already was, I mean. There was something cold in Juliet's tone; something in the way she said 'you used me' that sounded like she was making a decision. Something felt *wrong*. More wrong.

'That's the industry, kid,' Celestia said. 'Even being Juliet Stone doesn't mean it won't tell you it loves you when it needs you and drop you without ceremony the minute you're not useful any more.'

Juliet was calm as she reached into her pocket. My skin prickled. *What is she reaching for?* She pulled her hand back out quickly and uncurled her fingers to reveal . . . a lighter? I breathed out. What did I think she had in there, some sort of weapon? She couldn't do much damage with a lighter. It wasn't like that tiny flame could set the room alight no matter what she was planning to spark up. Nobody said anything as she moved to open the tall metal locker in the corner of the room, lighter still in hand, all of us just watching this strange piece of performance art. But something still wasn't sitting right. Something wasn't *clicking*. I wracked my brains, fast at first, speeding through everything that had happened, but when that didn't work, I forced myself to slow down. Replay.

And again, to check I was right.

Once more, even though I knew I was.

'Someone call the fire brigade.' I said quietly, and Juliet did not turn, barely even moved, as she said, 'You don't want to do that, Livi.'

So I'm right.

'Someone call the fire brigade.' I said it again, more forceful this time. 'Daisy, I'm serious.'

```
So am I. She really doesn't want
to do that.

JULIET: Livi, I will take you down with me.
LIVI: You can try.
JULIET: I'll tell.
CELESTIA: Can someone tell me what is
going on?

Well. What could make a more explosive
finale than fireworks?
```

Why were none of them listening to me? Why was Daisy still not calling?!

'The dangerous chemicals cupboard!' I said, and I was talking to all of them but I didn't dare take my eyes off Juliet. I didn't know what her move was here, what she was actually going to do with all the fluids and powders and tools I was now sure she'd emptied from the cupboard, but the lighter still in her hand told me I wasn't going to like it. 'She emptied it. God knows where she's hidden all the stuff, but I'd be willing to bet my life that some of it is in there.'

```
Nobody pays attention to LIVI when JULIET
is centre stage.


LIVI: Celestia, I'm serious.


CELESTIA pays no attention.


LIVI huffs out a squeal. Like that's
going to work.


Braces herself and wrenches her hand out
of SAM's.


Steps towards JULIET. Reaches out, right
as JULIET opens the door of the locker.
```

> *LIVI lunges as JULIET sparks the flame; grabs for the lighter right before the it makes contact with the makeshift firework JULIET has stashed in there.*
>
> *Like I said, it would have made an explosive finale.*
>
> *JULIET tries to stop herself; really, she does, but there's already too much momentum. She spins to fight back, but as she turns she hits LIVI. Hard.*
>
> *LIVI falls to the ground.*
>
> *I don't feel good about it.*

I came around on the dressing-room floor what could only be seconds later, but it felt like the world had changed. A police officer, dressed in full uniform, was leaning over me.

'How long was I out for?' I asked, and Celestia laughed.

'Less than a minute, Livi. Louis called the police the moment I left the room. He wouldn't tell me what was *really* going on... but he wouldn't let any of you go down either.'

I'd never been more glad that Louis liked gossip so much that he'd followed us into the woods at 3 a.m. in the hope of getting some.

Another police officer was leading Juliet out of the room, while yet another was swabbing her horror suite for fingerprints. If you asked me, that was pretty pointless. There was only one person whose handiwork this could have been, and I had a feeling she'd happily admit she'd been working alone. Wouldn't want to give anyone else the credit I was sure she still felt she deserved. I couldn't read the look on her face, but she was staring straight at me, as if she was trying really hard to tell me something.

I closed my eyes.

'Livi, are you all right?' Daisy asked from right beside me. She was crying. Why was she crying?

'I'm fine,' I said, or thought I said, or tried to say, but now I was crying too so I couldn't be sure how it had come out.

'Celestia,' I croaked, and she turned away from the doorway where she was whispering about the need for an ambulance with one of the officers and focused her full attention back on me.

'Livi, I'm so sorry,' she said, and I knew she was apologising for the fact that I'd been hurt, but it felt like she was saying sorry for something else too.

No need to ask the question I was going to. She just answered it.

Did it work? Did we get the funding? Is Camp Chance going to survive this?

No.

No.

No.

I closed my eyes again. I was so tired.

The way she told it is pretty much how it happened.

Just one thing, though.

Even now, even when all bets are off and there's no reason left to pretend, Livi Campbell is playing a part.

She really is an amazing actress.

Right before they put me in the police car, I slip my phone out of my pocket and navigate to the app I use to control the cameras. I turn every last one off.

End of footage.

CHAPTER 31

NOW

IT'S NOT EVERY DAY YOU SEE A WHOLE WORLD BEING carried out of a set of rainbow gates; not every day that the secrets of Camp Chance step into the light, right there, for anyone to see.

(OK, not *all* of the secrets.)

All of the campers are gone, the counsellors not too far behind, but the one benefit of getting hit around the head and knocked out, of catching a murderer even if that isn't what she intended to be, is that my parents are being *so* nice to me. So when I told them I had plans, would be gone all day, they didn't ask – just said yes. Of course, there was no coach to bring me. I took a train, and then another, and then a taxi with a driver so chatty that I was almost tempted to tell him the whole story, just to see what he'd say.

That would have shut him up, I'm sure.

Instead, I'd put my headphones in and looked out of the

window at the landscapes I'd never paid attention to before. Every other journey to Camp Chance had been full of singing, and as much dancing as we could do sitting down with a seatbelt on, and easing ourselves back into who we really were. Nothing happening outside the windows had mattered.

I listened to 'Let It Go'.

I thought of Chloe.

I didn't tell anyone where I was going.

The gates were open when I got here, the rainbow paint beginning to rust after weeks of rain. I'm only realising now that they must have touched them up before we arrived every single summer, to make sure it was surface-level perfect for us.

We all tried so hard, and it wasn't enough.

We're pretty out of the way out here, so there isn't a lot of foot traffic, and the few people who are walking past are mostly rushing by without a second look, then glancing back over their shoulders to confirm that yes, that man really was carrying out a fountain made of glass, a broomstick, a whole host of wigs and what looked like a dismantled tent, the kind that once saw magic.

I'm standing opposite the gates, my black hoodie pulled tight around my face as if I'm in mourning, which I guess I am. I don't recognise the men in red T-shirts, tearing apart a universe without a backwards glance to the gaping hole they're leaving behind. I know they're not Camp Chance staff. They must be people brought in just to destroy it. Nobody who was part of it could have done it with such nonchalance.

They carry out a bunk bed.

I see Daisy stretched across it, gossiping in earnest about who is dating who, and where they're gathering when they sneak out in the middle of the night. She belonged here immediately, but I have a feeling she'll be fine wherever she lands next, too. That's what happens when you're completely authentic – you find your place, or you make it. I'm so glad we got to meet.

They carry out a grand piano.

I see Aaron, draped across it with a smile on his face, taking a break from whichever song he's supposed to be rehearsing to fill us in on a true crime case from twenty-five years ago. I know how it feels to have something you love that much; know that when your face lights up like that, it's something worth pursuing. Hollywood royalty? Yeah, maybe. For now. But for the rest of time, when I look at Aaron Wilson I will only see my friend.

The majority of passers-by still aren't paying attention, but a small crowd have stopped and are looking on with interest as a three-pronged candelabra, once almost as tall as I am, is carried out in pieces, a tired remnant of a time that no longer exists, where it's no longer needed. At least, that's what the onlookers see.

I see Sam.

I see him lit only by those candles, right before we kissed, even though I know, logically, that there was emergency lighting in that room the whole time, hidden in the shadows, designed specifically for that space, and that moment. That's the thing about having me as your narrator. I do tend to theatricalise.

Doesn't matter. It felt real. I see his hand, as if it's hovering at my cheek, and I move towards it. I know it isn't real; that he isn't really here, but I *feel him*. Our atoms are in the air. We changed the physiology of this place just by being here.

I close my eyes.

When I open them, the candelabra is gone, and so is he.

'All right, I think that's the last of it,' one of the red shirts shouts.

The onlookers see four men walking through the rainbow gates holding a wishing well, like it's no effort at all.

I make a wish.

CHAPTER 32

THREE MONTHS LATER

IT'S AN OLD SUPERSTITION THAT YOU SHOULD NEVER speak the last line of a show before it is performed for the first time. I don't think anyone really sticks to that any more – it would make rehearsals pretty hard, for one thing, but I've always liked it. I like the idea of never knowing for sure how a thing is going to end, and the idea that even after the curtain comes down, the characters carry on.

Stories don't always work like that though.

Sometimes, you have to decide when you're going to stop telling them.

This is the end of ours.

I suppose I should tell you where we all landed. It's only fair, when you've come this far with us, isn't it? You want to know that we're all OK. That we made it.

It isn't that simple, but I'll try.

I milked the Juliet-attack-and-subsequent-emotional-trauma

for just long enough that when drama school auditions came around, my parents had no hesitation about sending me to every one I wanted to go to.

Did I talk up everything I'd been through just a little, to give myself the edge?

I'll never tell, but if you've got a skill . . . well, you learn how to use it.

Now all that's left to do is wait, but I'm not worried. I'm not as single-minded as I once was; not as convinced that formal training is the only way to build a life in the theatre. Not that I'd ever say that out loud to my family. I don't know if it's relief that I was so close to danger and made it out relatively unscathed, or the realisation that if it isn't acting, they don't know what to do with me, or simply the gift of time, but since I got back from camp it's like they're different people. Like they can see that the story I'm telling myself is that eventually, despite everything, I win. And I'm telling it *well*. What can I say, I'm excellent at spinning a narrative. At my best when I'm playing a part. Even when I'm nervous, even when I'm terrified it isn't going to work and I'll have to find some other plan, just like Sophia did, I can sell a performance. And that, at least, *is* working – they ask me every day if I know the results from any schools yet. I don't think it's lying when I say no if the envelopes have been unopened in my bedroom for days, right? I just want a few more moments of peace before I find out. A few more hours, or days, where theatre is a dream on the brink of coming true, because I know that once it *does*, it will never feel this pure and important again.

And it's *going* to come true.

Aaron, on the other hand, told his parents he *doesn't* want to act, and was surprised to find they're completely fine with that. He has no idea why he didn't do it sooner. He's still dating Luke, although it's a lot more casual than it was when their homes were two cabins about a metre apart, suspended somewhere out of time, where everything was possible. Trains and buses and real life and responsibility are making it harder, but they're trying. All they can do is try. He's applied to uni to study criminology. Have you ever heard anything more perfect? Daisy rolled her eyes when he told us, but even she has to admit it's a match. He's finally found his place.

Talking of Daisy, she's working with Celestia, which felt out of left field at first, but which makes more sense the more we hear about what they're doing – developing a new training programme for kids like Daisy who come to theatre later, to get them ready to be thrown into a place like Camp Chance and be able to hold their own. We speak most days. I tell her regularly to tell Celestia I say hi, but if you think saving a whole camp from going up in flames would make someone like you more . . . not so much. It's kind of comforting. There's probably only so much change a person can take.

Louis, really, was the one who saved us all. Who called the police *right* on time. Who never loosened his grip on our secrets until they weren't secrets any more. I told him, in the end, that I was interested in someone else. That I'd love to be his friend, but it wasn't going to be more than that. He wasn't surprised, he said. He'd known that all along.

Everyone had.

And yeah, what you really want to hear about is Sam, isn't it? That tracks, since he's the hardest one for me to talk about, and aren't those almost always the most interesting? The story I told myself about Sam was that we were going to be something – I had no idea what, but *something*. He'd changed when he met me. No more Prince Charming, even if that version of him had only really existed in my still-wounded brain, no more leading man – he was mine, and I was his, and we'd be happy. And it was true. For a little while it was *really* true. When it came to it, though, it was me who hadn't changed. Me who wasn't ready. Me who broke it off before it went too far – no body count, to quote *Waitress*, the last show we saw together before it ended. No body count? If that's true, those characters did better than us. It shattered me. There will always be something between us – I don't think you can go through what we did and that not be true. It's just a case of being in the right place at the right time. On the same page of the same script. He's studying drama at university, and I keep promising that I'll visit. One day soon I will.

I think I know how that story ends, and it's a happy one.

It's all in the timing.

But this story isn't *really* about me and Sam. From the first day, the first shot, the first page, the overture – the leading players were Juliet and me.

Her video never saw the light of day. Obviously. Even once

the police investigation was over, once Chloe's death had been ruled accidental, and Juliet's punishment – a hell of a lot of community service and intensive therapy which she's somehow managed to keep secret from her channels – was set, she didn't stand a chance against Aaron's family, who threatened to sue if even one shot of it ever got out. Turns out that while Juliet Stone (definitely not her real name, by the way – I've seen the police reports) does love art, she loves not being taken for everything she's got by one of the most powerful families in Hollywood more. She deleted the file. Didn't even keep a copy.

I know she didn't have a choice.

I know that's the right thing.

I know there was no other way it could have gone, but sometimes, when I'm alone in the dark, I watch the edit that she sent me before she destroyed the original.

I haven't told a single other person it exists, but sometimes when it's quiet I can't resist. I load up the file and I press play, and I'm back there. It's the time machine I wished for, when those men in red shirts carried out the wishing well. The way back I never dared dream I would get.

I love seeing myself on screen with them all. With Daisy, and with Aaron.

With Sam.

With her.

I'd never admit it, but I secretly dream of leaking it – as much as I'm loathe to give her any credit, Juliet deserves it for this.

It's funny. It's moving. It's perfectly edited, and the story arc is gripping.

It's theatre.

She made a piece of theatre the likes of which has never been seen.

It isn't just that, though.

It's *us*, too. I want the world to see how *good* we are; what a show we put on, even when we were just being ourselves. We *shone*, the camera loved us, and I can't feel guilty for that.

I'm too busy feeling guilty for other things.

Like what Juliet whispered to me, back in the star dressing room, right before Celestia barged in with the police.

Stop playing innocent. You've known all along.

While *all along* might be exaggerating, I know theatre better than anyone else I've met. Know storytelling. I knew, a long time before we *knew*.

```
RAW FOOTAGE.
REHEARSAL BARN, the night LIVI accuses
SAM. Watch as she looks up, right to
where the camera is planted. The glance
is fleeting, but it's there.


She moves SAM out of shot.
She doesn't want us to see this.


RAW FOOTAGE.
```

*MAIN STAGE, the night LIVI and SAM kissed.
Before she leaves, LIVI looks right up
at the camera. She looks embarrassed.
Not embarrassed enough to stop her
grinning right down the lens.*

*RAW FOOTAGE.
LIVI glances up at the camera as she
walks through the woods.*

*RAW FOOTAGE.
LIVI moves DAISY out of the way of
the camera.*

*RAW FOOTAGE.
LIVI swaps places with AARON almost
seamlessly, so he's in shot and she's
hidden behind him and can brush her
fingers against SAM's.*

*RAW FOOTAGE.
LIVI not even trying to pretend she doesn't
know — she'd worked it out a long time ago.*

I should say that I'll regret not telling for the rest of my life. I should be wracked with guilt and wondering if speaking up sooner would have changed anything.

I should be begging for forgiveness – from Celestia. From my friends.

The truth, though?

I did what I thought I had to.

I was just trying to save the place I loved.

Of course I knew Juliet was filming – she's *Juliet Stone*. I'd watched enough of her videos, gone far enough down the rabbit hole, that I knew before I even met her that she'd have something planned. And when I heard a whisper on the wind that Camp Chance was in danger? That the investors were threatening to pull the funding?

Well. I saw an opportunity.

I thought that if they watched Juliet's video, they'd see camp for what it really was – somewhere people became themselves. Somewhere magic. It began when she started vlogging after Chloe's death – that's what I thought at the time, at least. I had no idea about the edit suite from hell, or the extent of the hidden cameras. I spotted a few, but I thought they were just CCTV. Thought I was grinning down the lens at a bored counsellor, at best. So few of those cameras were working properly anyway that it never occurred to me that there was no feed for half the places the new cameras had sprung up. It wasn't until *much* later that I thought they might be hers, and by then . . . I just thought that if I kept my mouth shut and let her make her messed-up movie, it might be the thing that saved us all.

Sure, I still hate the idea of theatre on screen, but if Juliet capitalising on the murder with her vlogs could be the thing to keep camp open . . . well, it would never be worth it, but I could live with it. Of course, I know now what I missed – that the video and the murder were related. That the cameras were turned on before we even drove through the rainbow gates. I would have told straight away if I'd known that was the case. I never could have imagined that everything that was happening had been set up *for* the video.

```
Would you? Couldn't you?
```

Not in a million years.

```
This is where we leave her.
```

```
There's no point in pushing.
She'll deny it till her dying breath.
```

```
If you ask me, though? I wouldn't
be so sure.
```

```
We make a good team, the director
and her star.
```

```
And Livi Campbell never could
resist the spotlight.
```

ACKNOWLEDGEMENTS

WRITING A NOVEL IS MUCH LIKE MAKING A MUSICAL, in that it takes an entire cast and crew working tirelessly behind the scenes to make the leading player look like she knows what she's doing. (In this scenario I am the leading player. Go with me here!)

Some thanks, then, for the people who helped bring this book to life; who it could not have existed, at least in this form, without:

My agent Lucy Irvine, first on every one of these lists. The journey to *Exit Stage Death* has been long, and at times ridiculous, but it has also been the most fun I've ever had writing anything, because you always got what I was trying to do and encouraged me to do it. I'm glad that half a decade in we still make such a good team.

Jonathan and Rosie. 'Thank you for everything' doesn't feel like a big enough sentiment after the last few years, but saying it every chance I get is still the least I can do.

Everyone else at Peters, Fraser and Dunlop. I really love being a PFD author. It is a very special agency.

Hazel Holmes and the team at UCLan. I knew that *Exit Stage Death* needed a publisher who loved and respected musicals (and murder mysteries!) and who totally got what I was trying to achieve, and I struck gold. Thank you for really caring about this book. UCLan and everyone who works with them are so respectful of authors, and getting to feel part of the process outside of just the writing has been such a welcome breath of fresh air.

Kathy Webb, for your thoughtful edits which inspired some 11th hour plot twists that I now can't believe weren't there all along.

David Wardle and Becky Chilcott for my gorgeous cover, for taking my ideas on board, and crucially for telling me when they weren't going to work! You were, of course, right – I love where we ended up.

There will be many people I haven't even met yet who will play crucial parts in the life and success of *Exit Stage Death* – marketing, sales, publicity to name just a few departments. It doesn't stop when the author types 'The End' and I'm forever grateful to everyone working to make sure readers find this book.

Booksellers are such a fundamental part of getting books into the hands of readers. They are the magic of reading distilled into human form, and I'm so lucky to have been championed by some of the most brilliant there are. Particular thanks to Helen, who read *Exit Stage Death* before it found a publisher – when you said you liked it, I knew I had something good, because I trust your taste implicitly. Thank you, truly.

I was walking back to my desk through Troy town square (Woolwich, London) when Juliet's scripted voice came to me fully formed. Thank you Punchdrunk for the most inspiring playground to work and create in. I love spending my days with you.

The Screenwriting for Novelists group, who are so smart and supportive. We're all such different writers, but our chats always leave me feeling empowered and like you've all got my back. Goes both ways – I think you're all brilliant. Holly Race, you're a wonder and one of the most supportive assets UKYA has. Thank you for bringing, and keeping, us all together.

James Bailey, these past few years in publishing would have been a lot more challenging if everything (amazing and not!) that happened to one of us hadn't happened to the other first. Thank you for completely getting it.

My fellow Team Irvine authors. Celebrating your successes feels like a win for all of us, every time. Melissa Welliver, I rarely love this job more than when I'm putting the world to rights over a prosecco with you.

Lex Croucher, for the title and for the cult. The Hellions – I tried to list the reasons but there were too many. Last time I did this I didn't know any of you, and none of us were published authors. By the time you're reading this, seven of us are with doubtless more to come. I am so proud of this group, in matters of writing and everything else. Doing this with all of you is the best part. Special thanks to very early readers Alice and Zoe.

My endlessly supportive pals – The Boyband Girls, Rachel, Liam, Bernie, Lily, Siobhan and Philippa in particular.

My family. In the writing of these acknowledgements, I left this one for last because I couldn't find the words. Still can't. Nothing I could ever say would be enough.

Jesse and Oscar, who bring more joy than I think any of us knew was possible.

I couldn't write a book about theatre kids without mentioning Edith, who has exactly the theatrical energy I hope runs through this book, and who understands musicals on a more fundamental level than most adults I know. I think you're going to enjoy this one, but maybe wait a few years!

I've worked in theatre since I was 18 years old, which means it's how I know most of the people in my life. Of the very many who have been a special part of a specific moment, a few forever friends – Sharif Afifi, Chrissie Homer-Greenslade, Stephen Patry-Makin. If we're measuring in love, there isn't a number high enough for how I feel about the three of you.

IF YOU LIKED THIS, YOU'LL LOVE...

POPPY T. PERRY

Grab Your Zom-Stompers
And A Spare Pair Of Pants,
It's About To Get Real...

DEAD REAL